THE
UNCLEAN
SIX

THE UNCLEAN SIX

STEVEN ARCHER

authorHOUSE®

AuthorHouse™
1663 Liberty Drive
Bloomington, IN 47403
www.authorhouse.com
Phone: 1-800-839-8640

First published by AuthorHouse   11/30/2011

ISBN: 978-1-4678-7813-5 (sc)
ISBN: 978-1-4678-7814-2 (hc)
ISBN: 978-1-4678-7815-9 (ebk)

Printed in the United States of America

For Emma and Rachel with love.

It is easy to look at events and occurrences in retrospect.

This is especially true when retrospective time is not weeks, months or years but measured in *ages*.

I will try not to ramble too much during the telling of this particular story.

I ask only one thing of you: even if you do not understand completely what unfolds, at least recognise that there is another perspective to every story, yarn, fable, tale and of course . . . Truth.

Prologue

They had been seated in an outer waiting room for a long, long time.

None of them had uttered a solitary word to one another. There was no need to.

The walls were carved out of rock, which must have been a Herculean task given the immense size of the space. Also included in the work was a basic seating plinth that ran around the perimeter. Moisture ran and dripped down all four of the hand made curved, blackened, walls, it was as though they were sweating.

Due to the two torches that were supported on opposite walls and the orange, yellow flames that crackled from them, the air was heavy and parched, making it very difficult to breathe.

None of the six paid any heed. Each of them seemed to be lost in meditation or private reflection.

During the course of the last days, each one of them had been introduced to the room and left to wait. The first arrival had been nearly two days ago and the most recent, fourteen hours ago.

When each had entered, he had stood in the centre of the cave like room and looked around at his sparse surroundings. Except for the torches, the walls were bare and oppressive.

There were two heavy wooden doors with giant, rusted metal hinges and substantial iron handles and locks, although they had not had a key turn in them for many hundreds of years. The wood had aged and darkened, giving an unforgiving, solid, appearance that complimented the walls, perfectly.

The once jagged, rough edges to the floor had been smoothed away by the thousands of shuffling feet that had paced the room over thousands of years, blackening it in the process in a mixture of dust, dirt and blood.

Each of the six had then sat in a carefully chosen, statuesque position and began to wait. One at a time they had come into the chamber to bide time.

The only sound to be heard was the crackling of the flames.

None of them spoke, none of them looked around they simply waited for they knew that once they were all together, it would not be long . . .

Then it would begin.

*

As they continued to bide their time in the flickering light of the torches, all was still.

Eventually, one of the large wooden doors slowly creaked open, the opposite one to which they had used to enter.

Once it was fully open and the passageway outside could be seen, the nearest figure to the door stood and turned steadily toward it. One at a time the other five followed suit.

Each of them had on long grey, brown cloaks made from heavy, hemp like material that obscured their taut, sinewy bodies totally, with hoods that were pulled over their heads so that only darkness could be seen instead of features.

With their hands clasped tightly in front of them, their knuckles whitened they started to walk slowly from the smoky room, wafting the visible grey, smoky air as they moved.

The corridor was similar to the room in that it was also carved out of the same rock.

It was barely wider than the broadest of the six and about two feet higher than the tallest of them.

There were torches at random intervals to give just enough light for passage along the winding route and the dank atmosphere had an almost tangible depression to it.

Steven Archer

The surface of the floor was rougher to the touch as it had not been as well trodden.

If any of the six held any questions about what was to come, they kept them to themselves. Each knew that they had been summoned for a purpose and that it would shortly be explained to them.

The only sound echoing around the limited passage was the movement of their feet on the hard rock floor.

No other doors or access points were to be seen along the shadowy route, just the dingy passageway ahead.

For several minutes they walked along the path in front of them with no sense of direction having taken so many twists and turns, not that it mattered as they all knew where they would be shortly, even though none of them had been here before, they could sense it.

The corridor began to widen slightly as they rounded a left hand bend that had a large, solid wooden door at its end. The door was already open.

Without pause, all six entered a large open cavern. There was a long carved bench toward the rear on which all of them filed along and then sat upon once they had turned to the front.

Four torches flickered on the front wall that they looked to. None of them moved or tried to determine where they were. The door closed with a groan and they were left in silence, which after a while was finally broken by a disconnected, deep voice.

It is time . . .
Each of you knew that this moment would arrive:
Gadereal.
Armean.
Danyuel.
Azazeal.
Yetereal.
Tureal.

Each of you has served well, each of you has proved his worthiness and each of you now has your part to play in what is to unfold.

Now let us discuss the future . . .

Chapter One

1872. Wisconsin, USA.

The dry, cold autumn wind, although refreshing, did cause the young girl to pull her thin jacket around her in an attempt to get more warmth from it.

Her pace quickened as not only did she know that she was late but the biting chill gave her an added impetus that she wasn't conscious of.

Beneath the blonde curly locks of hair, her brow furrowed.

It hadn't been her fault that stupid Ernie Sidney had kicked her.

In fact, it wasn't her fault that stupid Ernie Sidney had kicked her and then denied it with such sincerity after the teacher had been informed of the deed that it ended up with both of them staying after class to explain themselves. It wasn't fair.

Miss O' Toole wasn't happy with what she had heard from either of them.

"This is *not* the sort of behaviour that I expect from my class." She had informed them, severely, from behind her giant wooden desk.

And now, hurrying along the thick muddy trail home, through the part of the woods that she wasn't supposed to be in, Louise Maynard wasn't happy at all.

Louise Maynard was not only unhappy at the fact that she had resigned herself to a punishment that she knew she did not deserve because stupid Ernie the eel was such a good liar, she was unhappy because now she was trying to get home as quickly as possible by using a trail that her father had expressly forbidden her to use so that she would not be too late home. Even using this trail, she was going to be late and she knew it.

This meant that her father would be mad and she knew what that meant too.

As she strode on, she briefly scrunched her eyes up and fought back the urge to cry, emotion almost overtaking her.

Even though she was in really deep trouble for being late home, she hurried to her fate and it upset her deeply, though she was just too young to make sense of both her predicament and her feelings.

The frustration of knowing what awaited at home wrapped in the fact that she felt compelled to try and limit the outcome by rushing so, made her want to weep.

Her vision became blurred as the thought of slippery, stupid Ernie the eel and his wandering feet caused the dam to break.

As soon as the tears streamed down her cheeks she felt two things, one physical and one mental: The cold tracks became almost hardened on her face as the wind blew against her and anger at the fact that she had been bested by a stupid boy.

The main reason for the tears was, of course, that the stupid boy had no idea how badly his actions were going to injure her. Far more than the original kick itself.

If only she had brushed it off and carried on playing with the other children. If only.

As the muddy trail narrowed at the right hand bend that would slowly bring her around to the copse, which was a stone's throw from her home, she saw the figure in front of her standing right in the middle of the track.

The combination of the weather and the maelstrom of feelings within her meant that she had to concentrate on the person.

She slowed and tried to wipe her eyes with her mitten-covered hands. The wool made her cheeks itch as she wiped.

Hadn't the figure been dressed in a brown coloured robe a second ago, she thought?

No, no it couldn't have been, for although she could still not quite make out who it was in front of her, the person certainly wasn't wearing a brown robe.

Steven Archer

Tureal had been following the little girl since she left the schoolhouse.

He could tell straight away that she was very upset, something must have happened to make her late.

It wasn't hard to keep a safe distance between them and as he concentrated on her thoughts, her swirling emotions and worries of the impending future, he had been able to tap into one tiny glimmer of brightness within her. That was it. That was the thing that he could use . . .

That was the edge that he needed and that he would now exploit. Faster than the naked eye could see, he moved ahead of her . . .

"Hello, Louise Maynard."

"Hel-, hello Billy. What are you doing here?" Although her heart virtually skipped a beat at seeing him in front her, Louise could not quite work out what on earth he would be doing across the village at this time of day. Shouldn't he be helping his father with the animals?

The boy who was about three years older than Louise looked at her with a bright, smiling and open expression.

"I finished my chores early and I wanted to see if you would like to come and play in the old Hanson barn with me for a while."

Louise stood rigid and tried desperately to remain calm. The wind whistled in the leaves of the trees above. All thoughts of slippery Ernie the eel had gone and most of the thoughts about her father too, all but one.

"I, I ain't been home yet. If I don't get back my daddy will be angry . . ." The last word was almost whispered yet resonated a point.

"Is that why you've been crying?" Billy pointed at her face as if to emphasise his meaning.

Still trying to work out why Billy would want to be even seen with her but at the same time hoping beyond hope that this was the first of many such get-togethers they would have, just as she had daydreamed so many times in class, she said:

"Yes. I should be getting along . . ." There was no conviction in her tone and they both knew it.

Walking the few feet that separated them and putting his arm around her gently, Billy carried on.

"Why don't you tell me all about it? I might be able to help. Y'know I've been watching you for a while now. I've wanted to talk to you and, well, I think I sort of like you . . ."

Louise whipped her head around to face Billy and look into his deep dark blue eyes. Could this truly be happening?

"It started with Ernie," she mouthed, although the words sounded as if they were coming from someone else.

As Billy motioned for her to sit back on a patch of lush, long grass, she continued as he sat to her right. "He kicked me."

"I know Ernie and if you want, I'll kick him right back for you. Would that help?" Sincerity was in his eyes, as he spoke.

"I'm not sure that it would help," Louise replied gazing into his eyes.

"Then tell me, what can I do? You seem so upset. What is it?"

Turning her head slightly, to hide the welling of tears in her eyes from him as she thought again of her father, she searched for the words.

Billy sensed her discomfort and moved a little closer to her, placing his left arm over her back, gently holding her left shoulder through her thin coat with his hand.

"It's your daddy isn't it? Not Ernie . . ." He had decided that the time had come to be direct and it achieved the result that he wanted.

Louise started to gently sob, her shoulders jerked as tears flowed down her rosy cheeks. They didn't hurt as much as earlier but she still felt pain inside.

"Shhh now, comon . . . I didn't mean to upset you." Billy squeezed her firmly and raised his right arm a fraction from his side.

Steven Archer

Louise rested her head on his shoulder and let her emotions flood out with her tears, the release was surprising to her. As he held her for a few more seconds she became aware that his grip on her was tightening slightly.

Just as she was about to speak, Billy moved his right hand and placed it squarely in the middle of her chest.

His strength defied his build.

"Don't worry Louise Maynard, no one will hurt you again."

His hand pressed on her chest and Louise felt a short, sharp shock. It was the last thing that she would feel.

Her heart jumped a rhythm and then stopped completely. She could feel it no more.

Although he couldn't see her eyes, Billy waited until the life and sparkle drained out of them before removing his pale hand and then pushing her forcefully forward with his left so that she fell forward and landed face down in the mud of the trail that she wasn't even meant to take. Her blonde curls blew with the wind.

Billy stood, wiped his hands and gave a snort.

Time to go.

*

Excellent.

A heart attack in one so young . . . still she had been warned about the trail . . .

Come back now Tureal, your work is done.

Nobody will suspect a thing.

"Maybe not in this time but there will be interest from ours . . ." Tureal kept his head bowed.

Yes there will. But we will deal with that interest at the appropriate moment.

No more talk Tureal. Leave now.

Chapter Two

A status quo had existed for many, *many* years.

This was a very delicate situation and very fragile. At any moment, one small fault or deed by either side could cause untold chaos.

That is how Light and Dark existed.

The Realm of the Good and The Realm of the Bad constantly plotted and conjured ideas that could be used to gain an upper hand, but after eons of one upmanship, which inevitably had one side at an advantage for only a period of time before a shift in power, a truce gradually developed that both sides were content to live with. Time meant nothing to either The Truth or The Lie and so an elongated period of introspection came about.

Although obviously different in many ways, this one common element had meant a peaceful time for man during which the Good and the Bad developed and had their notions and ideals used and abused by man, the years passed on earth were mere moments for Light and Dark.

It got to the point where the actual beginning was lost in time. The purpose of both Good and Bad was lost.

In many instances the very meaning of Good and Bad had been lost . . .

Man concentrated on that which he loved best: Himself.

And so The Realm of Good and The Realm of Bad went on through the mists of time, practically unnoticed by anyone.

*

Although Man indulged his many religious needs with many different Idols, texts and philosophies the ultimate point had been lost and now man did not even know of it. Nor did he

Steven Archer

know of the battles that took place on ethereal plains between the Angels of Good and Bad and their various troops.

They were just so many children, walking around on their little world with no idea of how they had been so viciously fought over, all of them blissful in their ignorance.

Chapter Three

1916. Normandy, France.

The orange and red glow of the flare illuminated the dark, cloud-covered landscape of the muddy, crater marked battlefield.

The night had been long and outstretched as it always was here, in the mud filled trenches, where the only breaks in the silence were the whistling of a random flare, followed quickly by the deafening explosion of the shell that had been fired immediately afterward as a target was sighted and fired upon in the eerie light that was shed.

Mud and debris, sometimes accompanied by body parts if the gunner had targeted well, were thrown up into the air, falling hundreds of feet in all directions.

This was how each night passed, filled with flying shells and tension.

Nineteen year old Stephan Olivires sat hunched in the corner of one of the trenches on a rickety old vegetable box and ducked his head to avoid being hit by any of the falling material that headed to the ground after the last explosion which had landed only twenty metres away in no man's land to his right.

He shivered partly from nerves but mainly because of the freezing temperature.

He was cold, dirty, wet and tired.

Not only was he physically and emotionally fatigued he was tired of the war itself. He had been fighting on this front for fourteen months with only one single break for R&R. Stephan was sure that he and the others were de-evolving into a kind of human sub-species in this cursed world they inhabited, filled with death and repetition.

Pushing his hands as far into his pockets as he could to try and stay at least a little warm, he cursed himself as he had done on many such nights, on many watches.

Stephan could still not quite believe how stupid he had been.

Instead of going to college to study math and physics as he had been going to, to the delight of his parents, he had instead got caught up in the fervour that was war and volunteered for the army, to the absolute disbelief of his parents.

This had not been easy of course, as occupied France was under strict German law but a resourceful and clever young man like Stephan had been able to access the resistance, who had spirited him away to England as fast as his head had spun and to where he had enlisted.

Stephan did not feel in the least bit resourceful or clever now.

He hated himself for making the decision to come to this war almost as much as he hated the war, almost.

Another flare cast its light over the trench and its mud walls, stabilised with wooden planks, the filthy, water drenched ground and the three miserable men within this short stretch.

The two other men with Stephan were on guard with him to ensure that nothing untoward occurred during these early hours, whilst the rest of the men tried their damnedest to sleep in the cramped, stinking rooms that acted as bunks.

Closing his eyes, Stephan felt a wave of emotion wash over him and had to fight back at the urge to cry as fiercely as if it was the enemy, which was across the field of battle above him.

Would he be able to survive this battle? Even if he did would he still have his wits about him, as at present, he was so strung out that mental exhaustion felt as if it were not too far away at all. The horrors he had seen would fill his dreams for years to come, instead of being confined to the odd nightmare of one who hadn't served in this man made futility.

If only he had stayed home and gone to college. His parents had not been rich but had managed to use their positions to bribe a few German officials to make sure that he was able to enter further education and take the subjects that he loved.

Shaking his head, he tried to make these thoughts disappear so that they would not torture him anymore.

Pulling his right sleeve across his face over his freezing, running nose, he looked up at Robert who was peering intently over the edge of the trench with his binoculars.

"They'll see the flare's reflection if you are not careful." Stephan spoke slowly and in a matter of fact tone.

Robert turned steadily, taking the glasses away from his head, and said: "I do not wish to die, what do you think I am, stupid? I check quickly between blasts, idiot. At least one of us is doing what we are here to do and not skulking in corners, waiting for relief, worrying over nothing."

Stephan did not even consider replying or rising to the bait. He was far beyond that. If Robert wanted to get himself shot, what did it matter to him? He did not care.

The heavy silence fell on them again as did the darkness.

After a few moments Robert spoke quietly to himself, Gerrard, the third guard and Stephan looked at each other and exchanged a shrug neither of them asked what he had said.

"I don't believe it." Robert leaned into the thick wooden, makeshift wall of the trench to try and confirm what his unbelieving eyes were seeing.

"This is a suicide. One of them has had enough! Pass me my rifle!" Still holding the binoculars with his left hand, Robert watched as the shadowy figure of the German soldier trudged with a purpose toward their lines, rolling the fingers of his right hand until they made contact with the rifle that Stephan had retrieved and now passed to him.

From time to time, soldiers on both sides of the field would clamber up out of the trench that they occupied and walk to the enemy. It was suicide, as Robert had said, as some men finally succumbed to death rather than carry on in the endless nightmare of the battle.

Steven Archer

Placing his gun on the mud in front of him, Robert looked to the left and right of the man coming to him, in the wide open, crater-strewn field.

He was alone. Robert was sure that it wasn't a trap.

"He has lost his mind and is looking for the peace that comes with death." Turning and smiling at Stephan and Gerrard, Robert continued, "I shall give him his peace!"

He dropped the binoculars onto a blanket and took his rifle up, quickly checking it and sliding the firing pin into position. Placing his right cheek on the butt behind the sight and pulling it firmly into his shoulder, he searched for his quarry.

Once the now larger figure was in his sight he gently began to squeeze the trigger. "Goodbye, friend, no need to thank me."

The crack of the shot echoed around them much louder than it should have been.

"Yes!" Robert shouted, a crazed expression on his face. "Right in the chest, he . . ."

Stephan looked up at Robert as he failed to finish his sentence and was about to ask what was wrong when he got his answer.

"He's got back up . . . he's coming toward us again!"

"You must have clipped him, you fool!" Shouted Stephan standing and grimacing at his aching legs through gritted teeth he spoke loudly.

"Put him out of his misery, for pity's sake! Don't toy with him, kill him!"

Robert spun around and fixed a stern look on Stephan, "I did aim to kill him, boy. Shut your mouth and let me finish this." Determination covered his features.

As the figure moved with what seemed to be a greater stride, Robert took aim again as Gerrard and Stephan watched, mindfully from either side of him, standing on their box seats, wary that this could still be a trap.

The rifle cracked again and the man twisted slightly to his left but carried on without missing a step. He was now about fifty feet from them, his pace quickening.

"I hit him again! He won't go down!"

"He must be either crazed or numb from drink you stupid bastard! Hit him again, quickly!" Gerrard spat the words into Robert's ear.

Shaking slightly, Robert took time to sight the man and could make him out with ease now even in the dark, as he was getting so close.

Crack!

Again the figure was struck, this time in the left leg and yet still he came, striding on, moving a little faster to thirty feet away.

"Oh, my God! I don't believe th—this can't . . ." The words fell from Robert's mouth, his face a mask of disbelief.

"Again! Shoot him again!" Screamed Stephan fighting the overwhelming urge to run. He looked down, panicked, into the trench to locate his own gun.

Crack!

With the fourth hit, it was as if the crazed German tired of the game.

He began to run.

He lifted his right arm and pointed the pistol that he held at the small amount of the men that were in view to him, above the trench.

"He's still coming!" Robert cried and fired off another shot, which went wildly past the German to his left.

Stephan had jumped into the trench near to where his gun was leaning against the wall. He heard the next shot and in the split second that he realized that it was not Robert firing, he felt the warm, sticky fluid on the back of his neck. As he turned to look back at his comrades, he was in time to watch Robert falling backward into the trench, as if in slow motion. The top right quarter of his skull was gone.

Gerrard had also fallen back in the trench screaming in terror, thick dark blood spattered on his face.

As Stephan tried to process what was happening and trying to force himself to reach for the rifle, the German appeared at the top of the trench. As voices in the distance began to shout at the commotion and Gerrard blew his warning whistle, frantically, the moment hung in the air for what felt like an eternity.

The German aimed his pistol at the scrambling figure of Gerrard and fired twice, hitting him in the chest, sending him falling back against the wall of the trench, dead before he hit the ground.

Stephan could only watch, mouth wide open, as were his eyes, in fear at the nightmare scene before him.

The German jumped down, never taking his gun off Stephan who could see the wounds that the man had sustained on his march over no man's land weeping blood, steam rising up off him. His filthy appearance and condition gave him an unnatural look.

"Hello, Stephan. Very nice to make your acquaintance," the German said quietly.

As Stephan felt his expression change to one of questioning, his heart raced even faster and he heard the bang of the pistol and smelt the smoke that came with the bullet.

Looking lazily down he saw the hole in his chest and blood pouring from the wound. Before he could gaze at his killer again, he was struck by a second bullet that shut him down. There was nothing left to think with.

The German dispassionately looked at the dead body that had been Stephan Olivires, took a step closer and as the voices from the bunks got louder and the rushing footsteps got nearer, he fired again into Stephan's body.

A thin smile crossed the German's lips.

Time to go.

*

Yetereal.

Yetereal, although that was somewhat more dramatic than I had anticipated, it was, never the less a job well done, well disguised.

"Thank you."

Perhaps next time a little more composure will be in order . . .

Still, your mission was successful; he will be unable to fulfil his destiny now . . .

Leave and make ready, prepare well . . .

Chapter Four

The dirt on the floor was something that was both interesting and dull at the same time.

In this standing position, which he had adopted so many times before, he had been able to determine the quality of dirt.

Of course, this was not by choice. Yet over the expanse of time, this was one of the skills that he had taught himself to maintain his composure, a balance if you will.

The first time that he had waited for instruction had been beyond him.

He had not even been given the task that he had been proposed to do, for before it was disclosed to him he had already begun to scream in agony, contorting his face as his mind had been contorted.

An agony of his own making, as all he was required to do first of all was to wait for the instruction, and he had failed.

That particular task had been passed to another with more experience. But at least he had learned a lesson.

Not everyone does.

It was after this abject failure that he had realized that if he was to be chosen to carry out a task he would be tested in the most simple and obvious of ways: How do you control yourself if all you have to do is stand still in a room in the darkness for an indeterminate amount of time?

Even the veterans of such a folly had found themselves stricken by the time. Time that was in most cases just out of reach, unobtainable even, and yet there for the taking, always.

This had been a lesson that he had learned well and still observed, because he wanted to serve . . .

Dirt had become something of a necessary hobby now, for it didn't matter where you had to stand or how long that you had to stand for, there would always be dirt.

Barely visible whether on the floor, the walls or the ceiling it was always there.

Concentrate on the dirt. Organize it. Think about where it could have possibly come from and then give it not only a story but a history.

Keep yourself occupied, keep your mind occupied.

Dirt was the secret.

This was why he now felt that he was the number one choice for the most difficult of tasks. This was why he knew he would be made to wait longer than any of the other candidates for the job, because he was the best and the best had to earn the right to perform.

From a simple thing like dirt came the greatness of servitude.

*

The time that he spent away from the service was of course monitored but that had never bothered him.

He realized that this was a part of the price that he had to pay . . .

Strange that it should give him some comfort in knowing that the longer he carried out the missions that were set before him, the sooner he would move on, and yet these where the crimes that he had carried out in another life that had merited discipline.

This was a parody that still made him smile.

Laughter was something that had long since been forgotten.

There was a familiar feel to the structure of the world around him, almost as if it had been designed around him to make him feel at ease. This in itself had taken many years to get the hang of and yet this again was a task in itself and one that he felt he had done very well on and that was why he was given the hardest roles to act out.

A cop is a cop is a cop.

It doesn't matter where you carry out the role and it does not matter who else is involved as long as you understand that you have a case to crack and a timeframe to do it in.

After learning the way that things worked here, there was now an understanding of how to carry out a role for which he was best suited. And the environment seemed to mould itself around him as though he was in some sort of simulation but with very serious consequence should he fail to carry out the task at hand.

And so he waited to receive his instruction.

Jophiel stood and waited.

Oblivious of his surroundings he stared at the dirt. Briefly his mind wandered to a time long ago, before he was Jophiel. His previous name when in life evaded him like a phantom of his imagination, a name that had belonged to another.

The thought dissipated as quickly as it had come and the floor returned to focus.

The sound of the voice made him twitch involuntarily. He had not been expecting it so soon.

"There is a task that requires your abilities. Will you accept it?" The dismembered voice echoed around and inside his head.

Jophiel did not hesitate or need to think.

"Yes. I accept the task."

Chapter Five

1465. Pistoia, Italy.

The spacious workshop had at one time been a barn.

The whitewashed walls, now dusty with cobwebs, ran for forty feet at the longest stretch and the heavy oak beams were twelve feet from the ground.

It had been converted for a different use four years previously by Sanzio Tassoni who had inherited the land on which the farm stood, several outer buildings and the barn with it. Sanzio had moved from the outskirts of Milan to this part of the country when his father had died and he had brought his work with him. His work was why he had needed a workshop and the workshop was why the locals thought him to be quite mad.

To say that the profession of alchemy was frowned upon would be an understatement, in not just this area, but across Italy and most of the known world also but to allow fourteen acres of the best farmland and vineyards in Pistoia to go to ruin was unheard of and unforgivable in a time of strife for many folk.

Sanzio was not liked (not that he had ever really been loved) but he did not care. He did not care for he had become used to the taunts and jibes of the commoners and the illiterate and also he knew that he was close to reaching his objective.

The enormous stone hearth in the centre of the room raged red, yellow and orange with the fire within and the light and heat that it gave off filled the room.

Sanzio sat at a desk scribbling furiously in his journal, occasionally looking up at various tools, measuring devices and chemicals on the shelves in front of him.

"Is it ready yet?" He shouted over his shoulder whilst still writing.

"Nearly master," the young apprentice, Anton, paused in the performance of his task to steal a glance at his master, who, as usual ignored him completely and carried on mumbling to himself, sometimes tapping his lips with his index finger as he wrestled another part of the experiment that needed clarification in his mind.

Anton returned to the pestle and mortar continuing to grind the powder within further still.

"Hurry up boy! I am almost ready!"

Finishing his notes and shutting the journal with a flourish, Sanzio stood, stretched and yawned. He rubbed his weary dark eyes with aching hands. He had not slept for two days but inside he felt vibrant. Pacing along the stone floor he looked at the worktops checking the instruments, staring at the gently boiling potions and adjusted a small oil burner. He was pleased.

He was nearly there. He was so close.

The boy finished his preparation and emptied the fine dust like powder into a second bowl, which already had a yellow powder within it. Taking up a spatula, he gently began to mix the two together.

"Almost ready now master." He said with a tone of achievement.

"Good! Good!" Sanzio replied distractedly.

He was about to prove himself a genius.

He was about to be able to show all of those who had scorned, ridiculed and laughed at his work exactly what he was capable of. He was about to become one of the few great men who fulfilled their enormous potential.

A glow of pride grew within him, his moment beckoned.

He chastised himself for the momentary lapse in concentration and made one more mental check of the preparations that had been done, turning slowly on his heels pointing at various stages of the process and registering their readiness.

Striding over the straw and sawdust that covered the floor, Anton carried the powder to Sanzio.

Sanzio turned, looked at the boy and then at the powder.

Steven Archer

After scrutinising for a second or two he said "Good work." As he moved to the workbench Anton let loose a sigh, Sanzio was a hard taskmaster but brilliant with it.

"You know what to do now boy." Sanzio confirmed to Anton his next move.

Nodding his head in servitude, Anton stepped back to the workbench that ran along the longest wall of the room. He turned once he had backed into it and stood slightly to one side observing what his master was about to do. He knew that his master had been working on this particular experiment for many years before they had met, refining the process and getting getter closer to his goal as he did every time. Anton knew that this was going to be a very special moment and he allowed himself a tiny smile.

Sanzio took the heavy leather gloves from the side of the hearth and pushed his hands into them. They were cumbersome of course, but vital at the last stage of the experiment to withdraw the raw material deposited at the conclusion of the experiment.

Looking once again from left to right along the length of the apparatus that combined to create his destiny Sanzio Tassoni gritted his teeth and took up the bowl that Anton had placed on the side, ready for use, ready to begin the experiment with this the last component.

Now was the time. Now was *his* time.

Holding the bowl in one hand he gave the liquid in the metal cauldron one last stir before adding some of the powder in delicate measures, satisfied, he took up a clean spoon and gently scooped the remaining powder into the boiling liquid.

Once it was all in he watched as the reaction began.

Once the boiling liquid reached its high point, some of the precipitation would be filtered off and on to the second stage of the process via a glass tube.

The seconds crept by agonisingly slowly and as they did Sanzio almost hopped from one foot to the other in anticipation. He prepared himself for the small step to the left to retrieve the resulting element.

All of his time, all of his effort was about to come to fruition.

As he watched, the liquid bubbled furiously and turned a deep mustard colour. Sanzio leaned in a little, as this was a darker colour than he had seen during his many previous trials. He was about to brush off the happening as a small change in the nature of the chemicals being used when he noticed something else.

There was an odour emanating from the cauldron that was familiar and yet far from his conscious mind, he couldn't quite place it. Curiosity at this tiny change in the experiment drew him closer to the hearth, his brow furrowed deeply.

The last thought that crossed Sanzio's brain was recognition of the smell.

He didn't have a chance for further thoughts or actions as the explosion that emanated from the liquid in the cauldron was sufficient to blast him backward for ten feet, into the wall behind him with such force that he shattered many of the bones in his body and ruptured many of his internal organs. The impact was enough to kill him instantly.

Sanzio was dead before he hit the floor in a pile of disfigured limbs like a rag doll a child had tossed casually into a corner when playtime had ended.

The flash of the explosion was instantaneous. The hearth had sustained serious damage and small fires and smoking embers littered the room and set more fires going as the straw on the floor caught light.

Anton dropped his right arm, dusted himself off and walked to the alchemist.

Looking upon the head twisted at an extreme angle, blood trickling from his mouth, nose and ears Anton stared for several seconds ensuring that his master was indeed dead.

The crackling of the fire in the room as it began to take hold and spread urged Anton into movement.

Once he had approached the end of the workbench that he had leaned against, he knelt and opened up a large double cupboard door. An arm fell limply out as he did so.

Steven Archer

The body of the real Anton was pulled from its home of rest for the last ten hours unceremoniously and dragged to the hearth by the shoulders. The gaping wound across the neck had long since stopped bleeding and was caked in darkened, hardened blood. Once hoisted into the air the corpse was thrown into the fire in the centre of the hearth and was immediately engulfed in flames that licked at the clothing, skin and hair lighting it slowly. There was an almost hypnotic effect in viewing the deterioration of the body from the flames that seemed to smother the boy like a lost lover.

It was done.

Walking away from Anton's body and through the fire, causing his clothing to singe, Anton the doppelganger headed for the big wooden doors. After removing the large beam that kept them closed, he pushed them open and enjoyed the wave of fresh air that rushed at him.

Without pause or reflection Anton strode away from the workshop.

Time to go.

*

Azazeal.

Patience is truly one of your finer traits as you have shown here. Waiting to the very second that success was within his grasp . . . that was very nearly too cruel. Or did you want to have a glimpse at what could be before removing him?

"No, Master, I simply thought that this way would be best." Azazeal kept his head bowed and his pace steady. His voice was emotionless and simply confirmed his conviction.

Of course. The simplest way is often the best way. Now come back Azazeal, we must continue to ready ourselves . . .

So far everything is going according to plan but we must not take anything for granted.

Chapter Six

Jophiel was on his way to receive word of his next action.

He wondered why he had not been left alone for as long as he had been before.

Although there was no doubt of his will now, he still expected to be waiting for an age at least but who was he to question at this point and questions came so easily to him . . . strangely, he realised that he was a little disappointed and suspected that this was because it was the only time that he was totally alone, alone with his thoughts, quiet and happily alone with his own thoughts and, of course, the dirt.

Now he was back in the fabricated reality that surrounded his every move and breath.

The building, offices, furniture and accessories were replicas of a run down precinct house in the early nineteen thirties of Chicago. Perhaps there were less people. Perhaps the air was a little warmer and staler but this was, as he had known it in life and almost how he lived it in death. Jophiel had taken the time to wonder which of the people that populated his made to measure fantasy were real and in some sort of penance or how many were there to keep a watchful eye on him.

There seemed to be a fake quality to the whole environment that he was very aware of, especially the colours, which were more muted and dark. It was a shame as he would have enjoyed being blissfully ignorant of his surroundings meaning and simply enjoy it as best he could but his inner self held that possibility back, he was in effect partly responsible for his own purgatory, an irony not lost on him.

Jophiel was beyond caring about this anymore, he had moved past emotions and into acceptance. Yes, it had taken time but now he understood his role in this place and realized that this was for his benefit to make him comfortable, or at least as comfortable as you can be in death.

Upon entering the large, mainly wooden room that was the Captain's office, Jophiel perused the room and then took a seat in the wooden chair that faced the large paper laden oak desk in the centre of the room. As he eased down onto the seat he slowly relaxed his body. Ironic how such an every day function could be relished so now.

The din from the rest of the building blurred in his ears and he tried to extract any one to pass the time; a typewriter being bashed by a one-finger typist, a telephone ringing, pleading to be answered, and a distraught woman crying for someone to help her.

That was when the door opened and the Captain walked in, stiffly.

Jophiel was always wary of the Captain that metered out his tasks.

He was tall and bulky but not heavyset. He wore slacks, braces and a crumpled white shirt that had seen far better days but it was his face that set him aside. It was as if an unseen force was gripping the back of his head and pulling at it. Some sort of Sprite that rode piggyback, invisibly, never releasing its grip on the body that he owned. This not only gave a mask like quality to his features and narrowed his eyes but also meant that his head sat back on his neck, like a boxer avoiding a jab.

"I have your next action." The Captain, Sorrence, pulled the chair from behind the desk that was his from where he had never worked a single moment in time and sat squarely facing Jophiel.

"Good."

"There have been several disturbances detected by some of our agents. These were very difficult to determine, as they seem not only to be random but spread across time. We have not been able to isolate one yet but it will not take too much longer. The agents are sure that these . . . incidents, are not taking place in chronological order, however, and that was how they were first detected subtle as they were."

"How many have been detected?" Jophiel slipped straight into his role, comfortably.

"Two of them so far. The tracking agents are sure that there will be more, of course we don't know how many more or what purpose they serve." The pink smooth mask of Captain Sorrence was emotionless.

"It's not possible that they could be unconnected and simply isolated occurrences?"

After a pause, a glance to the top right of his field of vision and a returning stare Sorrence replied. "Possible of course but the agents think this to be unlikely, they are sure that they are connected somehow."

"How soon until we can lock on one incident and investigate?"

"As I said, soon. You may confer with the agents working on this from Trace Room Four. I need not stress that time, as always is a factor, so do what you do and report back to me. You will be given the usual movement clearances, anything else?"

Sorrence stood to his full six feet four height and looked at Jophiel with black bottomless eyes.

"No. No questions."

Sorrence had started out of the room before Jophiel had finished speaking.

Collecting his thoughts and placing his next moves into place in his mind he started for the Trace Room. He could now relish being productive and serving a purpose once more even if that purpose was served for a master he would rather not be party too but he was here now and it was time to act, time to do what he did best.

Chapter Seven

1958. London, England.

Geraldine Whithey had been waiting for some time now and the creeping thought that Pete wasn't going to show up was becoming more of a weight on her mind.

Her feet had begun to hurt both from the shoes that were too tight for her but, all that she could afford, and the unforgiving surface of the cobbled street corner on which she stood, waiting.

She had only known Pete for a couple of weeks. They had met through a mutual friend who had thought that they may hit it off (Sandra had in fact practically forced Gerrie into the blind date as she had known how long she had not been with anyone and her work colleague from the bank, Pete was a stand up guy and not unattractive. Gerrie had not taken too much persuading.).

Now, under the flickering streetlight with its harsh glow that seemed to act as a psychic x-ray and expose her worries and concerns, she idly rubbed her slender hands together. Darkness was becoming heavier and it was about time to give up this, which would have been their third date, as a bad idea, when she heard the footsteps.

Turning her head slightly to the left, she glanced up toward Tottenham Court Road were she thought that the footfalls were coming from.

The sounds of the clumping feet came ahead of the person that made them and for a second, Gerrie felt a pang of fear, alone in the dark. Not another soul to be seen at all even though it was not too late in the evening.

Fear gave way to relief and relief to happiness.

It was Pete. As he came into view under the hazy lighting she could make out his thin frame. She smiled to herself as he saw her and immediately stopped running and began to walk, albeit briskly instead. It wouldn't do to appear uncool.

He was dressed in dark drainpipe trousers and an even darker overcoat that flapped open at his side revealing a white shirt.

He wasn't handsome but neither was he ugly, far from it. He had an honest and smiling face.

Pete got nearer and his breathing had begun to slow, although sweat still forced its way from his brow. He wasn't smiling.

"Gerrie. I'm so sorry. The bloody car wouldn't start. I had a Hell of a job getting the bus and it stops miles away. His apologetic expression won Gerrie over straight away.

She had the thought that this was a man that she could grow to love.

"It's okay. Don't worry, there's no harm done. What are we going to do now?"

They had been going to go for a quiet drink in a small pub that she knew but it was a drive away.

Pete put a hand on each of her arms and looked into her green eyes.

"I know a place not far from here and it's on your bus route. We could go there and then there's no fretting about getting home later."

The look they exchanged seemed to act as a magnet and Gerrie felt herself leaning, slowly, into Pete.

"That sounds fine . . ." She almost whispered as they kissed.

Their lips pressed together, hers moist and soft his firm and gently forceful.

They locked together for a long moment and then pulled, reluctantly apart.

Gerrie opened her eyes slowly and gazed at Pete who smiled down at her warmly. His eyes sparkled mischievously.

Steven Archer

Pete took her hand and led her back the way he had just come from. The grip was firm and his thumb rubbed her hand gently.

"Have you had a good day?" Gerrie winced at the formal line that she had taken but the kiss had flustered her slightly and she wanted to regroup, hoping that the darkness hid her blushing cheeks.

After a pause Pete replied.

"It's not the most stimulating business, banking, but it was quite busy today so it went quickly . . . I was looking forward to seeing you tonight . . . and tomorrow?" Gerrie bit the smile on her lips. This date hadn't even started and he was angling for another. She enjoyed the warm physical feeling that her emotions afforded her.

"I was looking forward to seeing you too."

"I'm sorry I was late, stupid bloody car. I'll have to get it fixed as soon as I can. I got into a bit of a panic tha- . . . I, er thought for a second that I might be a bit late." His voice was low and trailing off.

Gerrie allowed Pete his appearance of composure and liked the fact that he had almost blurted out his concern at missing their meeting.

"I said not to worry, there's no harm done." They looked at each other as they walked and smiles spread slowly across their faces that changed to light laughs.

Pete slowed and stopped, again taking Gerrie by the arms. He pulled her to him and she moved into him willingly, reaching around him to clinch an embrace. The evening was getting much better after a slow start, she thought.

They kissed and moulded into one another. Gently moving hands over one another and taking small steps into a side alley that was conveniently close to where Pete had stopped. He gently guided and she followed freely.

Gerrie was lost in the moment, caught up in the intoxicating atmosphere that surrounded them as though they were in a tunnel of light within the dark of the night and the gloom of the damp brick and cobbled alley.

As his grip tightened around her and his tongue gently pushed its way between her parting lips, Gerrie's eyes quickly opened wide.

His hands had moved up her body and were now cupping her face. The pressure increased as they kissed as though he did not want to let her go again.

Closing her eyes again she gave in to the moment and wondered for a split second how much farther into her mouth his tongue could get, it felt as though it was probing the very back of her mouth near her throat.

Pete's hands pressed on her cheeks a little more making her open her eyes again as a panic began to grip her also. She couldn't see his eyes as they were closed but she could feel his warm soft tongue pushing further down her throat. Gerrie tried to pull back.

This was wrong.

Pete held her fast and as he did she felt his tongue swell within her as it continued its journey into her body, invading her being and blocking the movement of air as it did.

Her eyes were wide and she tried to struggle free but the invading organ carried on swelling and moving inside of her. Pete gripped her tightly. She couldn't breathe let alone scream and could feel a strange sensation in her chest as part of Pete still grew within her.

Gerrie's thoughts stopped tumbling in her mind and as she started to cloud over her struggles became weaker as his tongue reached into the very centre of her body, pulsing, tasting and feeling as it did so.

After one final effort, Gerrie was overcome. The clouds deepened into an oblivion that she was hesitant to enter but could not avoid . . .

Pete supported her dead weight for a few minutes more, enjoying the different tastes within her and the warmth that surrounded his tongue.

Finally, he began to retract himself. He could feel, even through the clothing that her body shrunk a little as he did so. The swelling went down and his tongue came back up to its rightful place, back inside of his own mouth.

Steven Archer

Pete licked his lips slowly and purposefully then looked at Gerrie's inert form. He laid her on the ground softly then brushed himself down.

Having first checked the far end of the alley, he exited from the way that they had entered.

Time to go.

*

Well done Danyuel. The delivery of the execution was superb, just as I knew that it would be.

"Thank you."

Now it is time to come back. Our plans are coming together perfectly.

"Will it be long now, Master?"

No Danyuel, not long at all, be patient for a little longer and you can be free to explore and destroy all.

"Very well, Master." Danyuel shook off the disguise of Pete as he strode on through the shadows like an unwanted overcoat.

Once we complete the final phases, we can confirm our positioning for the final push of all. Come back now Danyuel and help with the preparations . . .

Chapter Eight

Trace Room four was unremarkable.

It was no more than a canteen with one very long, pristine serving surface running along nearly the full length of the far wall and tables and chairs covering the rest of the room's floor space and also acting as cover for the hundreds of cables and wires that snaked from one piece of equipment to another.

Some of the tables had been pulled together to make greater space for the masses of gadgetry and computers that buzzed with an energy that was almost living.

Technicians also buzzed around the room, flitting from table to table, comparing notes with one another and pointing out relevant information with rigid, purposeful fingers and pursed lips. The fact that they were dressed in casual clothing belied the air of authority that they held.

Jophiel stood at the entrance to the odd canteen and took in the scene before him. Men in slacks and shirts with braces, women wearing skirts and blouses with high heels all sharing pensive expressions and furrowed brows as they went about their business.

Jophiel let his eyes look upon the centrepiece of the room.

Above the long serving station with its many compartments baron of food but stuffed with flashing equipment was a vast set of three screens reaching to the ceiling. The technology was a stark contrast to the wooden room that contained it and again made him shake his head slightly that the need to keep his small fragile mind from shattering with full exposure meant that this environment was deemed necessary to make him feel comfortable, his past contrasted with the technology of the future. Although putting him at ease, he supposed, it also imposed its surreality upon him.

All it did now was irritate him slightly.

Shaking off the feeling to concentrate he looked at the three vast screens and their flat screen displays.

The first showed a computer-generated simulation of the Earth, rotating on every axis as information was fed into it for it to compute, ruminate over and update. Red dots were being joined by fine indicating lines and then deleted as each computation was checked and pursued as far as possible, before being logged, saved and then filed. It showed, he thought, the transgressions that were happening all over the globe at an incredible rate. Each transgression had to be checked and eliminated as a simple happenstance or confirmed as a tampering with and in time. The world rotated and spun furiously one moment, slowing the next whilst keeping up with the events that were taking place throughout history and ensuring their legitimacy.

The second, middle screen had data scrolling down in several columns detailing the events that the first screen was detecting. This information was a timeline projecting from the conception of the event to its natural end, if that were the case. Major points in history that were known to be true events were constantly referenced to assist in the confirmation of another true event or the exposure of a fake timeline and the chaos that would be caused by it being left unchecked. The green writing was a blur to Jophiel and he knew better than to stare at it for too long, he left that to the readers, the eight figures linked by a force greater than telepathy to the screen that only they could read, decipher and understand at that rate.

The final screen to his right was relatively clear.

This would normally be the screen dedicated to re-checking timelines thought to be fake or engineered to source them back to the perpetrator for recriminations at a later date, another timeline in itself, and one of the issues that Jophiel had long ago stopped trying to understand. It caused his head to ache when he attempted to follow and comprehend the intricacies of space, time and multi-dimensional space. He had learned to simply accept that this was beyond him.

At the moment there were only two halves to the screen. Each represented a file that had been opened on an event that must have been verified as fraudulent. Taking two steps forward on the varnished wooden floor, he was about to read the files and look at the pictures more closely when he became aware of the person coming toward him.

The smile on the face of the blonde woman was as forced as her happiness to see him in the room.

He ran the rule over her: five-ten, long legs, straight back and lifted hairstyle. Her skirt was below the knee and the tweed jacket completing a tutorial appearance although she did have what could be a forgiving face, if given the chance.

Jophiel reprimanded himself as he broke off his stare and gazed at the floor for a second. It was an illusion just like the room and the building, covering the reality perfectly.

"I've been expecting you." The blonde stated flatly, her actions almost calculated.

"What do you have for me?" It was time to get down to business and complete his task. All else was irrelevant.

"Please come this way." She motioned with her arm and he followed toward the third gigantic monitor.

She stopped at a table that he presumed was for the moment her workspace.

"You've been here before, yes?" She raised an eyebrow.

"Yes. I don't need the orientation lecture again."

"Good. Let me show you what we have so far."

The fact that she got straight down to the task at hand and did not offer a name was not lost on Jophiel, indeed, this would have irked him in a previous life but now it was another thing that he took for granted. Names were for the flesh and blood slaves, the first method of detracting from uniqueness.

Her fingers moved over the keyboard at an incredible speed as she spoke.

"If you look at the monitor, I'll show you what we have been able to deduce so far."

Jophiel turned his back on the technician and viewed the screen awaiting the information to be imparted.

Steven Archer

"We have detected these two events and believe them to be frauds. The first is the death of a young girl in Wisconsin, of the United States of America in 1872 . . ."

"How old was she?" Jophiel interrupted and noted from the stern expression on her face as he half turned toward her that he had best save any further queries until the end of the briefing.

"Does that really matter?" Her head moved left to right slightly in emphasis.

"It might."

After pausing, looking off to her left and then deciding better of what she was going to say the technical agent replied:

"Seven. She was seven years of age."

Having waited for a few seconds to pass, she regained her authority and began to speak again.

"The second incident took place in 1916 in Normandy, France. A young soldier approximately nineteen years of age," she cast him a sideways glance "was shot and killed with two comrades in a trench. Now the last one in particular, on first viewing does not seem to be out of the ordinary but we are currently confirming further data to illustrate that these two people should have lived longer lives, however, we think that there is more to this and that a third or even fourth event may have to take place before we can truly begin to pull apart the threads of the tapestry to get to the truth, this isn't ideal, of course, as it means that we allow time to get away from us as we wait. The reporting and historical documentation that follows each death is solid and unassuming. There is nothing to indicate cover up as yet."

Jophiel thought that the loss of time to her and not life was cold, almost clinical but disregarded it as useless as the agent had no feelings one way or the other.

"So why are you onto these events and why do you think that there will be more to come?"

"The manner of the deaths was the start. The girl's death, a heart attack, causes concern in one so young even in the timeframe. It seems too clinical and we are tuned to follow every aspect of a possible problem. The soldier was shot by a foe that crossed the no-mans land region as if on a suicide mission, which again, we are pursuing. The fact that both were relatively young raises the theory that they could have gone onto great achievements whether infamous or not and that leads to possibility that other deaths may occur, if they haven't already we may not have detected them yet, relating to otherwise average persons who would have had a hand in the changing of history."

The fact as Jophiel saw it, was that there was hardly anything to go on, and certainly nothing solid. He would only be able to really take the task forward when he had more information. He knew from experience that the agent would impart anything else relevant if there was anything and so follow up questions were pointless.

"Is there somewhere here that I can work from?" He enquired.

"Yes, we have a station set up for you with all detail of the brief that I have given you, access to records of the time and the entry level of four, should you wish to do some . . . research of your own." As she told him this, the agent indicated to the corner of the room with her arm and began walking to his station, careful not to tread on the wiry snakes and eels that lay frozen to the floor.

"Thank you." Jophiel followed two steps behind and realized that this could be harder than he had anticipated. He would find it difficult to discover anything that the technical agents couldn't but then, one of the reasons that he was here was his ability to see the invisible, to play a hunch.

His thoughts were distracted for a second as he became aware of the sense of being watched, which was idiotic as he was being monitored always, but this was something else, a shadow lost in a fog that he couldn't quite grasp.

Deciding to ignore the feeling, Jophiel tuned in to the work to be done.

Chapter Nine

1966. Prague, Czech Republic.

Because it was winter it was cold, in fact it was freezing but that was not why Vaclav felt the chill in his heart, like an icicle dagger had been thrust into his chest.

With one of the most beautiful cities in the world around him, he had chosen to encapsulated himself in this tiny, dank mould ridden room for his final hours. How could it have come to this? How could a life that was once so full of promise and possibilities have dwindled to one that was as worthless as his was now?

The path from optimism and hope, love and fulfilment to the end with desolation and loneliness, fear and loathing had been rapid and disastrous.

No person could live through what Vaclav had in the last six months.

He certainly didn't want to and that was why he was here.

The last of his money had been spent on three things:

Enough medication to stock a small chemist, a bottle of his favourite Jack Daniels liquor, and, finally, his own plot in the cemetery next to where his beloved wife now lay to rest in peace for all eternity.

From the edge of the uncomfortable bed on which he sat he peered around the room and his shoulders hunched forward slightly.

He looked down into the palm of his right hand at the assorted coloured tablets. There were about ten of different sizes for different ailments and had taken him trips to four different pharmacies to have his black market prescriptions filled without raising too much concern. It had in fact been all too easy. The only worry that he had about being caught was the delay in carrying out this final act.

He was tired from the lack of sleep over the past few months and the mental exhaustion that had taken its toll on what had been a very happy, if average person.

Gazing into his palm, he began to drift back over the recent events that had led him down this single-track path to where he was this night.

As he stared the pills melted into a kaleidoscope of colour and swimming patterns set against the deep lines of his palm.

Firstly, there had been the loss of his job. Vaclav had never excelled as an accountant, but prided himself on a high professional standard and a thoroughness that had not gained him the promotions that he would have liked but he had been happy in his work, until the day that he was called into his manager's office, out of the blue and, along with two colleagues from the audit section and a fraud squad officer who stood ominously behind Mr. Kracov staring at him with cold eyes, to inform him that they had suspicions that he had been embezzling money from the company.

He, Vaclav Palacky, an embezzler! If it were not so real, it would be laughable.

Boxes of paperwork had materialised, along with box files and brown envelopes stuffed with the fruit of a thorough internal investigation that had led to police involvement because of the sums of money that had been discovered to be involved. This was no laughing matter.

As his head swam with both the shock and the speed of this turn of events, he had been escorted out of the building unceremoniously, taken to the police station, questioned for several hours exhaustively by several different officer's working in shifts until he could barely remember his own name.

After two days, a brief court appearance and bail being set, his wife Roslyn had come for him.

They had talked and talked and tried to make sense of what was happening to them, but to no avail.

Tears had spilled from both of them, she in exasperation of the situation and he out of concern for Roslyn's health and that of their unborn child.

As the days followed and more interviews were taken with the police and the solicitor that he had engaged, they became aware of how little their own financial position could withstand. Although their little apartment off Narodni near Vaclavske Namesti was modest, it was in a sought after part of Prague and so, reluctantly, easy to sell, their security for the future now gone.

The move back to his parent's house had been traumatic for them both as their world began to unravel before their very eyes and although the support of his parents helped it was not enough.

The swiftness with which the machinery of law moved was breathtaking, protesting innocence seemed only to raise eyebrows and lower his standing. The movement back and forth from his Counsel's offices to the police station ended when a court date was set for Vaclav to stand and defend himself against the charges brought against him.

The pressure of attrition had taken its toll on both Vaclav and Roslyn in very physical ways and also mentally. They would lay in each other's arms in the single bed that he had used as a boy and try to ease each other's fears for the future.

Then the unthinkable happened.

Roslyn had not let Vaclav know just how much strain that she had been under, as she did not want to worry him any more than he already was. She broke.

Having survived the rush to hospital and the blue light journey that nearly took her from him, she was immediately taken into surgery upon arrival in a critical state. Not only had her own heart begun to falter but also the baby within had felt the strain and had to be induced if it were to have any hope of survival.

*

When the pills hit the wooden floor, the small noise was enough to wrench Vaclav back to reality, such as it was. He realized that he had been crying and wiped the tear traces from his hollowed, stubbled cheeks.

After leaning forward to pick up the dropped tablets, he stood and walked into the bathroom where the rest of the bottles were next to the bath. Once in front of the bathroom mirror he looked at his haggard reflection with soulless eyes and as the last thoughts of his wife's death, his baby boy's death and his subsequent disappearance after the funeral, whilst he had been granted a brief stay of execution to grieve at home before the restart of his trial, he emptied all of the assorted pills into the sink and took hold of the glass on the cabinet's shelf.

He filled the glass with water and his mouth with pills, swallowing as he threw back his head and swigged from the glass to flush them down.

He repeated the routine four times, pausing only once to avoid the reaction of vomiting. He had to get this right the first time, he didn't want any mistakes.

He had no idea of how many tablets were making their way to his stomach but it was a lot. His eyes skewed in and out of focus. He had to be quick.

Grabbing one last handful from the sink he returned to the open room with the bed and steadied himself on the doorframe as he entered.

Taking the open bottle of Jack Daniels from the bedside cabinet, he swallowed the rest of the pills and washed them down with the fiery liquid.

Taking five more large slugs, he lifted his leaden feet onto the bed and tried to shuffle into as comfortable a position as he could. Drinking from the bottle again he thought of how heavy his arm had become and then the darkness fell.

He could not see through the thick black cloak that began to envelope him. Although he couldn't see, he knew that Roslyn was near. She was weeping but she was near.

The half empty bottle dropped to the floor and gave its contents freely.

As the liquid gently ebbed onto the carpet as Vaclav's life ebbed from his body, a figure materialised from the shadows in the corner of the room. He had witnessed everything, not just in the room this evening but all that had come before because it was he who had painstakingly, almost lovingly, prepared the death of Vaclav Palacky with the finesse of a play-write, it was appropriate that this puppet in the play of life should meet his end in such a dramatic manner. Now it was time.

Time to go.

*

You seem distant Armean, has the work taken its toll?

"No, Master. I was thinking of how fragile they are . . . how very fragile."

Do not allow sentiment to enter your thoughts Armean. Remember what they have done in the past. Do they all not deserve the same fate?

"Yes, they do, Master."

Do they not all deserve the outcome for which we have planned so long?

"Yes, Master."

Now that your part is done we are one step nearer to our greatest time. Be ready and be steadfast.

"I am, Master and always will be. The fragility simply compounds my hatred for these pathetic things. I will be ready to serve as you wish."

Good, Armean, good. Now go and prepare yourself.

Chapter Ten

Although he did not have to sleep for very long now, if ever, Jophiel realised, unusually, that he was tired, physically tired as if he ached to his very core.

Having gained access to the main computer network and pored over the reports that had so far been amassed relating to these and other instances, his eyes ached. The two known shifts in time had been difficult to break down and taken his full attention. He had tracked several different threads that had developed from each of them to ensure complete understanding of the situation and to seek more clues. Pausing for a moment to rub his eyes again and ponder the irony of still feeling the fatigue he did without actually experiencing it anymore caused him to crack a wry smile.

This was part of the transition period that he would undergo, his body had been glad to give up the human physicality's that were routine such as eating and needing the bathroom, aging and tiring but his mind found the transition harder to overcome.

This was an element of transforming from once being alive to now being dead.

It could take decades in some cases and at this point in time Jophiel doubted that he would ever really be rid of his human self, his humanity, maybe he never should be rid of it, perhaps it made him good at what he did.

Snapping out of his reverie, he sat back and glanced around the bustling room from his corner and wondered how much of the activity was actual and how much was simply for his benefit. He had to stop thinking like this, he thought to himself. Acceptance in full of his situation would make his time, and life, such as it was more tolerable in this place.

Steven Archer

Stretching in his seat he viewed the notes that he had made from the four reports that were now in front of him.

As he had been locked in thought and concentration with the first two shifts in time, reports had filtered through of two more occurrences and maybe even a fifth.

The third was the death of a scientist in Pistoia, Italy around 1465 and the fourth was the death of a young woman in 1958 London, England. As more information had become available as it had been extracted from the computers, the voices of those involved in the assimilation of the data had become shriller and more emphatic.

At first, Jophiel had continued to work on his own, realising that he would at some point be made aware of the discoveries if they panned out and concentrated on the task at hand.

The workmanship of the first two time killings was masterful, each a testament to their author and executioner. The dedication was incredible and the trace left behind, negligible.

As there was more to read over from the Normandy event, he had started there and studied the descriptions of the soldier responsible for the action carefully. This had stirred something deep within Jophiel to the point that all other material, although important, paled a little, the feeling he had was uncomfortable. The young girl that had died in Wisconsin had been taken by a boy but the early dateline had left no really solid description, but it was the fact that they seemed so far removed that touched Jophiel . . . and there was something else, something just out of reach.

Once he had been made aware of the other two events and gained access to the small amount of data gleaned so far, he had tendered the seed of an idea that had sprouted within his subconscious. An idea that presented itself slowly from behind the fog in which it was hidden.

All of the killers were male.

Not an Earth shattering discovery and in fact so obvious as to almost seem irrelevant, almost, but it stood out beyond all other information to Jophiel.

This was the one element that would lead to a conclusion. Yes, the other detail would help in tracking the route, but this was the unique point and one that Jophiel followed through on.

Tracking down a multitude of possible life times for an individual is an arduous task, although not impossible, it just took time and application.

The alchemist, not scientist as first thought and that in itself was relevant was the easy one. He must have been on the verge of a discovery.

This led to the idea that all of these events were linked and that they could be part of a bigger picture.

The young woman, whose boyfriend had been thought to have committed the crime of her murder although never proved and had always pleaded his innocence with vigour, could have been straightforward. A child of the future snuffed out before conception to prevent . . . of course that was the hard part, what would the child have done? Or was it, in fact the woman who was due for greatness?

There was a bigger picture here and Jophiel knew it.

The boy at war instead of at college could have been productive in an alternate reality and finally, the suicide. This one was too good. Too perfect and that's what raised the alarm within Jophiel, quite what the reason for his death could be would come later. For now, Jophiel was sure he knew part of what was happening. With his hands spread wide on the table top in front of him, the hubbub of the room swirling in his head, Jophiel felt two emotions: excitement and apprehension.

He had to seek confirmation of his pursuit.

He would go to see Sorrence and explain in very little detail that he thought the coming of the Unclean Six was at hand.

Chapter Eleven

2004. Benalmadena Costa, Spain.

The park was very busy with a mixture of tourists and locals. As it was Sunday, there was no work and it would seem that everyone had thought to enjoy the sunshine and the gentle breeze that blew in from the coast and stroll around the large open spaces with its grass area's, lake, animal enclosures and restaurants.

Only the small play park, situated at the top of a slight rise was not well attended.

Whether that was because it was the smallest of the three within the park's perimeter or because it was the farthest from the entrances but nearest the toilets, was anyone's guess.

At the moment there was only one small boy sat on one of the six swings that rocked himself back and forth, staring intently at his feet, smiling.

His legs dragged on the ground, scuffing his shoes, but he did not seem to care. He was lost in his own thoughts, daydreaming or simply enjoying his own company. The brown haired child lifted his round face and stared into the distance with eyes that didn't take in any of his surroundings.

Paco Fransisco watched the boy with a careful intensity, as he had done for the last hour, ever since he had seen him wander in, alone through the tall, ornate metal gates nearest the beach entrance.

The boy had nothing with him and no adult supervision, he was certain of that.

Paco lowered the newspaper from behind which he studied the boy in the red shirt and light brown combat style cut off shorts. Rustling the pages as if still reading the print he was now beginning to think of how best to make his move.

Strategy and planning were all important at these opportune times.

He mentally checked off the tools of his trade:

The old dogs lead . . . check.

The bag of Euros . . . check.

The packet of sweets bought fresh in the market this very morning . . . check.

These were his first choice accessories, he did have others in the small shoulder bag that he had with him including a cuddly bear, a broken kite and a light blue shirt with matching hat, a baton and a silver shield, although this was his more risky approach, being a policeman in the eyes of a child had reaped rewards before.

Latex gloves, duct tape, KY jelly, condoms and a length of rope filled out the bag.

Today, however, there would be no need for the uniform, thought Paco.

He had appraised the situation and had decided that the boy would be alone for at least another few minutes, which would be all that he needed to begin his adventure.

A shiver of excitement started in Paco's lower back and travelled up to his neck where the hairs began to stand on end. As the boy gently swung back and forth, so Paco's anticipation rose.

Folding his newspaper with deliberate action and placing it back in the bag at his feet, Paco felt around for the lead as he continued to watch the child. He scanned the immediate area and checked himself as he saw that it was as clear as it would be, hopefully, for the next few minutes. The nearest people were a couple sunbathing on the grass a good fifty metres away. Now was the time.

Paco stood, took up his bag and placed it over his shoulder and then began to wave the lead in his right hand.

Instead of standing at his full six feet, Paco stooped a little and bent his legs to appear smaller and so less intimidating.

Steven Archer

As he began to walk toward the small park and the boy he started to shout.

"Nesta!" He cried through cupped hands.

Closer to the park now, he enjoyed the rush that his racing pulse and blood gave him.

"Nesta, where *are* you?" He shook his head.

Sure enough the boy stopped his reverie and looked at the stranger with concern in his eyes. His body went rigid and Paco was quick to act and allay the little ones fears.

"Have you seen a little dog come by? He is brown and white with a red collar?"

The boy hesitated and looked along the path in front of the park as if to check the route that the dog could have taken.

"No." He said quietly.

Paco leaned on the fence that was between them, looking frantically up and down the path for poor Nesta, whilst ensuring that he was still in a position to act. Still none of the crowds up here, it was his lucky day.

"I only turned my back for a moment and he was gone, I hope he isn't too far," he wiped his eye to reinforce his mock distress. "I don't know what I'd do without him."

The boy stood and took a step nearer Paco.

This was when Paco knew that he had him he controlled his tremors and pushed on.

"He must have gone this way I suppose," he pointed up from the park towards the toilet block. "I'm sure I would have seen him coming to me otherwise."

Gazing up the path, the boy nodded his agreement, his body relaxed now. Supple.

"Would you mind helping me look? I could give you a reward when we find him. Please?" Leaving no doubt that the dog would be found and a reward given, the boy hardly hesitated.

"Okay. My friend is late but I could look for a few minutes." He shrugged as he walked to the play area's entrance and the two of them began the search in earnest.

"Thank you, thank you so much." Paco averted his gaze just before the look had been held for too long. Now was not the time for uneasiness.

"Nesta!"

"Nesta!"

They shouted and looked, raising hands to their faces to block the sun at times and bending low to check under benches. Where was that silly dog?

"Nesta!" The child shouted again, pursing his pouty lips and shaking his head a little.

As they got to the toilets, Paco swallowed hard and readied himself for the final phase.

"I need the bathroom. Will you wait a moment in case he runs by?" Paco's expression of sincerity carried the adventure on.

"Sure." Shrugged the boy once again looking over the park for the brown and white dog.

Paco smiled and only hesitated slightly before walking into the men's bathroom.

He stood for a moment and viewed his own potential play area. The main room was clear and as he took a deep breath and moved forward he saw that only one of the five stalls had its door closed.

He stopped at a sink and rinsed his hands. "Cleanliness is next to Godliness." He thought as he listened intently for any sound coming from the cubicle.

He had to hurry, as he didn't want the boy to become bored or see his little friend, at least not before they'd had their fun.

Kneeling down to see if there were any feet in the cubicle and satisfying himself that there were not he stood again and breathed deeply.

As Paco took a step closer to the door he lifted his shaking hand to try the lock it flew open, sending him backward a step.

The sight in front of him made no sense. Paco was speechless, his mind racing.

The boy that should have been outside looking for his dog was standing on the toilet seat, knife in hand.

Before being able to make any sound or move, the boy leapt on Paco.

Steven Archer

The knife entered Paco's neck on his left side just above the shoulder.

"AAAAAGGGGHHHHH!" Warm metallic tasting blood started to enter his throat.

He stumbled backward trying to fend off the boy with his right hand whilst reaching for the wound and the knife with the left. The shock of the pain blanked his mind.

The boy twisted the knife and then pulled it across slightly. Blood poured from Paco's artery and some had the force to spurt over the boy and into the cubicle from which he had come.

As he hit the sinks behind him and slipped on the floor (was that water or blood beneath his feet?) Paco slumped to the ground. He could only think of the fire in his neck and how strong the boy was, he was like an animal.

Pulling out the knife, the brown haired boy readjusted his grip and thrust the knife into Paco's jaw and up into his mouth, piercing the tongue and sticking in the roof of his pallet. A gurgling sound was all that could be heard now as more blood covered the boys red shirt and combat shorts.

Like holding onto a funfair ride, the boy had kept hold of Paco as he had stumbled back, slipped down and now lay on the tiled floor. Holding his grip for a few moments longer as the body of Paco twitched and contorted away its remaining life, the boy had purpose in his eyes. He looked to his right and watched the pool of blood slowly moving outward on the tiles, running away in rivulets along the edges of the tiles. The trance and the body broken, the boy stood and took one last look at Paco.

The job done, and just as the tiny face of the boy appeared from around the entrance of the toilet, his look questioning as he gazed upon himself, standing over the man who had lost his dog, it was time.

Shedding the skin of the boy was a relief; he moved to leave, as it was, indeed time.

Time to go.

*

Such a shame that one of our own should need to be eliminated.

"Yes, Master."

Yet there will always be sacrifices during such a venture as ours . . . they cannot be avoided in times such as these.

"Yes."

Now, Gadereal, come back swiftly and let us make final preparations.

"Are we ready?" Gadereal asked, not knowing if an answer would be forthcoming.

We are always ready, Gadereal, it is only ensuring that we take care before we act that takes the time. Soon, soon we can move on . . .

Chapter Twelve

The six shadowy figures had gathered in the cavernous hall once again.

All of them were together having completed the individual duties that they had been tasked to do.

They sat on the wooden bench facing forward in the dim light of the torches.

Their return had been unheralded the journey through the unforgiving halls of rocky darkness was free of both conversation and of any other being, although the oppressive surroundings and atmosphere were lost on them as they trudged to their destination, each of them looking down at the flinty pathway in front of them.

None of them spoke and none of them felt the need to. Not even to confirm to another being that they'd had success in the task that they had been chosen to carry out.

Pride was one of the many emotions that now meant nothing to any of them.

Confirmation came only from one source that mattered and had any of them failed they would have been more than aware of it by now.

In being here it was apparent to them that the next phase of the mission was about to start.

They waited for the command. They waited to serve. They wanted to serve.

As the walls seemed to undulate like rivers with the flickering of the flames from the torches, they waited in the gloom, each of them rigid and still.

It was difficult to guess just how much time had gone by before they heard the voice. Time was a concept lost upon them in this place and everyone else in this domain.

Having travelled to different years throughout human history to complete their sanctioned killings it was an irony but, again, one that none of them had concerned themselves with commenting on for centuries.

Finally, the silence was broken.

The voice was deep, thoughtful and almost seductive in tone . . .

Each of you has carried out his task to perfection.

Each of you has done as I asked and eliminated the target that had been sanctioned.

In the eons that have gone by since the Fall from Grace, we have been part of the select few who are above the others that inhabit our domain.

We have been the ones to guide the masses and the troops to ensure that they never waiver in the effort that has been required to get to this point, a point that perhaps even some of you thought could not be reached . . .

It has taken ages and has not been without trial, tribulation and loss, but you six are the selected few from the ones still able to carry out this mission, this sacred task, the one to which we have all strived to achieve.

In having our minions, ghouls, messengers and cohorts carry out thousands of deeds over thousands of years, in thousands of places, to not only create the opportunity that we now have but to also throw up the smokescreen of diversion in the human world and beyond, we have an edge that has not been contemplated or spoken of since the Fall.

In having scripture, Angelic seals and Sigils pored over and scrutinised over the Millennium that have passed, we have reached a point unique in our history. Our combined effort in action and enlightenment will bring us all success.

There was a pause and the six Fallen Angels began to realize what it was that they were about to embark upon. There were questions, but none of them asked, there were milliseconds of what could have been happiness or disbelief, yet none of them celebrated nor scorned.

Each of them now appreciated how weary they had become over the ages, how worn down and how close they had come to an apathy so deep and consuming as to be irretrievable.

The goal was so close now and yet they had tried so hard for so long to get to this objective that they had almost forgotten what it was that they strove and fought and believed for.

Their Master could, of course, sense all of their reeling emotions and questions and doubts. Now was the time to put them to rest and reach out for the ultimate prize.

The final pieces of the jigsaw have been put into place. In carrying out these specific orders that you were given, each of you has contributed to all of us standing on the threshold of a new era. A new Dark Dawn . . .

You have all carried out tasks such as these before, they also have contributed to a change in the human timelines or have acted as initiations and training. You have all endured and survived in both body and spirit.

Each of you has become used to travelling through the Portal that allows access to time but denies access to walk with the humans out of the Angelic Hours. Many have attempted to do what you have achieved and failed for many different reasons, but now you six have proved what could only be whispered of in the beginning.

The six sat and took in the information being imparted to them.

Travel through time had been available since the Fall from Grace, via the Portal but how to use it took in itself decades to understand.

Many actions (mainly unsanctioned then) had been carried out in the human world until the formation of an idea . . .

The restraint of having to inhabit certain times of the day and night whilst on Earth had been a restriction imposed by the Creator after the Fall. This simply meant that any Angel could indeed travel through human history but had to remain within a timeframe whilst there, any Angel that did not remain in the designated time span suffered the punishment of non-existence.

This meant that not only did the spirit die, as was inevitable, but also the body and all that it had achieved ceased to exist, only the Creator would have any recollection of the unfortunate victim and even then his love would not be felt.

Yetereal and Danyuel shifted slightly where they sat, not through nervousness but through anticipation. They wanted to hear the actual words confirmed for them to hear, then it would be true to them. They were experiencing a burning within them that had lain dormant for a very long time. They all were.

The flames in the torches seemed to brighten and glow more fiercely in the cavern.

The dry heat and smoke vanished.

Even the sound of the crackling fires seemed to fade.

The six listened intently.

All preparation has been made. As soon as the first of you embarks on his journey through the Portal, the Angels who have policed the night and day hours will cease to exist. They will be no more . . .

These will be the first genuine casualties of the next step in our evolution, the first casualties of this next step in the war . . .

Michael, Sachiel, Cassiel . . . Aneal, Sameal and all of the others? All of them gone?

The Guardian Angels of Day and Night, gone!

The words had the impact of physical connections to each of the six, they had heard it and had *wanted* to hear it but now this was a reality! They could move in the human world at *anytime*!

It was now that the burning within each of them was fanned like a small flame waiting to grow into an all-consuming inferno. It rose inside all of them giving each a new energy and strength they had not felt for an eternity. Each was revitalised, rejuvenated . . . reborn in hope.

But more importantly, they would have a direction.

Steven Archer

Now is our time . . .

You have all come together to become . . . The Unclean Six.

You will be the vanguard that leads the way into the human world to do, as we have always wanted . . .

We will not only destroy the physical, we will ensure that the human monkeys finally understand that there is nothing after life! They will finally realise that there is only the service that can be performed whilst on Earth! Services for our Dark Dawn!

Any who choose to serve the wrong Master have only one destiny . . .

Death and the oblivion that comes with it.

The Unclean Six bowed their heads and relished the challenge in front of them, the power within them and the satisfaction of knowing that they could soon eliminate as many of the monkeys as they wished. They rose from the bench and stood shoulder-to-shoulder keeping their heads bowed in reverence and respect of their glorious Master, who had led them to this great time, this great Prophecy.

Chapter Thirteen

Jophiel had been halfway to Sorrence's office when it had struck him. He had been running through his search thus far in his mind and it had leapt out at him from the haze.

How could he not have seen it before?

He had taken time out to check over the files that he had with him and then he had continued on to see Sorrence. His pace was quicker and he felt more certain of his findings than he did before but he knew that it would still not be enough, yet he had to try.

In back tracking at such a pace Jophiel had become aware of just how few of the individuals around him were in fact keeping him under surveillance. He ignored them as he had done so far and as he had done so on previous actions. The fact that he would always be watched played on his mind for another second before he pushed it to one side to concentrate on the discovery that he was putting together in his mind.

The cops, administrators, hookers and criminals inhabiting the corridor down which he strode and the offices about seemed, for an instance to give up their fake forms and be seen for what they truly were; minions, cohorts, troops and lackeys but, again, Jophiel put this down to his heightened state of mind and the fact that he was becoming more and more used to not only these deceptive surroundings but also his part and place within this Realm.

Sorrence sat behind his desk, chewing a large unlit cigar, whilst looking over some paperwork before him.

As he stood at the door, Jophiel's comprehension took another leap as he realised that Sorrence was always at his desk and always chewing a cigar when he had needed to see him. He wondered momentarily if he sat without motion until he was within distance of seeing him, what had been the old adage about trees falling in forests?

Sorrence looked up with a weary, glazed expression over his tight features.

They were in silence for a moment until he almost jerked into action and grunted, "Well? Whaddya want?"

Jophiel gathered his thoughts and laid out his strategy of explanation, right or wrong, he new his participation in this case hinged on this offering. If he was wrong he would be off the action and back to the waiting game he played between jobs, but if he was right . . .

Pushing some paperwork across the desk and placing his files there, Jophiel sat and took a second to appraise Sorrence. Was he a go-between or the Master?

"Well? I ain't here for the good of my health . . ." Sorrence shook his head slightly left to right and held his hands up, palms open.

"I've looked at the information available so far and want to give you a broad stroke."

If Jophiel thought that there would be a reaction from Sorrence, so far there wasn't.

"I don't want to go into great detail as that will not only come later and flesh out this lead that I have, it will also, if you think that I am wrong, give you the chance to get someone else to investigate the problem at hand. As you'll see, I'll be useless as I see no other solution and so would waste your time and . . . mine." The concept of wasting time seemed almost laughable.

Sorrence reached behind him to retrieve a dusty glass tumbler. He placed it on the desk in front of him then leaned down to his right and took a bottle of bourbon from the bottom drawer.

As he poured he spilt some on the papers under the glass, never taking his eyes from Jophiel.

"Very nice speech." He stretched back in his chair and gazed at the ceiling fan for a moment. "Now, you gonna tell me whatcha got already or do ya need to spout some more?"

Now was the time for Jophiel to take the next step.

"All of the killers were male." He blurted out the information like verbal bullet points.

"There will be six connected actions, there are the first two, three more that are being looked into that have promise and there will be a sixth." The conviction in his tone lent weight to the words.

Sorrence took a slug from the glass and gave Jophiel a "Is that all you've got," look.

"Each of the killings was carried out by one individual. In some cases the time was brief and the contract carried out quickly within the allowed time on the day or night as is written, however, there are at least two of the actions that would appear to have taken longer than would be allowed in one visit to a time span. It is usual in these instances to have two or more involved in the elimination of a given target, but I am sure that one individual did each killing, even the killings that would need repeat visits.

Each individual leaves a residual trace in time and I'm sure I'll have this theory confirmed later rather than sooner, but as this is a time critical action, I'm laying my cards down now."

Sorrence rubbed his head with both hands then smoothed his thinning hair over his scalp.

"Go on." He waved a hand, impatiently.

"This means that there are definitely six hitters on this job. This leads me to believe that not only is it organised and has been for some time but also that these guys have been around the block a few times, they're veterans."

Jophiel paused before delivering the final piece of information that he had come to trust as true.

Sorrence swirled his glass of liquor around in his right hand and stared blankly at Jophiel, awaiting the punch line and ready to react accordingly.

"I think that these six males have been designated as the Unclean Six to carry out the prophecy of the Dark Dawn." As he finished and took a step to the wall unit behind Sorrence and grabbed another glass, he did not get the response that he had expected. He had played his hand and now played it cool.

Sorrence gave a thick laugh and coughed.

Steven Archer

"Ya gotta be kiddin' me right? That's what you've come up with?"

Jophiel ignored the Captain's stare of unhappiness at him helping himself to not only the glass, but some of his booze too and poured a large measure.

"The Dark Dawn is about to begin. The Unclean Six will enter the human world, being able to travel anywhere and anytime that they wish. They will cause chaos by confirming to man that there is no life after death. Man will not be able to handle the thought of this and two things will then happen: Firstly, they will be plunged into a dark lifetime of servitude to the Dark Dawn and its Master and secondly, millions will simply give up and die. Either way, the human battleground will be lost to the Dark. Humans will either be dead or enslaved for eternity and when they are all finally gone . . ."

The phone on Sorrence's desk rang cutting Jophiel off and causing Sorrence to jerk upright in his seat.

His hand hesitated over the receiver. Jophiel took a drink and sat in the chair opposite the captain, taking in his reaction.

"Yes. Yes bu-, no. No I don't. It would take some time . . . I agree we cannot afford the tim- . . . Yes. Yes. Right away." Sorrence's hand shook as he replaced the receiver.

He sat for a moment and colour drained out of his smooth face.

"Get back to trace four. You're gonna need some help . . ."

Jophiel's brow creased and he stared at Sorrence for several moments. Just as the fidgeting Captain was about to blow his stack and shout him out of the office, Jophiel stood, drained the glass of its contents, looking at the telephone as he did.

"How many do I get?" Jophiel asked.

"One." Came the curt reply. It was obvious that the Captain was not convinced of the answer that Jophiel had supplied but had been instructed to allow him to carry on.

Rather than argue the issue, Jophiel accepted the single operative to assist.

As their eyes met before he left the room he could see something behind the anger in Sorrences eyes.

Doubt.

Chapter Fourteen

"Gabriel. I haven't seen you for some time . . ." Jophiel did not look up as the woman entered the trace room and strode purposefully toward him, ignoring every other being in the room and every piece of equipment.

A smile stretched across the oval face of the black haired woman accentuating the fullness of her lips.

Taking a small step nearer to Jophiel's desk she raised her arms from her sides gracefully.

"You knew it was me in a second, didn't you? Even in *this* form . . ." Gabriel slowly indicated to her tall, slender, athletic body with a sweeping motion from shoulders to thighs. "I thought that I might have given you cause for at least a moments pause."

Leaning back in his chair, Jophiel looked at Gabriel, slowly taking in the raven black hair, the almond eyes, the slender figure, long legs and the ever present smile . . . but what was behind the smile? Jophiel did not want to linger and so would have to wait to find out.

"It's not the body that I recognise, although you have really outdone yourself this time, really, you have . . . it's your aura. I'd know it anywhere . . . I always have and always will. Using a female form is new but then you always did like your surprise entrances." He saw Gabriel's brown eyes harden as he spoke. "I should have guessed that they would give me you to work with, even after the last time."

Gabriel walked forward, took a chair and turned it to face Jophiel. Sitting slowly and crossing her legs even slower, she replied in a terse voice.

"It doesn't matter about last time. This is all that matters now." She wafted a hand in the air to indicate her surrounding's. "I was chosen to work with you and so we must make the most of it, there must be good reason for it as always. I have been briefed on your theory and the investigation so far . . . interesting isn't it and somewhat prophetic that it should be you and I who track the Unclean Six. I have to say that although I do not completely believe your theory as yet, I am keen to be converted to your thinking and assist in any way that I can." The disarming smile that crept across Gabriel's face was obviously practised and lost on Jophiel.

"It doesn't matter what you do or do not believe. We have a job to do. Until we are told to redeploy elsewhere, we must pursue this action with conviction. Anything else would be a weakness."

Gabriel clasped her hands together and studied Jophiel. He was a little different than she remembered. He had earned respect in the deeds that he had managed to carry out with his limitations as an ex-human, an ex-primate, but now he seemed beyond confident. He seemed assured, bold.

"Of course, you are right. Now, tell me. How do we proceed?"

"It couldn't be easier." Jophiel returned to the file on his desk.

After perusing the activity in the room around her and checking out the ever-changing screens, Gabriel asked nonchalantly, "well?"

"We wait. As soon as any or all of the Six enter the human world we will detect it and so follow to intercept them." Jophiel nodded toward the three large screens.

They sat in silence as the room full of people busied themselves.

"They have the ability to cross Day and Night . . . what do you think has become of the Guardian Angels?" Gabriel spoke in a hushed almost reverent tone, which was most unlike him.

Jophiel understood the gravity of the question and paused before answering, giving himself plenty of time for thought.

"I think that for them the end has arrived. I think that without realising it, they have fulfilled the prophecy and will now try to influence the balance between the Light and the

Dark. They will stop at nothing to ensure their success and that success can mean only one thing for man . . ."

Gabriel nodded slowly she had known the answer before she had heard it.

"Then the primates are about to suffer as they have never suffered before . . ."

"*Humans*" countered Jophiel quickly, deliberately avoiding eye contact.

Gabriel's thoughtful expression changed to a wide-eyed smile.

"Humans, yes of course, humans. They really have no idea of what could be about to befall them . . . you still have feeling toward the world of man . . ." Gabriel prodded the issue taking a delight in the opportunity to do so.

"No . . . no I don't *feel* anything for the human world anymore . . . for better or for worse. But that doesn't negate the fact that I used to be one of them and so do have a respect for them, as well you know."

Gabriel sat back and smiled, deciding that there was nothing further to gain from the encounter, as Jophiel *was* different. Holding her hands palm down she began to study her long nails carefully.

Jophiel took hold of a thick file of data that was to his right and threw it into Gabriel's lap. As the file landed, it caught Gabriel unaware and the long legs unwrapped themselves as the paperwork fell to the floor.

"Sorry. Thought you'd like to bone up on events. "Jophiel said without a hint of humour.

Gabriel stared at the papers and thought better of any comment. She huffed instead.

Chapter Fifteen

It had only been a few short hours since Gadereal, Armean, Danyuel, Azazeal, Yetereal and Tureal had sat and listened intently to their final instructions and yet the power that each of them felt inside had swollen to a point as to be an almost physical entity to be used for their own purposes.

Beyond confidence, far from arrogance they all simply knew deep within themselves that they had indeed been chosen from the many in service to carry out this most sacred of missions and they each knew that they would not fail either themselves or their Master.

Now they stood in front of the portal waiting the time to go into the human world.

A large granite block wall surrounded the cobbled courtyard, in which they stood, forty feet high and very imposing. It was like standing on the inside of a very large, heavily fortified castle turret.

Above them grey, heavy clouds sped across the gloomy sky, pushed by a wind that whipped and rushed creating all manner of sounds.

The occasional lightning bolt spread its tendrils across the greyness and illuminated the figures standing below for a brief moment under the flash.

They all stood silently looking at the portal, the time for entry getting closer.

There was no anticipation only assuredness, no concern only belief.

The portal was as simple as it was powerful. Set back in the huge blocks of the circular wall, it was twenty feet at its widest point. Looking for intent and purpose like the entrance gate to a castle keep, its massive wooden doors were thousands of years old. The bolts, hinges and lock had all rusted with time but were as sturdy and strong as the door itself.

Around the door were granite blocks of a slightly lighter grey than the rest of the wall with a spattering of what seemed to be a crystalline substance that reflected white and purple when the lightening struck above in the sky.

Each of these blocks, although smaller than the others in the wall was still at least two feet in length.

All of them had been hand carved with an individual letter, symbol or word from the old text that the Angels had used long ago. Read right to left by those that still possessed the skill it revealed a mantra. The markings came in and out of focus as the lightening flashed, becoming part of the moment only to fall back into the shadows when darkness reclaimed the skies.

Finally, the massive wooden doors began to creak and groan as if under immense pressure. They slowly parted to reveal a shaft of light so bright that it illuminated every fissure and crevice that it fell upon as it widened.

The doors opened further and the brilliant light of white, blue and purple spread further into the courtyard, flashes of light like static electricity glowed and grew as the doors completed their movement until fully open.

The Six had not moved but did sway against the force of the wind that pushed out from the light, from inside the portal.

A rushing sound began to compliment the wind, the light and the glare that emanated from the doorway. Tentacles of the coloured light reached out and seemed to beckon them forward but for another instant they stood firm, it wasn't quite time to enter.

As the crescendo carried on the Six raised their arms to the heavens as one and shouted the mantra, then moved forward into the light, embracing it and becoming a part of it.

Once all of the Six had entered the doorway the two colossal doors slammed shut behind them shaking the wall of the courtyard and sending dust and dirt drifting and falling to the ground.

The noise had gone.

The light had gone.

The Unclean Six had gone.

Steven Archer

The red brick alleyway with wrought iron fire escapes and grimy, sightless windows was the same as every other in the city . . . until tonight.

The brightness of the mid afternoon sun seemed to dull a little.

The carefree atmosphere of the weekend seemed to get a little heavier.

The air cracked, as newspapers began to float and swirl, whilst empty drinks cans rolled to find cover.

It only took an instant. Anyone who had been passing the alley would have missed it unless they were staring right down into it at the time from the sidewalk some two hundred feet away.

The purple white flash was over as quickly as it had begun. Smoke wafted up to the tops of the tenements roofs in big bulbous clouds.

The loud crack that echoed around the walls died out and could easily have been mistaken for a car back firing.

Once the brightness, the noise and the smoke had disappeared, all that was left was the Six figures.

After an initial second to acclimatise to their surroundings they began to look around, taking in the environment and all that it contained.

Danyuel blinked and looked skyward, shielding his eyes against the sunshine.

Gadereal brushed down his clothing as if trying to remove dust.

Tureal turned and stared down the alley to the entrance to the city that awaited them. The city of humans. The first city of human primates that they would visit and destroy. He smiled and glanced at each of his colleagues who stopped taking in the immediate area and the clothing that had been chosen for the task and returned his look and his grim smile.

"How the fuck did you guys get in here? Ah sure as hell hopes that you ain't thinkin' about tryin' ta take ma gear . . . where'd ya come from?" The derelicts voice and questions were strained.

He stared with wide red-rimmed eyes that were glazed over from the booze that he had consumed at the six figures now standing in close proximity to not just him but all of his pathetic worldly possessions. He was nervous and scared but tried not to show it, he was wishing that he hadn't said anything at all now, maybe they would have just gone away.

Danyuel looked down at the filthy tramp wrapped in several ripped and holed blankets and his dark expression and piercing gaze lightened visibly into a laugh.

A laugh that got louder with every breath.

The tramp shuffled up into a seated position and thought about joining in with the unmade joke but decided against it, instead he simply looked from one of the men to the next, beginning to fear that he was about to receive yet another beating at the hands of a group of suburban straight men.

Danyuel ceased his laughter and cleared his throat. "It seems appropriate somehow that the lowest that this world has to offer, the ugliest, loneliest monkey of all should be the first to choose his side . . ." Turning to face the tramp Danyuel asked; "do you believe?"

The vagrant could not work out what was going on but knew without doubt that the answer that he was about to give would determine his immediate future.

"I don't know what you mean. Believe in what?"

Danyuel took a step forward and looked down on the filthy, disgusting man. "Exactly." He said in a quiet, firm tone and raised his right hand.

As he did, the man was lifted from the ground as if pulled by an invisible puppeteer. As he rose against the brick wall, his feet kicking uselessly in the air for a purchase that was not there, his eyes began to bleed. Tears of crimson streaked down his cheeks and splashed drops onto his grimy brown jacket. He began to scream as his head began to pulse and throb.

The louder the scream the harder the throbbing pressure became inside of his head, causing his veins to stand out on his forehead and face like snakes on sand.

Danyuel raised his arm above his head and then stopped. The tramp waved his arms and legs in a futile effort to move from

Steven Archer

his position fifteen feet above the deck. His body temperature climbed as his blood started to boil in his arteries, his heart pushing the heated life force around his body in booming pulses, the pressure becoming so great from within that the blood coming from his eyes flowed quicker but also spouted in tiny arcs, spraying the alley below. His screams got louder and more panicked, all sense was lost to him as all he could focus on was the excruciating pain that he was in.

Tilting his head slightly to the left, Danyuel took one more casual look at his prey and then clenched his fist.

The tramps head crumpled inward like a paper bag devoid of air. Blood squelched from the open but restricted orifices of his mouth, nose and ears. He hung limply in the air above the floor, his screams silenced, his puppeteer bored.

As Danyuel wiped his hands together as if brushing dust from them the inert figure dropped at pace to the floor with a bone breaking crunch and came to rest at a grotesque angle, lifeless red rimmed eyes asking a silent question of his attacker. Why?

"It's time that we really got started with our task." Danyuel said as he strode off toward the waiting, unsuspecting city.

The rest moved off after him exchanging looks and grim smiles.

Azazeal approached the dead vagrant and nudged him with his left foot, watching as the corpse lolled over. "They really are weak aren't they?" He said to himself and to nobody as he too walked with a purpose away down the alley.

Chapter Sixteen

As Gabriel studied the information within the file, Jophiel looked under his eyebrows at him. He hadn't quite gotten used to the female form that had been adopted yet but that was simply a matter of adapting and wouldn't take too long.

His mind drifted back over the encounters that he'd had with the Angel Gabriel. He remembered how he had been in awe of him on their first action together, albeit that his part was small, he had still been very much aware of the reputation that Gabriel had, whilst carrying out his duties.

During the time of the casting out of the Fallen Angels, the rebels, Gabriel had been at the forefront. He had been resolute in his duty and steadfast in his service. Once all of the rebels had been outcast and Lucifer had taken the form of Satan, Gabriel had been instrumental in setting the boundaries and conditions of the Angelic Hours, using the Seals and Scripts available to him to ensure the Day and Night would be secure.

Gabriel had, indeed, been one of the first to volunteer to be part of the Angelic Watch, serving with distinction for many eons.

Now, his skills and abilities were used elsewhere and had been for a time longer than Jophiel was aware of, taking on individual actions and seeing them to resolution.

Jophiel had encountered Gabriel in the time since that first nervous meeting and watched as Gabriel seemed to change slightly as he himself grew more accustomed to the new lease of life that he had been chosen for, so Gabriel seemed to tire of it. Not that another soul had noticed it. Only Jophiel had and this was why they now had the delicate relationship that they had for each other, a begrudging respect had formed, although the last incident had almost seen both of them in peril that could not be escaped.

"Thought that I'd find ya here." Sorrence boomed as he barged into the room and walked directly toward them. He looked at Gabriel, raised his eyebrows and shook his head a little from side to side. Jophiel and Gabriel shared a split second of silent humour between them.

"It's happened. Don't even start with the *I told you so* looks and get to it." Sorrence boomed and pointed a finger in Jophiel's direction.

Jophiel didn't even consider casting the look as he was more concerned about the fact that he and Gabriel had not moved from their station and had not detected any unusual activity on any of the boards, when each of the screens lit with a red glow and a droning alarm tone began to sound.

If Jophiel was perturbed by Sorrence's anticipation, he didn't show it and Gabriel seemed to fend off a yawn at the drama of it all, perhaps for Sorrence's benefit.

"It is the Six. The data gleaned from combing through records of every time frame that was disrupted by the deaths that have occurred have yielded some interesting facts, but events have advanced beyond deduction now, the time of the Unclean Six is now. Follow me." Sorrence took his hands from his hips, turned on his heels and walked back toward the entrance to Trace Room Four.

"Aren't you going to tell us?" Gabriel ventured.

"Tell you what? Didn't you just hear what I said?" Sorrence countered in a grim fashion, even his stretched features looked a little worn.

"About events overtaking deduction, yes." Gabriel continued unabashed. "But what was the info, I'd like to know out of interest." Trying to keep pace with the Captain in his high heels was a new challenge for Gabriel and he looked at his feet as he spoke.

Sorrence stopped in his tracks.

Gabriel did the same to avoid him and Jophiel almost knocked into him.

"Change." Sorrence said with a stern look at Gabriel.

"Why? I like this form."

"It's not going to make a difference with this action now, so change." Sorrence spat.

"If it doesn't make a difference, why should I bother? As I said, I like this form." Gabriel returned.

The Captain sighed and said under his breath: "We really don't have time for this."

Then to Gabriel again: "This is the time of the Prophecy. This is the time of the Unclean Six. I don't want there to be any doubt on your part as to the gravity of this situation, you know what could lie ahead. I want you to realize that these chosen ones are not going to be easy. I do not want them to have any doubt that they are up against *you*. *Gabriel*. Not a female *form* of Gabriel. Gabriel, straight up and down. Got it?" Sorrence emphasised his point by leaning into Gabriel slightly, who returned his stare with composure but also with understanding.

"Alright," was all that he said in return.

"Good, now let's get on with it." Sorrence carried on walking down the corridor, waiting for Gabriel to morph before carrying on with his talking.

Jophiel followed behind Gabriel and watched as he began to shake as he walked.

It started slowly and then increased to a judder encapsulating his entire body, although it did not interfere with his forward motion.

The shaking became faster and faster until it was more like a rapid vibration moving every particle and atom of Gabriel's being.

Jophiel skipped a step behind him to avoid any possible contact. He had seen a being get in the way of a transmutation and it had not been pretty.

Gabriel was fluctuating so quickly as to blur at the edges of his body. Colours moulded and mixed, limbs contracted and retracted. His head shook so much as to give the appearance of spinning at great speed.

Gabriel had become a whirlwind of movement.

When the agitation reached its peak and a low hum became audible, so the transformation began.

Steven Archer

From the form of a woman there were millisecond flashes of a winged man, stretching and extending before that body also changed into that of a man. The activity began to slow and what had taken mere seconds was accomplished. The hum stopped. The shaking ceased.

Gabriel had reached his true form.

Once he had changed totally into a tall, lean raven haired man with angular features and an arrow straight nose, he turned back to Jophiel and winked an almond eye, then turned back to fall into stride with Sorrence who had ignored the whole spectacle but knew when to begin speaking again.

"Now that we're straight on this, let's get on. The actions that happened over the six time frames were, of course, all connected. These events have led to a focal eventuality that has allowed the Dark to eliminate all of the Angelic Watch and send the Six into the realm of man without restriction. Each of the Six has been able to carry out an action that has meant remaining in the human world for longer periods than usual. They have gained a kind of immunity over the expanse of time and the exposure that they have had in the human world, but this final connecting of dots has added to the power that they have and pulled them, inevitably together to fulfil the Prophecy."

"You sound as if you were expecting it." Jophiel said and instantly regretted the statement.

After sighing, Sorrence said: "Of course we're aware of it. Every soul is aware of it, but time distorts . . . It's simply that nobody thought that it would happen so soon."

Jophiel couldn't help but ponder for a second the fact that some thought that this had happened too soon, when in fact the Light and Dark, the Truth and the Lie had been operating in tandem for a time beyond comprehension.

"This is the time that we have prepared for, what you two have prepared for." Sorrence said as he stopped again in the corridor outside a closed office door.

"Even if you haven't been aware of it," he indicated to Jophiel. "You have been readying yourself for this." He dropped his head for a second and both Gabriel and Jophiel caught a glimpse of a side to Sorrence they had not witnessed before. They exchanged a quick look and Gabriel shrugged.

"Now it's time to send you on your way." Sorrence reached for the handle to the door next to which he stood and turned it.

*

Sorrence had opened the unremarkable door and allowed Jophiel and Gabriel to enter, without another word he closed the door behind them leaving them alone in the darkened room.

There was no discernable source for the little light that did permeate the room, which was totally empty.

The only other part of the room was a second door at the far end of the space in front of them. They knew that Sorrence had gone and they also knew that they must make their own way from now on. Neither spoke for a few moments, each running through the last few hours and indeed the last few centuries, trying to piece together individual histories that had led them to this place and time.

"Have you ever seen anything this like this?" Jophiel asked in a hushed tone.

Looking straight into his eyes, Gabriel said: "No."

"Have you ever been involved in anything as . . . serious as this?"

Gabriel raised his eyebrows.

"Sorry . . . stupid question." Jophiel walked after Gabriel as he moved toward the second door.

As with the room, it was unremarkable, also. Set slightly back from the wall itself in a small alcove, the frame was wide, wooden and a deep brown with age. It was plain and so helped to highlight what little there was to look at on the door itself.

This was eight feet tall and four feet wide. It had a simple brass ring on the right for opening and no hinges could be seen.

The only oddity was the carved symbols and emblems that adorned it.

Steven Archer

They covered the doors surface in there hundreds and had been carved by hand long ago. Some were so deep and old that dust had settled and become part of the material.

There was no pattern to the way in which they had been carved, and in some cases scratched, into the wood.

Gabriel ran his fingertips over some of the elaborate designs.

"I have heard about this . . . a long time ago. I didn't think that it could be true back then, but over the years in-between I have heard other whispers and stories of the door that has the sacred seals inscribed on it."

Gabriel looked at Jophiel and carried on as Jophiel gazed back at the door and listened intently.

"There have been accounts of a doorway to the human world that is unlike the ones used to carry out our actions and investigations. A door that has had ancient scripture and sacred seals added to it over hundreds of thousands of years as they were discovered, either by accident or with intent, by others who have gone into the human world. Even I was not given the text that was distributed on the Earth as a reminder of what had happened." Gabriel's eyes seemed to glisten with a new edge as he took in the writing, "I can't quite understand how these fit together, it would take an age to decipher each symbol and put it into the greater context, even for me."

Gabriel stood and stared, taking in the enormity of what was before him.

Jophiel tried to grasp what his comrade was saying. He too had heard of these yarns, but being that much farther down the pecking order, had heard mere snippets.

Resting his forehead in his fingertips, Gabriel took a moment to comprehend what they viewed.

"In this darkened room, forgotten and left for longer than anyone can remember, this has been hidden. Not guarded and so lost and not celebrated and so easily denied . . . this . . . this assemblage of written treasure is the actual word of God from the time of the casting down of Lucifer, His feelings. His anger, His disbelief, His regret, His angst and His fury over what occurred, recorded to perhaps unburden Himself or perhaps to let others know the depth of the revolution that took place."

Jophiel shook his head in wonderment, staggered by this simple door with the actual word of God upon it, but heartfelt and personal words, words that could reveal emotion . . . feeling.

"What does it mean? What do we do?" Jophiel asked.

"We go through. We go through into the world of man and stop the Six. This is the way through . . . His way through. We must try to save the humans, perhaps when the prophecy is over once and for all, this can all be put into context and all remaining sides take a step forward in true harmony."

Jophiel nodded and took a deep breath. "Okay then. Let's do it."

His thoughts still raced at a speed that made thinking difficult, so he focussed on the task at hand; stopping the Six. Then this could start to make sense as man and the Light moved on. The Dark had brought the time and events upon them to seize an opportunity made over the length of time itself and born of a poisoning hatred that would enslave man for the rest of eternity should they succeed.

Gabriel took hold of the ring tenderly, then increased his grip and began to pull the door open.

Chapter Seventeen

Having exited the alleyway, it had not taken too long for the Angels of the Prophecy to split up and begin the mission with which they had been tasked.

Although each of them had found it strange to be in a human form, even though they had all been on many visits to the human world and taken various human incarnations, they had never had their forms imposed upon them. Vanity meant nothing to them, of course, and as long as the body functioned well enough to be able to carry out their purposes they were all content but there was more security in choosing the form that is to be taken.

The city was as grey as the sky above it and just as distant.

The traffic flowed ever onward in streams to various destinations.

The buildings were filled the activities of the working day.

And the people went on about their business, the vast majority of them an island in their own right, isolated, alone and happy to be this way.

Gadereal and Armean had paired up and now stood on the sidewalk in front of a smoke glass windowed skyscraper. The edifice had an almost tomb like appearance to it.

The sign in front of the main entrance hall at the top of a flight of overly wide steps rotated to ensure that everyone could see it from every angle.

The Bassingburn Bank was one of, if not the major player in the financial world market of the Pacific Rim. Its resources and assets ran into billions of dollars and its annual turnover was as high as many European countries.

Armean began to walk up the steps to the large glass doors, his overcoat flapping in the slight breeze.

He paused and looked back at Gadereal who was taking in the milling pedestrians, one at a time in the way that an auctioneer would appraise a fake painting.

"They really are simple beings aren't they." He stated rather than asked.

Armean did not reply but understood what his companion was saying clearly.

"They truly do not understand the opportunity that was afforded them. They barely seem to even have life anymore. Most of these . . . sheep seem only to . . . exist."

Gadereal took one more look around and then caught up with Armean on the steps and grinned tightly.

"All the more reason for us to release them from this torment and where better to start than here?"

"Yes," replied Armean. "We have much to do and this place is only the beginning, let's get on."

They turned and took the steps two at a time, their cold eyes not meeting with any of the people around them. It was as if they were invisible to all and sundry, an irony that was not lost on either of them.

*

Seven miles to the east, Danyuel and Azazeal were having similar thoughts to Gadereal.

As they had ridden on the subway, each of them had looked on at the monkeys with contempt and disgust in equal measure.

Neither of them could wait to start the cleansing process that would remove so many of these pathetic beings from existence or have them serve their Master and them.

After exiting the subway at the required stop, they had made straight for the vast complex in the heart of the metropolis. It was one of the countries largest televisual empires, supplying more than half of the nation with the mind-numbing programming that had helped raise the laziness of those that watched, had helped dismantle the communities that had existed before this invention had and made apathy the norm for the majority

Steven Archer

that tuned in each day, making the primates slaves to it and boxed in their own homes by the leaders who wanted placid conformists as voters. The apes had truly speeded up their own downfall and the anticipation was almost as sweet as the taste that dominance over them all would bring for the Six.

Once the message that they had was played to the millions of zombies watching, the word would spread quickly indeed.

*

The room was dark as the light was out. In the gloom of the office, Yetereal and Tureal sat on their haunches in two of the corners. Yetereal rubbed one of his small horns that sat just above his eyes, lost in concentration.

"Capture your form again Tureal, this is not the time to be seen for what we are. Not yet." Yetereal said without moving.

Tureal turned his head and looked at Yetereal in the shadows for a moment, then closed his eyes and the horns that were part of his true form slowly moulded themselves back into the face that he had been told to take. It had been a long while since they had entered the communications conglomerates offices and found the office to stay in until all had left. The building that housed the company that supplied telecommunications and internet services to millions of humans all over the country was enormous and held within much of the technology that allowed the stupid monkeys to while their time away in the useless pursuit of online pleasure or babbling to one another about the mundane issues that were strewn across their pathetic lives.

Entering the facility had been so easy as to almost be an insult to the two of them, but it did mean that so far there had been no chance of any problem and they knew that their Master wanted this quest to be faultless.

In a couple of hours it would be time to begin the re-education of the human race and witness the storm that it brought.

Rubbing his now smooth forehead, Tureal thought of what it would be like to see the human primate's struggle with the enormity of their new existence with the new revelation that was upon them.

Chapter Eighteen

As Jophiel stepped out of what was blinding light swirling with faint hues before him, he began to see a blurred, dark figure. A shadow in the purples, pinks and blues that streaked around him, the colours actually making him feel warm, which he knew was only his mind playing tricks on him.

As he took a few more steps through the shining aura, he became aware of two things:

Firstly that it was, of course, Gabriel who stood before him and he seemed dazed, with a far off look in his eye although he were trying to see into the future via the brick wall that he faced and secondly that the positive sensation he realised that he had felt whilst within the aura he moved through upon entering the door was wearing off like an old comfortable jacket being hung back up not to be worn for a long time.

These thoughts were stupid and useless.

Jophiel chastised himself for getting carried away for a moment in the transportation to the human world but just as he was about to disregard the feelings that he had he remembered what it was about them that made him want to push them away so quickly. It was not the fact that he had a role to perform, a duty to carry out. It was because, for a moment he remembered what it was like to be human again.

Shaking these thoughts off like cobwebs, he looked attentively at Gabriel and understood that he should wait until he was addressed as Gabriel was receiving instruction.

Usually when on a mission, a sensation very similar to the hairs on the back of his neck rising would warn him that he was about to be contacted telepathically. The passing of information in this manner was commonplace for the agents that had a task to complete and were always brief and to the point. The agent receiving the data simply stood and took on the look of someone lost in a personal reverie whilst it occurred. It had taken Jophiel a couple of times to get the hang of the process and at first he had seen it as something of an intrusion, but now he took it in his stride.

Jophiel took the time to view his surroundings having first of all checked that his pistol was in place in his shoulder holster, a hangover from his human life.

The room was large and vacuous. Dust particles could be seen wafting down in front of the shafts of light that shone through the windows of the warehouse in which he stood. There were only some empty boxes at the far end of the floor space, other than that it was bare.

He wandered slowly to the double door that had a bar across and chains around securing it from intruders. He closed in on the gap between the doors and looked outside.

He could just make out a side street with red brick walls, trash cans and a streetlamp at the end of a wall that ended where, presumably, the street would begin. Before he could adjust his position to gain a closer look, the doors flew open and outward, startling him into taking a defensive stance a step back from where he had stood.

Gabriel shook his head and a raised index finger at him in mock disgust.

"There was a time when I wouldn't have gotten within ten feet of you. You're either losing your touch or you're reflecting again on the old life." Gabriel said as he moved into the alley, standing sideways on and leaning out to view more and more of the locality in which they found themselves.

Jophiel brushed the comment aside, he knew better than to rise to Gabriel's baiting about his living years.

"Well?" was all that he said as he too looked down the alley but in the opposite direction to Gabriel.

Gabriel looked at Jophiel for a second and then flinched into action, beginning to walk at pace to the end of the alley and the street ahead, his footsteps sounding gently on the paving.

"We need to get to the bank." He said over his shoulder. "Please take the hat off, it doesn't suit you at all." He added.

Jophiel responded by reaching for his head, being unaware that he had been wearing a hat since leaving the door he removed the brown baseball cap and threw it down. He didn't like hats. The rest of the ensemble that he had been given seemed comfortable enough, jeans a long sleeved grey top and a short denim jacket.

Looking up he saw that Gabriel was dressed similarly.

"The bank." Jophiel repeated.

"Yes. They've paired off and the nearest two are in a bank in something called the financial district. I know the way. We can be there shortly."

They entered the street and neither looked out of place in the bustling concrete sprawl that was all around them.

Both fell silent as Jophiel took up position just behind Gabriel, they surveyed their new environment as they walked, each checking for not only threat but also absorbing as much as they could to become comfortable in the new place as soon as possible.

"What's the plan?" Jophiel asked after several blocks.

"Simple as usual. Find them and vaporise them." Gabriel communicated the words without emotion and Jophiel processed them the same way.

Chapter Nineteen

Gadereal and Armean had made it to the Bassingburn Bank without incident. They had blended into the crowds without any problem at all, the world in which they now inhabited carried on moving forward in time and had no effect on them whatsoever.

Both of them had been oblivious to the people, the noise and the hustle.

The entrance to the bank's main building was massive and immaculate, in keeping with its monolithic external appearance.

There were four aisles that led from the main entrance doors to the hall that then allowed the dispersal of personnel to various parts of the building and to the various roles that they performed therein.

At the beginning of each aisle was an airport style metal detector gate and x-ray check with a security guard stationed by them, observing the entering masses with the same glazed expression between them.

Gadereal and Armean did not even hesitate in their route into the building. They mingled easily with the throng and nobody paid them any heed as they passed through the detectors.

Neither of them had given any cause to be noticed, their appearance was smart and simple. Dark suits and ties covered by calf length black overcoats and black shoes.

As they stood and waited for the lift to the blue zone of the business, which contained all of the operating systems, file back ups, security protocol computers and data retrieval storage and assessment, they perused the hall and the humans within it with dispassionate looks.

The journey up in the lift with three other people took mere seconds but the close proximity to the chattering apes distracted Gadereal a little. He found the primates to be an irritation at best. Armean caught his eye and held his gaze for a second as if to calm him.

The number indicator lit orange and the low sound of the bell indicated the exit from the already opening, silver doors.

Gadereal and Armean allowed the three people to leave and noticed immediately the size of the floor that they were now on as they slowly left the lift to stand side by side as the doors swished closed behind them.

The floor space was divided into five sections and although each of them was laid out in an open plan format, to give the illusion of space, this was countered by the two guards that stood at the front of each section, discreetly standing and sitting as if trying to blend in.

It was obvious that they were not there to catch the employees doing anything untoward but to give them piece of mind in the middle security level that they worked on.

Without a word, the two accomplices walked toward the first of the portioned areas that had a large sign indicating that it was the Operating Systems Section, hanging from the ceiling.

As Armean entered swiftly and passed the guards before they had the chance to react to him he headed for the nearest bank of computers. Gadereal who stepped to the closest guard and placed his hand on his chest squarely caught the turning guards in mid movement.

A loud crackle of electricity and a brilliant flash of light erupted simultaneously at the contact and sent the guard flying off the floor for eight feet, until his flight was stopped suddenly by the partition to the zone.

He impacted with a thud and crumpled to the deck in a motionless heap of twisted limbs.

Heads began to turn and the other guards started to move forward to Gadereal.

"Don't move!" He shouted at the top of his voice.

Most of the people paused, looking scared and bewildered except for the nearest guard who carried on and reached for his side arm.

With a rapid twist and an outstretched hand, Gadereal sent a bolt of energy from his right palm straight at the man. It struck him in the centre of his chest and sent him spinning and reeling backward onto the floor near his fallen comrade. He did not move anymore, only the faint wisp of smoke that rose from his wound gave an indication as to what had happened.

Armean studied the computers in front of him, ignoring the events that unfolded as if removed from them.

Among the shrieks and gasps Gadereal spoke again.

"Now, every one of you pay attention this time. Do not move or you will die!"

He looked around the room as the tears began to flow and the colour began to drain from the faces of the people who could still not quite grasp what their eyes were telling them. Even the remaining guards stood still in the face of such a display of unusual power.

Armean satisfied himself that he had found the point that he wanted and placed his hand upon the cool metal of the whirring computer.

An energy surge caused glaring sparks of electricity, light and smoke to emit from the machinery, which quickly became inoperative.

He repeated the same procedure, scrutinising the machinery, moving from zone to zone, stepping past the humans, who flinched and avoided his gaze as he caused the acrid smell of burning plastic and metal to fill the air as he shut down each piece of equipment that he chose to.

In doing so, data from the millions of customers was lost to oblivion.

Account details, monies in credit or debt were wiped out and all information from every transaction vanished and thrice removed back-up systems with individual lock down files also evaporated.

Gadereal kept an eye on the people who stared stunned with wide expressions as Armean carried out his work.

"It's done. This is the beginning. They can never recover the lost information." Armean smiled grimly as Gadereal nodded his approval.

They moved off back to the lift in unison, leaving the gaping mouths, the blank expressions and the ringing phones behind them.

*

Danyuel and Azazeal had taken the exact same steps to control the people and the scene at the television production studios and offices that their accomplices had.

There had been some who had thought that bravery was a better option than living and so they had paid the price, the cheapness reflected in the faces of the two Angels.

One second they were living people with choices, hopes and dreams and the next second they were dead simply to turn to dust.

The serene expressions of their assailants gave rise to the terror that each of the people unfortunate enough to be caught up in the unfolding events.

They had been dispatched in the same manner as all of the others, with a pulse of energy that extinguished life instantly. One flash and it was over.

The corpses of the fallen lay where they had been struck, the crimson of the blood a contrast to the grey of the smoke that rose ever upward like a departing soul from each victim.

Danyuel in particular had known that there would be some of the humans who would want to try and halt them and although he took no pleasure in eliminating the monkeys stupid enough to try, even after an albeit hollow warning not to, there was a flash of relish on his calm features as he did so.

It hadn't taken too long to destroy the transmitting equipment for all of the stations both cable and satellite feeds for all of the broadcasters and some that provided for the outer areas and boroughs of the massive, sprawling city.

Hacking into the system had been child's play, so that no signal could be sent and would not be able to for a considerable time.

Danyuel had placed his hands upon the main servers and watched the monitor to the side of it dispassionately as words, text, codes and commands flashed on the screen at such a speed as to be a blur to the naked eye. Once he had accomplished his goal, he looked down the system and planted a code so intricate that it would take the simean's years to even understand how to approach it, even using their limited technology. Starting from scratch would be a better option than that for them.

Only one channel had been left to transmit.

The emergency broadcast channel that was frequently tested in the early hours to ensure that it was fully functioning, had been retrieved from its buried programme within the data stream and was now being utilised by the Unclean Six for their own purposes.

As hundreds of thousands of frustrated viewers punched buttons on remote controls with rigid fingers and rising anger, they stumbled across the only channel that was not displaying rolling static like a polar blizzard.

It was crystal clear and had one simple message:

Today is the day.
Today is the day of Prophecy.
The choice is yours.

THERE IS NO GOD.

Bear witness to what is to follow.

It was simple, direct and informative but still Azazeal felt deep within himself that there would be many who just would not get the context even in this basic form. He knew the Master was aware of this but his angst, although slight, was there within. There would be those who would not believe it and those who would laugh it off as a bad joke. Some may even think it to be terrorists.

There were, however, some that would be stricken by the words and believe in them completely.

They were the ones that would spread the word somehow. Even in the isolating communications near blackout that would surround them, the word would spread . . .

And so would the fear.

*

The final pair of the Six had met with no opposition, save for two goons passing themselves off as security guards.

The InterNational Communications Corporation that operated the facility which housed the vast complex and the mega-machines therein ran and monitored the feeds for the internet capability and mobile phones communications for the city and large areas of the country did not man the building with too many staff at this time of night. The security systems were state of the art and, of course, although there was the threat of terrorist's trying to close down or damage the operations the likely hood seemed remote.

Entry was secure for all staff only and during office hours there were many more security guards about the building, checking the monitors and detectors.

It had been straightforward for them to gain access because to everyone and everything that looked at them or searched them or scanned them, in those moments they were employees of the InterNational Communications Corporation and so above reproach. It was too easy, so easy, in fact that whilst entering the facility both of them had to focus on maintaining a high level of concentration.

After finding an appropriate and vacant storeroom Yetereal and Tureal had hidden for a short while until the staff had gone home for the day.

They were beyond most of the security and only the two people patrolling the halls had been unlucky enough to come across them.

The guards weren't even given the opportunity to surrender or run, they were killed, quickly and without emotion, like the irritating insects that they were and so, they now lay with unseeing eyes as Yetereal and Tureal went about their business undisturbed.

Neither of them passed any comments as they resolutely carried out the first stage of the mission.

Along the rows upon rows of servers and databanks lined in several aisles that filled the air-conditioned room to its capacity, they located the necessary equipment. Once they had ensured that the message was posted so that every workstation, home computer and laptop received it, Yetereal then configured and injected a virus which would then freeze their words on that screen, making sure that the station being used was unable to perform another action or command that the user tried to input.

The message was the same that was transmitted on the emergency broadcast channel:

Today is the day.
Today is the day of Prophecy.
The choice is yours.

THERE IS NO GOD.

Bear witness to what is to follow.

Once it was posted, all other systems were crashed and the virus activated sent at speed through the communications and internet world infecting all that it came across, the machinery was then rendered useless causing untold numbers of people either working or using the net at home to scratch their heads in puzzlement and gradually get angrier and angrier.

The two companions left the sterile room and moved silently to the next floor, taking the stairs they located the second room that contained the telecommunications systems.

The room itself was similar to the one that they had just exited with only slightly fewer banks and aisles of humming equipment. These allowed the mobile telephone users to make calls, text messages or use web service connections across the same area as the Internet services, which was millions of users covering all of the major networks.

Once the correct machine was located, it was a matter of moments before Yetereal was able to guarantee that every person got one final message, which was the same again, before their mobile telephone was rendered useless, stuck on that screen.

With a satisfied nod and pursed lips, Yetereal turned to Tureal who remained expressionless.

There was no need to utter a word, they both sensed that theirs and the others' missions were being completed as planned. They knew instinctively where they had to go and walked to the elevator without any concern for the alarm that would be raised alerting the guards in the foyer.

The Dark Dawn had begun . . .

*

Like a pond in the stillness of the night after a stone has been thrown into its centre, the ripples of the actions carried out by the Unclean Six began to take hold of the city.

Time seemed to have lost its meaning as the acts of violence and destruction occurred.

Word started to spread about the problems that were being encountered throughout the city and outlying areas.

Television screens left without signal except for the abstract message that had been placed on the emergency broadcast channel, no mobile phone use, the same ambiguous message sent by text message to millions of mobile customers who were left perplexed with no answers as to who had sent them but more worrying was the loss of immeasurable amounts of banking data with both the institutes themselves and the customers perplexed, concerned and angry about where it could have gone and who could have done such a thing.

Landlines were now the only form of communication readily available to the population to access and utilise to pass news.

Radio channels desperately tried to keep up with what was happening at what seemed to be a minute by minute rate,

Steven Archer

new information coming in from hundreds of different sources including the public, employees of the businesses targeted, the police and the city authorities.

The fact that these terrorist attacks had been carried out by five or six men who had not been described very well never mind apprehended or followed and that no political agency or group had come forward to take credit for the pandemonium spreading rapidly through the streets added to the confusion and whispers that they were still under threat.

What was starting as inconvenience to some began to develop into a frustration. People got angry at the lack of solid facts as to what was going on around them, what they heard and what they could find out for themselves.

Chinese whispers took hold.

Arguments between family members, colleagues and strangers on the street began.

Minor squabbles turned into shoving contests and then into fights as the pressure of the situation tightened. City inhabitants reacted with acts of violence born out of the rising hysteria.

Some went to the banks to find out what was happening with their accounts, their savings, and their money!

As the day drew on, more and more of the population experienced extremes of emotions: rage, anger, anxiety panic and fear.

The close-knit communities of the city began to question the leaders that they had installed in the search for answers.

The media attempted to assess the problems and regain not only the ability to reach the audience but find out what had happened.

Was there more to come?

Who were the terrorists?

What did the message mean? Was it a joke? A code?

Churches began to experience people coming in from the streets to ask about what they had seen, confused priests, clergymen, rabbi's and other religious leaders tried to calm the scared, the meek and the enraged for they knew that this was the beginning and that should things get worse, more would come.

As the first ripples of discontent washed up on the shore, the larger waves came ever closer.

Chapter Twenty

Gadereal and Armean had not been too distracted as they left the bank.

It was an indication of the world that the primates inhabited that no sooner had they walked four blocks and turned only two corners they were free of any of the stragglers that had been idiotic enough to pursue them. Armean wondered briefly how they could evolve to such a state.

As they had strolled through the main hall again to the outside world, they had stopped momentarily, partly to take in the rising hysteria that they had caused and the screaming emanating from a few people around them, though most were cowering in offices behind desks and cupboards like the cowards they were, and also to make a point which was simply: don't follow us.

To make this as clear as possible to the stupid humans, Gadereal and Armean took the time to pick out some of the people around them. Once chosen, they were dispatched to emphasise compliance using fear of death.

The air crackled with electricity as the bolts of energy sped from their palms, to such an extent as to make the nearest human's hair stand on end as if raised by static.

The bolts struck the targets and sent them crashing backward into a wall and part of the security checkpoint.

Arms and legs were wrenched out of sockets and out of position as they hit the floor, like dolls stuck with pins by a voodoo witch doctor.

The screaming died as the two victims did and turned into pathetic whimpering and sobbing as the Angels turned their attention to the metal detectors. As the bolts hit them, they exploded in a flash of sparks and noise, pieces of debris flying, smouldering in every direction.

Point made.

Now as they walked leisurely along the sidewalk Gadereal could sense something.

Just as he turned to face Armean and ask if he felt it too, they were both forced to the ground with a crushing impact from above that was forceful enough to crack the paving slabs that they hit.

People nearby in the thin crowd, gasped, pointed and having paused for a second retreated hastily to safety, fear on every face as more violence erupted in their city, before their very eyes.

Jophiel and Gabriel, falling literally from the heavens had caused the collision.

They had positioned themselves on the fifth floor of a building and as the two Angels approached, they had leapt to challenge them.

Even though every Angel has a heightened awareness of not only their surroundings and environment at any given moment, they also sensed other creatures.

This ability had not assisted Gadereal or Armean, whether distracted by recent events or concentrating on their next task, they were caught cold by the element of surprise.

For Armean in particular the completion of the Prophecy would have to be fulfilled without him.

As Gabriel slammed into him and sent him sprawling to the deck, he had managed to manipulate the fall so that Armean landed on his side. In that instant of impact, he had forced his hand onto his chest over his heart and fired the most powerful bolt of lethal power that he could summon directly into Armean's abdomen.

Whether for better or for worse, Armean was killed immediately. He did not even realise what had happened.

An Angel's life force is strong and they may have the power to regenerate themselves over time, depending on the wound, but they are not infallible and the shock of the bolt did its work, taking a life that had endured countless centuries.

Armean became limp, his eyes frosted over losing all colour and as he passed he lay still.

At the same time, Jophiel tried to subdue Gadereal. As he had flown through the air toward his impact, he had held his gun tightly in his right hand. Upon impact he had been able to fire a shot that had struck home, catching Gadereal in the right temple.

The direction of the bullet was shallow and as it shot through from temple to exit from the forehead it took part of Gadereal's skull with it.

Bone, brain and blood exploded into the air.

On impact Gadereal had still been able to react quickly to the onslaught through a combination of reactivity and anger that surged within him like a river of molten lava in his veins.

He thrust himself up and off the deck in a flash, sending Jophiel reeling backward, sprawling and desperately trying to find his feet quickly.

As Gadereal shot ten feet into the air and stopped, hovering over the scene, the moment elongated. His vision was blurred from his left eye from the impact of the bullet. His right eye only partially remained in its socket, blood spurting from the gaping wound in his head, which burned with the most intense pain.

He held out his hand and as he witnessed the demise of Armean at the hand of Gabriel he sent a bolt of thunder toward Jophiel.

Watching as Gadereal rose into the air, Jophiel had twisted his body to avoid the blast, the shot was slightly wide also, as Gadereal had not adapted to losing his eye. His face reflected the hatred that he felt in that second and was given a grim contorted appearance due to the damage of the bullet.

As Jophiel raised his arm to fire, Gadereal roared, and accelerated toward him like a banshee. The bullet fired struck him in the shoulder, ripping through his flesh, but did nothing to slow his descent.

As Gadereal hit Jophiel he fired another bolt, crackling with power.

The impact never happened.

The bolt struck the deck inches from Jophiel's side, blasting a hole in the concrete.

Gabriel had also reacted after looking up from Armean and had timed his rush with Gadereal's. The blow smashed them both over and onto the pavement, allowing Jophiel a second to recover from the blast that had gashed his neck on the left side from flying pieces of concrete.

The searing pain and the smell of burning flesh passed quickly and the blood that sprayed out from the wound began to stem rapidly as his body began to regenerate and deal with the injury.

Gabriel and Gadereal clutched each other tightly in knuckle white grips that held like vices.

They stared deep into each other's faces as they rolled, trying to gain an advantage.

Gabriel had a cold and icy depth to his gaze, whilst Gadereal's good eye reflected raw hatred; their faces became distorted in tension.

No words were spoken between them in the moment but both were certain that conflict, this war of which they were part and that they had engaged in for so long was coming to a conclusion.

There was almost sadness and a flicker of regret that it would soon be over for one of them. Eternal warriors that would either be dead or without service . . .

Jophiel moved with a purpose.

He strode after the rolling Angels locked together in a hateful embrace.

He took aim carefully. He was sure to target the right spot.

Before Gadereal could reposition himself to evade the fire that was to come, Jophiel had shot.

The collision jolted Gadereal as the bullet hit him in the throat. Gabriel took instantaneous advantage and forced the fatal blow to his heart, thrusting with all of his might, Gabriel pushed the now inert and lifeless body of Gadereal off him.

Gadereal's face, which had been reconstructing itself, was now forever frozen in a severe expression, like a waxwork that had been too close to a flame.

Knowing that it was over, Gabriel composed himself, before standing and slowly brushing himself down.

Jophiel scanned the area and was pleased to note that the streets were deserted but he could hear the wailing and wining of distant sirens.

"We should move." He stated rubbing his neck as it itched its way back to normal.

Gabriel didn't respond. He reached into an inside pocket and retrieved something with his hand.

Approaching the corpse of Gadereal he knelt and placed a gold coin over each of his frosted and half destroyed eyes.

As he moved to Armean, Jophiel watched as he repeated the action taking great care.

Jophiel had never seen such tenderness from Gabriel before; he did not see fit to question it but did wonder as to the meaning.

Having stood in silence with his head bowed for a second, Gabriel jerked to life and started off along the sidewalk, brushing himself down.

Jophiel followed, a yard behind, taking only one glance back at the scene they had left, as they moved onto the next.

*

There are some factors that will contribute to the fall of a civilised society in a very short space of time. Throughout history there have been examples of a community moving from sanity and stability to self-destruction and war, turning on themselves in frenzy before looking further to the actual cause of their plight.

So it was that the city selected as the best viable objective for the Unclean Six to begin the fulfilment of the Prophecy in the most effective manner because of its infra structure, its geographical position, the number of major and vital services that had their operations situated there and, possibly as important, if not more so the hedonistic and savage underbelly that flourished just below the surface of the civility that existed in this place.

The shade that contrasted the light.

The people of the city still had food and water supplies, which really should be two of the major factors for civil unrest to take root and yet the mass population still shifted uncomfortably as events unfolded about them. The incidents had been relentless as was the savagery of that accompanied them, yet not too long a time had actually elapsed since the first act of the Six but the degree of violence being reported and the specific nature of the targets chosen caused consternation.

As news of the attacks were communicated between individuals by landline or by word of mouth having been heard on the radio news updates spread around the city and beyond, so did the rise in dread and fear. The banking networks that had been crashed were already starting to have a rolling effect not only around the city but now around the country as well. Many more systems connected to the main source were being disrupted, meaning that more and more information was being lost and so far, the banks had not been able to stop it.

People trying to query what was happening got little in the way of explanation and so tempers and tension rose as the thought of being without funds for everyday, mundane purposes such as paying bills, rent and mortgages and no one accountable continued unchecked as the problem spread like a virus through the banking network.

The simple acts of not being able to watch television, use the internet or make a call on a mobile phone caused temperatures to shoot up at an alarming rate. The gap between a mild annoyance and anger at the related problems that not being able to communicate with others at anytime or find out what was going on was an unpredictable mark of how much people relied on these devices and how low patience had gotten.

As thousands upon thousands of people complained, argued and shouted at suppliers of these luxuries, moaned to each other about how typical the situation was and got angrier as every minute passed, there was also the feeling within everyone that there was something else, something sinister that ate away deep in the subconscious.

The authorities and the media services not being able to get information out to the masses did not help the situation.

The killings that had occurred at the three buildings defied belief at first.

The method of the slayings was contradictory and surely blown out of proportion by those purported to have seen it.

The deaths at each location had happened in quick succession, the police had so far been unable to track down any of the culprits, of which there could be many, as few attackers could not have covered the ground between each place in time, so there must be multiple perpetrators. The speed and efficiency with which the attacks had been carried out and the way that the terrorists had vanished caused issue in the media and reports expanded on hearsay, conjecture and eye witness accounts distorted by third party comments and opinions.

The authorities quickly understood that civil unrest was a possibility in the immediate future, not days away, due to the fact that there was still a sense of being under attack, which would make people think twice for a short time longer. The fact that nobody knew who the aggressors were worked in their favour for the moment.

The message posted on television and sent by text caused question and debate, tapping into an uncomfortable mindset, adding to the physical threat at hand.

Many did begin to take to the streets.

Small squabbles got out of hand. Some crowded around radios for news and argued among themselves.

Some started to decide that locking themselves inside was the best option available, others thought that taking the chance of running out of supplies would be stupid and so panic buying began even after this short time.

The frail psyche of the city and the country began to fracture.

After the reports of a disturbance involving four or five of the aggressors turning on each other mushroomed through the community, matters got worse.

The confusion was rising and so the city leaders met to discuss possibilities on how to deal with this unique situation, the police tried to maintain the status quo by swelling their numbers and visibility on the streets whilst some of the population simply began to leave.

It was the calm before the storm.

The crisis was about to get worse.

Chapter Twenty-One

The streets of the city were becoming more manic as time went on and no resolution or explanation to the disruption and danger were forthcoming. In the limbo of the unknown more and more people were venting their anger.

Danyuel and Azazeal had walked through the darkening streets, roads and avenues without incident, only the occasional siren and passing police car causing them to pause. Azazeal had considered briefly what pathetic things these humans were, these thoughts had to come to him on previous tasks in differing time frames and always ended up with the same conclusions.

He had served with trolls and minions with more integrity than these creatures.

On one hand, some of the primates were losing their control, their tiny little minds already unable to maintain a level of normality in the presiding circumstances, instead deciding that chaos was a better alternative and so they cut the slender thread holding them to rationality.

The only ones who had any saving grace were the ones with no pretence, who were simply taking advantage of the situation and stealing for their own gain. These would be the ones who started the conversion to servitude whilst on Earth in others of their kind.

Odd then, that in the same circumstances, some of the humans carried on as normal and hoped that all of the ugliness would just go away, lost in their own little bubble of existence, they did as they normally would in oblivion. These would be the converted in the new order.

The only thing that they all seemed to have in common was the fact that all of them were ignorant of Danyuel and himself.

Of course, their altering appearance had everything to do with not being recognised and yet Azazeal couldn't help but think that at least some of the humans should be sensitive enough to sense them on an instinctive level.

Now, they stood in a small, white baggage checkroom in the airport, waiting for the others to arrive.

Their entry through the heightened security of the airport had been straightforward as most, if not all, of the extra guards and police were deployed to wander around and look busy, ready to *react* to any unforeseen circumstance.

"Can you feel that?" Danyuel asked, gazing up at the ceiling but far into the distance with his gaze.

Pausing and tilting his head slightly to the left before answering, Azazeal replied, "Yes, I think there may be a problem."

They waited in silence trying to gauge what could be wrong.

"Someone's coming." Azazeal whispered a little later, realising that it was two of their colleagues.

Yetereal and Tureal entered the room cautiously and nodded at Danyuel and Azazeal.

Without debate, it was Yetereal that took the lead.

His expression was calm, though his eyes had a grey, granite look.

His tone was even as he spoke. "Gadereal and Armean have gone . . . they are no more." He raised a hand to stop the questions that were about to be asked. "Let me finish," he carried on looking at each of them in turn and then continuing on with the information that he needed to impart.

"We all knew that it would be unlikely that we would get through this task without opposition and even without losing some of our number that would have been short sighted. So far there are two agents for definite seeking to thwart what we seek to achieve, but there could be more. This means that we have to be more vigilant, more alert. It doesn't affect what we have to and still can achieve. Gadereal and Armean are gone so we move on and that is it."

Yetereal took the time again to search the eyes of his comrades' one at a time. All he saw was a hard-edged determination from each of them. Mourning was not something that they would consider; it was calculating the logistics of what they had to do without letting the urge for revenge to cloud them. Each of them was now even more resolute and, truthfully, opposition could have come earlier and possibly in greater numbers than this and also, Gadereal and Armean could quite easily have been more careful, confidence can be distracting.

"We are still on the right track to complete our mission, now that we are in this world again, we have to accept the limits of communication and get on with the final phase. The more of their pilots that we influence, the more targets we hit and, obviously, the more disruption we cause. This method will also strike a strong chord with their weak psyche after recent historical events. This is all in our favour. Make sure that you plant the message deep within each one you get to use and be sure that we are going to succeed with the monkeys that you choose. Remember, discretion will bring the reward that we seek. The time of the Dark Dawn is nigh. Do not falter and do not hesitate."

Yetereal's voice rose as he emphasised his point and as they stood closer in a circle, he held his right hand out, palm down, the others placed their hands on top of the other and bowed their heads.

"This is our time now. The Prophecy will be completed and man will finally have all that he deserves, no more blind faith to see him through. No more apathy to while away the days, just one decision: to serve or to die. This is the chance that we have worked toward, we will not fail now . . ."

The four Angels remained silent for the next moment, each contemplating the immediate future and their role in the long-term existence of man.

"Let's go to work." Danyuel said gravely.

"One at a time." Yetereal said over his shoulder as he moved to the door and opened it slightly, looking out.

Tureal stepped to his side and Yetereal placed a hand on his shoulder, nudging him gently through and into the corridor when the coast was clear.

They all left within the next few minutes, into the bright, neon lit lounges and arcades ready to set in motion the final piece of the jigsaw.

*

The remaining four of the Unclean Six moved among the humans like wraiths, identifying pilots as they discreetly passed between the throng of people in the various areas of the airport's terminals. The humans' minds were so open and easy to tap into that each of them had to take precautions during the searching process, as the depth of the banality that occupied their simple minds could be distracting. Complete concentration was needed to firstly, ensure that a successful implant could be carried out and secondly, continue to be aware of the surroundings.

Threats from both humans, although minimal, and the more serious opposition agents existed.

Tureal sensed another pilot as he casually walked around a bookshop in the main quadrant of one of the terminals large departure areas. There were so many people around now that he could practically stand still and sense where the prey were and move to them, homing in on them and stalking like the predator he was.

This one was going to Mexico City. Perfect.

The flight was in less than an hour and of all things, the pathetic human had decided to try and buy his wife a gift to try and cover the guilt of an indiscretion that he had committed whilst on a layover last evening. Tureal wasn't sure if the fact that this pathetic animal felt remorse for his carnal actions was outweighed by the ridiculous attempt at appeasement. The gift was obviously more for him in way of soothing his own guilty conscience.

As he approached the monkey Tureal looked down at his own hand. For some reason he was finding it difficult to touch the humans. It had never bothered him before, but then again, most other times were to deliver a fatal blow and end the life in question. He had not had to carry out this kind of action too many times before and he felt that the dirty primates were disgusting. Touching them almost repelled him.

Sliding past a couple linked arm in arm and eye to eye, Tureal put these negative thoughts to one side and prepared himself for the contact.

All he had to do was focus his mind. The power that he had was beyond anything that a human could even understand and so this exercise, although uncomfortable, was straightforward.

He concentrated on placing the message. These would be the pilot's final words to ground control, his co-pilot and passengers as he reached descent upon final approach. The trigger in this case would be reaching an altitude of 5,000 feet. At this point the pilot would disable the co-pilot with a blow to the throat and a beating that would be as frenzied as it was unexpected, tapping into the monkey's inner rage and basic instinct. Some may be stopped at this point, that was a possibility, but unlikely. Tureal had seen what a truly enraged human could do to another, any colleague in the cabin would be subdued.

He would then relay the message to ground control:

Today is the day.
Today is the day of Prophecy.
The choice is yours.

THERE IS NO GOD.

Bear witness to what is to follow.

His next action would be to secure the cockpit, reseat himself and choose a target. This was where the monkey had the chance to be creative, if that were at all possible. A well-known landmark, a building, a highly populated area or even the airport itself would do. As long as the plane struck its target and caused the maximum amount of damage, the mission was a success.

The human would not even know what he was doing.

The hesitant man had stopped and was looking at some romance novels, Tureal pushed his disgust to one side and eased closer to him, picking up a cheap cop novel and thumbing through it he was able to stand side by side with the pilot without being noticed. Now was the time. There were other people around but none close enough to notice what was about to happen.

Tureal replaced the book he held as the primate reached to choose one and quicker than the blink of an eye, touched the man's forehead with his index finger.

A tiny arc of blue electricity crossed from his finger to the man's head. The transaction was complete.

More potent and deeper in his mind than any brainwashing technique that they could muster, the man was primed.

His only reaction as Tureal whipped his hand away was to blink repeatedly, reach up to scratch his forehead and refocus his eyes. It was as if he had merely been overcome with giddiness for a moment.

Content that the next sleeper was set, Tureal quickly scanned his mind to ensure that all was in place, he then set off in search of the next victim.

Chicago.

That was only a few hours away, now, where was that little monkey . . .

Chapter Twenty-Two

It hadn't taken long for the first domestic flight to reach and hit its target.

The scheduled flight itself was a mere forty-five minute journey to the city which was, incidentally, the closest geographically and part of a regular shuttle service that ran in and out as the airport and the city was near to the coast and one of the stopover points used by many of the major airlines as a layover point for commuters leaving for foreign shores whether on business or for pleasure.

Everything had gone without a hitch; it was the perfect flight until the final approach.

That was when the pilot had snapped.

It took only a split second for Captain John Steadman to change from a thorough consummate professional, to a brain washed zombie, devoid of all emotion and with only one goal in mind.

He had rendered his co-pilot unconscious with a vicious blow to the head, as he had leaned closer to see if his colleague was alright, using a flashlight that he kept by the side of his station (he had once had to check a problem in the fuselage and had had a major trauma trying to find a torch to use).

Once that was done, he had engaged the autopilot for a few moments, ignoring ground control when they had radioed in asking if all was okay, and locked the cabin down. It would be nearly impossible for anyone to enter now after the upgrades that had been made, post 9/11.

He had then calmly contacted the tower and after emphasising the need for them to listen to him, he had proceeded to repeat the words that flowed through his mind like water over a fall.

Once he had satisfied himself that the message had been recorded several times, understood and pondered, he cut all communications.

Taking over the control of the plane again, he did two things.

Firstly he chose a target. He decided that the best option available to him, giving maximum casualty and damage chances was to hit the airport itself. He would fly the plane into the control tower. This would knock out all communication with all incoming flights and restrict the take off for those still on the ground until the secondary station could be brought online and take over.

The second thing that he did was to speak to the passengers. He wanted them as calm as possible for the run in. In an even, monotone voice, he explained to them and the staff that there had been a slight engine problem, nothing to concern them, and that as a precaution they had been re-routed to land beyond the control tower with immediate effect.

Captain Steadman, who had flown with the navy and had been a commercial airline pilot for fifteen years, then successfully guided his plane to the control tower.

All pleas to change course went unheard. The fighter jets stationed nearby were scrambled, but would arrive too late to do anything.

The collision wiped out the tower completely in a fireball of yellow and orange flames and blackened metal, killing the few people who had remained to try and secure the flights for planes still in the air, as they tried to flee at the last moment.

The impact was felt and seen, throughout the airport sending cracks shooting across the walls of buildings nearby and shattering every window on the site from the outside in, spraying hundreds of people with thousands of shards of glass.

The emergency services responded quickly to get to the scene but were overwhelmed by the enormity of the damage that had been wrought and the fire that raged both from the building and from the fragments of the plane which had broken into three pieces and flipped over and over before landing on the runways, smashed like a discarded model, belching smoke into the blue sky. Part of the plane had struck another stationary aircraft behind the cockpit and in front of the wing causing that too to break into flame.

Every passenger and crewmember on the plane was killed. Seven people in or near the tower on impact were killed. Five people in the surrounding buildings were killed and hundreds suffered various minor injuries.

The news of the horror swept across the nation and then the globe.

Disbelief at such a tragedy changed to rage when it emerged that the pilot had repeated the same message that had been on television for hours.

People couldn't take it anymore. The violence escalated rapidly from the city where it had all began, to the country and then onto other parts of the world. More and more reports of hostility, brutality and cruelty were heard. Countries far and wide had rioters in the streets, looting, stealing and destroying all that they could in waves of unbridled emotion. The authorities of the major nations held emergency discussions to try and reach an agreement on how to stem the tide.

As other people heard about what was happening at the centre of this destructive force, they too lost control.

The loss of bank data continued unchecked.

The television networks shut down save for the one and only channel still broadcasting.

Mobile phone and internet providers had their services cut and no sight as to when it could be repaired.

The carnage on the streets of the city returned people to their primitive form, not looking for answers anymore, simply looking out for themselves.

Fires raged, cars were overturned gunshots rang out accompanying the screams of terror and rage. Control turned to carnage.

Society was being lost and the plague of viciousness that had started in this city by the Unclean Six was spreading ever further.

Chapter Twenty-Three

The city was in the grip of an intensifying hysteria that Jophiel and Gabriel viewed impassively but this was tinged with a slight feeling of unease.

Gabriel, certainly, was determined to see this mission through as he had been tasked to do, as it was the most important conflict of all of the ages. Assisting the humans was distasteful but merely a by-product of the situation they found themselves in.

He was carrying out his Masters wishes to the very best of his abilities, for this is what he did, he served without question and with faith. It almost didn't matter what the problem was, as he was dedicated and loyal in the extreme, nothing would stand in his way. Service was everything to him, but to be a part of this was a challenge he was proud of.

Any thoughts that he was having about the humans were kept to himself.

Jophiel was slightly different in that he had an attachment with them but after so long in the other world that he now inhabited and being so far removed from his previous life, loved ones and acquaintances his detachment was all but complete, yet being around these souls again, walking among them, resurrected hints of feelings long since gone.

Both of them were unaware of the first strike by the plane and the other impending attacks. Both sensed, even without this information that the situation was as dire as it could be.

The dull, cold concrete grey of the surroundings struck Jophiel as they made their way to the airport. Although Gabriel hadn't said where they were heading, it had not taken too long for Jophiel to work it out given the road signs that were everywhere.

The decline of the people was here in this monolithic place for all to witness.

Skirmishes had broken out in varying numbers all over the city, looting was becoming more obvious and brazen as some decided to help themselves to what they didn't have and the police were beginning to find it difficult to spread themselves around the districts to maintain control, especially as those in their own ranks were not immune to what was going on about them, and even joining in with the carnage.

Walking, even at a pace had taken hours, now that they had arrived, they stood on the tarmac of one of the main runways. Dusk began to fall and hide the terrors that existed all around, even as some of the populace tried to carry on as normal, like automatons.

Gabriel leaned against the damp wall of the storage facility they were next to and spoke quietly.

"The other four are all definitely here but spread out over the area, I can sense them but can only pin point one the rest are too far away. They must be trying to cover more ground by working independently." He paused and turned his head to the sky as if listening for a far off sound.

"I can guide us to the nearest one, and enable us to position ourselves to be able to surprise him. He hasn't detected me yet . . . he seems to be concentrating on something else . . . he's paying close attention to the humans, as if he's trying to single them out, to pick some of them . . ."

Jophiel watched as he tried to focus on what was happening, his face relaxing as he did and almost becoming peaceful.

Gabriel didn't speak any further and moved off past Jophiel, his direction decided upon and his look stern once again.

The night helped add to the darkness of the already long shadows that had crept along the ground and afforded Jophiel and Gabriel cover as they silently covered the ground between buildings, big and small, with workers in limited numbers and distracted by events around them so that they were not seen in motion, they seemed to mould into their surroundings like dark chameleons.

Taking the lead, Gabriel pointed the way with hand gestures that Jophiel picked up on immediately. They were a good team and had so far managed to gel together well in little time.

Gabriel was pleased because, as with Gadereal and Armean, the prey that they stalked so cautiously had not yet sensed them. Gabriel was using all of his will to ensure that this remained the case by projecting limited thought and disguising it in human thought form. This would, however, only work under a casual scrutiny and not at all at close range but it would be enough to give them an edge, a slight advantage.

Gabriel stopped and raised his hand.

It was Azazeal.

Gabriel could pick him out clearly now, only twenty metres away . . .

It was just moments later that the confrontation took place.

Gabriel and Jophiel had positioned themselves at either side of an alley between two hangars, one of which housed a mess room of sorts that appeared to act as a flight crew debriefing room.

Azazeal was walking down the alley, to the left hand side, having stopped to discuss something with a uniformed man who had come from one of the hangars from a vast roller door, toward the exit point by which Gabriel and Jophiel now hid.

Jophiel pressed his back against the wall, trying to blend into it, listening intently as he did so, his senses heightened by the approaching danger.

Gabriel was behind a rubbish container that he had gently wheeled nearer to the alley.

He had focused himself totally and did his best not to reveal their presence, whilst trying to work out what exchange Azazeal had just had with the human.

Azazeal was taking his time peering into the large security windows of one of the hangars, glancing forward he looked at the main complex of the airport, illuminated with various fluorescent lights that came from within and without, flashing randomly at different speeds and in several colours that gave a clinical and unearthly quality to the buildings.

Just as he was about to exit the alley and move into the open, Jophiel stepped from the shadows and out in front of Azazeal.

Taking a step back, for an instant, Azazeal was caught on the back foot but he soon regained his composure, having chastised himself quickly for not picking up on Jophiel, with a spreading grin he spoke through tightened lips, distaste on his tongue.

"You are what they have sent to stop us?" He lifted his arms in an open, unbelieving fashion as if insulted by the very presence of Jophiel, who maintained eye contact whilst casually taking steps back toward the open ground behind him.

Azazeal shrugged, dropped his arms to his sides and shook his head with a heavy, exaggerated sigh.

"I can't understand why you would be the one to try and stop us. There must be more, I'm sure," he hesitated as if trying to hear something and, once satisfied, returned his attention to Jophiel, content they were alone.

"Yet here you are," he continued his dialogue. "Here you stand . . . I thought that there would be a deadly threat, it seems our mission has been underestimated, unless you are some sort of advance spy. No matter . . ."

Jophiel took two, small steps back and then stood firm, keeping his hands by his sides as he held the advancing Azazeal's inflexible stare.

"Don't think that any of that matters right now." Jophiel said after a second, his words drifting skyward on wisp's in the cold air.

The millisecond that Azazeal moved toward Jophiel, with his right arm raising, a calculating look on his face, both Jophiel and Gabriel reacted in unison, as if symbiotic.

Jophiel's hand sped to his gun and Gabriel swiftly shot from his position behind the container.

The blue bolt that flashed from Azazeal's hand zipped through the air and caught Jophiel on the left shoulder, burning into him and forcing him backward with the force with which it came. Jophiel grimaced at the impact, staggered but still held his gun, retrieved from his jacket, up into the closing gap between himself and Azazeal, firing as it levelled out.

The blast struck Azazeal in the chest at the same time that Gabriel rushed up on him and thrust his hand onto his back, sending a bone-shaking jolt of power through Azazeal's body with a lethal force that caused Azazeal to scream out in pain, surprise and shock at the unexpected attack he desperately tried to move away from.

His face stretched into a grimace of agony, a cry like a wolf's, dying out in his throat as his horrified eyes rolled back into his head.

Jophiel moved backward again, as Azazeal tried to reach out for him, beyond the gun still held in his outstretched arm, his fingers clutching the air frantically. He staggered forward, falling onto one knee, Gabriel moving with him continuing to press the electric death into him.

For an instant, Azaeal appeared to take on his true, winged form, flickering between the body he now occupied and his own.

The power of the discharge fired through Azazeal had its affect in spectacular fashion, blowing his earthly form apart into limbs and body parts that transformed into charcoal and ash. The explosion of debris and dust flew in all directions, covering Gabriel and Jophiel who were thrown to the deck by the silent flash.

As they lay for a moment, ash and small particles drifting down to the ground like a grey snowfall, they breathed heavily, taking in gasps of air as they started to return to normal, adrenalin slowing after the event.

Jophiel pushed himself up and winced as he brushed himself down. Although already repairing itself, his shoulder was an angry red welt.

Gabriel stood and looked down at what remained of Azazeal, his jaw and face tense. Reaching into his pocket, he tenderly took out two gold coins, looked at them with blank eyes and knelt next to the largest deposit of dusty grey matter. He placed the coins with reverence.

After a moment of reflection in which Jophiel waited patiently and silently Gabriel spoke in a hoarse voice.

"They're moving to the final phase. They're trying to gain control of as many pilots as possible to cause as much destruction and chaos as possible by crashing their planes. They're going to push mankind over the edge . . ."

Jophiel gazed down at his companion and wondered if it was too late to stop the fulfilment of the Prophecy.

Chapter Twenty-Four

Turning, turning, turning.

With all that had happened recently, all that was happening at the present moment and all that would happen in the future, the world continued to inevitably turn.

The world continued to turn and its human inhabitants continued to tear themselves apart, piece-by-piece and in the middle of it all was the three that were left of the Unclean Six.

Tureal and Danyuel had paired up, drawn to one another as they both followed their senses.

They had been able to pick up on Azazeal. In an instant his presence had been both intense and strong but then it had simply disappeared. Both of them knew that there was something wrong. It was easy to guess that they were being hunted down and eliminated before they could see the Prophecy to fulfilment and that Azazeal had become the latest victim of the struggle.

Having met in a departure lounge, both having enlisted the help of several more pilots, they now pushed their way through the people in the direction of the last place that they had sensed Azazeal.

The people that they shoved past were mixed. Some were frantic and active in trying to get out of the city to see loved ones or try to escape the ever-growing violence.

Some sat and held their heads in their hands, weeping, as they wondered what to think or believe of the situation surrounding them.

Others were angry and lashed out at all around them.

There were tears, shouting, begging, pleading and cries of rage and pity.

Steven Archer

Some of the monkeys hugged, some of them fought, some tried to stay calm, and some stood silently listening to one human pray.

All of this went on as Tureal and Danyuel forged on through this repulsive sight, to get to where they wanted to be, not caring who they hurt on the way, simply wanting to find the agents behind Azazeal's termination.

From the massive window at the end of the lounge, they had seen across the runway to the figures in the distance. Although they couldn't make out whom they were, they knew that they had to stop them.

"Do we contact Yetereal?" Danyuel asked as they ran down the escalator.

"I can't sense him, he is too far away. We must take care of this, of these two. We can contact him then or he may come across us, but we cannot afford to let these get away, we must stop them." Although racing at full sprint, shoving people out of the way, Tureal's reply was measured and assertive.

They barged on toward the nearest exit to the runway.

*

Jophiel and Gabriel had reached the main building. As they entered and passed each other, scanning the area as they swept it with their eyes, they remained vigilant. Moving fast and in steady covering formation they worked their way down a long corridor toward the populated terminal departure and arrivals lounges. They had to find the last three and as they were looking for pilots, it made sense to search through places with more people and of course, being in a large crowd of writhing, frustrated and emotional humans would help not only physical cover but mental blocking also.

The idea was a good one but had, unfortunately, been put into action too late.

They opened the emergency exit door just a crack, peered through into the peopled room and then stepped in to become part of the throng and to seek out their enemy.

As soon as they were in the room a scream erupted from the right, so high that it threatened to shatter the windows. A body, deformed and bent out of shape came sailing through the air from the source of the noise. Now just a gargled sound spewed out with the blood that poured from the flying man's mouth.

For a split second there seemed to be quiet and then bedlam broke out as people watched in horror as the flying man neared his destination, They ran, everyone in every direction, trying to escape from the terror as another figure was grabbed, battered with repeated furious blows to the body and then sent flying and flailing in the air toward Jophiel and Gabriel.

The first body hit the floor before them with a loud thud and a crack, Gabriel stepped over and beyond the dead man and started toward Tureal who, red faced with anger had grabbed a third person trying to flee, like an insect to be tortured.

As the body of the woman hit the wall between Gabriel and Jophiel, leaving a red smear as it slid to the floor, Danyuel took his opportunity.

As Jophiel moved to follow Gabriel, Danyuel grabbed him around the neck with his arm, wrenching him backward and off his feet. Jophiel reached up and grabbed the arm with his hands, his eyes bulging in their sockets as he watched Gabriel fire a thunderbolt of blue at Tureal.

When Danyuel tightened his grip, closing Jophiel's throat and restricting his breathing, Jophiel marshalled his thoughts and acted. He thrust back with his feet, using what little purchase he could gain to push Danyuel off balance and send him crashing into the wall behind them. Danyuel grunted and seemed to roar but did not let loose his grip. Jophiel crouched as best he could, pulling Danyuel over him and almost off his feet, still gripping and crushing as he went onto Jophiel's back.

That was when Jophiel focused his strength as his vision began to blur and his blood rushed around his head, booming in his ears. He quickly fell to one knee and pulled Danyuel as he did so, taking him off balance and over the top of him.

Danyuel let out a cry of frustration and anger as he hit the deck on his back, trying to roll as he did.

The third of the people grabbed and hurled by Tureal, landed at Danyuel's feet, obstructing his movement for a second. As he kicked out at the inert figure hindering his progress, Jophiel reached for and drew his gun. Breathing heavily and fighting off the light-headedness and the flashes in his vision, Jophiel aimed and fired four quick rounds at Danyuel, expecting to be rushed and forced back by an impact that didn't come.

Danyuel flailed around on the floor like a dervish, screaming and writhing in a fiery agony that would not let him alone but forced him into frantic action.

One of the bullets had hit him in the chest, entering his stomach because of the position he had been in when fired upon, one hit him in the right arm, shattering his elbow, another bullet hit him in the neck just below his right ear and the final bullet had struck the left of his head taking part of his skull off.

He spun up and around as Jophiel tried to fight back the waves of nausea that he felt and fire again, leaping at him with a rasping yell of blood and guts, arms outstretched, reaching again, desperately, for Jophiel's throat.

The blast of energy that left his good hand and arm forced Jophiel back and to the floor, reaching for his chest as he did as if it would stem the intense pain that he felt.

As Danyuel landed on top of him, forcing his hand onto Jophiel's chest they both acted together, Danyuel forcing a bolt of energy through Jophiel's body and Jophiel firing off the last remaining rounds in his pistol.

The simultaneous acts had the same results.

These blasts into Jophiel's body were too much even for him to withstand and the final shots into Danyuel's head were too much for him.

Both body's slumped down and twitched sporadically; the crimson fluid that spread from them across the smooth tiled floor in an expanding pool was the last movement that either of them would make.

As the remaining people that had stayed or been too slow fled the scene in panic as some of their number were attacked, mutilated and then hurled across the room whilst the fight and the shooting had broken out, the conflict continued.

On top of the level of hysteria that existed and the nervousness within the building, let alone everywhere else, these events had been enough to tip more of the humans over the edge.

Pushing and shoving others in their attempt to get as far away from the melee as possible, the scramble went on.

Tureal had grabbed the three nearest monkeys to him in turn, hardly moving as so many of them rushed around in alarm and, without prejudice, incapacitated them by shattering their weak bodies and then flung them, like discarded toys at Jophiel and Gabriel.

Now as Gabriel sprinted to him, dodging the running people as he went, lifting his arm to aim at his target, Tureal reached out again, only moving a fraction as the thinning herd of human cattle stampeded past him, grabbing the man to his left by the collar, this very action stopping him in mid-motion.

Gritting his teeth to subdue the roar that he wanted to expel, Tureal held the man around the throat and gripped hard, whilst at the same moment releasing some of his pent up fury by punching the overweight business man in the middle of his back with such force as to fracture his spine between L2 and L3 of his lumbar region, effectively severing the vertebrae.

Hoisting his victim up, he held the screaming man in front of him like a shield.

The bolt that Gabriel fired as he neared Tureal made no provision for the human that was in-between them. The thought of removing Tureal was the paramount thought that Gabriel had.

The blast knocked Tureal into the hardened safety glass, causing him to lose his grip on the limp, moaning man that he held so closely.

As he tried to both fend off Gabriel with a hastily fired bolt from his right hand whilst moving his makeshift shield again, he left himself open to opportunity.

Gabriel saw this and took the shot without thought or pause. He was only eight feet from Tureal now and once he had fired

Steven Archer

the electric charge, which hit Tureal in the right shoulder, he leapt into the air, his arms stretched out in front of him.

Tureal could not roll with the blow that hit his shoulder and instead was caught immobile for an instant, in which time Gabriel impacted on both him and his unconscious makeshift shield.

The jolt sent all three of them sprawling to the floor, the human falling forward at an angle which meant that he struck the first of a row of seats and landed in an inert heap on the floor, another life extinguished.

Gabriel clutched at Tureal with his left hand, holding onto his clothing for purchase as he forced his right hand up and onto his chest for the best possible target.

Tureal scrambled to try and get hold of Gabriel, one hand grasping on the ground as he tried to push himself up into a better position, whilst his right hand made contact with Gabriel's side.

As Gabriel fired into Tureal, he screamed at the shock of the power and the force due to its close proximity but still managed to fire himself.

Tureal felt Gabriel tense as he fired into his side, with as much energy as he could summon but neither the grip nor the electrical force let up.

Both of them attempted to get the upper hand, each of them desperate in their own way to be the victor, each of them catching fleeting glances at each other's distorted faces and in trying to move, each of them simply tightening the bind that they had on one other.

Both of them had the same purpose and pushed to carry it out, reaching deep within. Both wanted the other dead so badly that he could sense it and almost feel it and so, both forced more energy into their attacking bolts.

The increase in power from both of them caused them to cry out in effort and pain causing them to shake at the effort and the agony yet fight on through the barriers of physicality.

The surge that flowed from them finally erupted in an explosion sending them both soaring into the air.

Gabriel landed some twenty feet into the room and the wall that he crashed into with such a force that bones within him smashed and the plaster and masonry around him disintegrated only stopped his tumbling flight.

His head was full of flashing and pulsing lights, his arm and shoulder hurt with a pain that was so intense it felt like fire and he trembled with a combination of exerted effort and adrenalin still coursing its way through his veins.

His mind prompted him to move and move quickly, but his body took seconds to respond. He rolled to one side and pushed himself into a seated position, grimacing as he did so.

The room was quiet now, save for the sound of engines whining in the distance, a mechanical scream and the wind that carried it.

Focusing his blurred vision he saw Tureal.

Gabriel gained strength from within, pushing himself that little bit farther, and pushed himself up, grunting with pain and moving closer to the shattered window through which Tureal lay motionless.

The blast had sent Tureal through the protective glass window, but being so strong he had not been thrust through it; instead he lay at an angle on his side, practically severed through his waist, his innards exposed, steaming and raw.

Blood had drenched the floor beneath him as it poured freely from him and down the shattered glass and shards that were left.

His head lolled from side to side, his neck unable to give it any support, his face free of expression, blank of emotion but his eyes burning with pure hatred.

Tureal's hands held onto the edges of the glass that pierced him, torn and bloodied as he attempted to push himself free so that his body could begin to repair itself.

"It's time to let go Tureal," Gabriel said quietly, conscious of the body in front of him and the controlled shouts and movement of the armed police that were behind him.

"No matter, it is done, you can't stop it." Tureal coughed the words out and as he did he spat blood from his mouth, his lips covered in it like a nightmarish clown's lipstick.

Steven Archer

They exchanged a split second look that seemed to span the ages and then Tureal was gone, dispatched by one more shocking bolt from Gabriel.

The police moved rapidly on and Gabriel knew that he didn't have time to waste.

He turned, targeted two of the officers still brainwashed enough to carry out their duties, moving in a standard covering formation down the lounge and fired three quick bursts of snaking blue energy that blasted them backward and sent debris flying everywhere. There were shouts as the others ducked for cover and wailed at the loss of their two comrades, the smoke made the confusion too much for a few moments and that was when Gabriel acted.

He took two gold coins from his jacket and placed them on Tureal's eyes once he had dragged the lids shut, covering the blank eyes.

He then spun around to check for Jophiel.

He hesitated before running to him.

In that instant he knew that he too was gone.

As he covered the distance to Jophiel, Gabriel fired again and again at his pursuers, who entrenched themselves to avoid harm.

Gabriel pushed Danyuel to one side and felt something that he hadn't felt for many, many years; sorrow.

He gazed at Jophiel and everything else seemed to melt away for an instant as he bowed his head and fought back the choking sensation in his throat. He reached into his coat with his left hand, and wiped blood from Jophiel's face, smearing it as he did, with his right. Life, any life, comes to an end eventually, but although Gabriel knew this better than anyone or anything, he was still taken by the emotion that he felt for his friend. He placed two coins over Jophiel's eyes, cupped his face and held him for a moment, feeling the compassion well up within him.

He forced himself into action then moved to Danyuel, repeating the ritual that he had carried out before with two more coins, placing them carefully on his practically severed head.

Standing, he looked again upon Jophiel and for a second wished that he could stay with him, but he couldn't, he had to go.

The police had galvanised themselves and started to fire at him again, although Gabriel ignored it, taking one more moment to think of Jophiel.

As the police moved in, Gabriel clicked into action and fled through the door that they had entered, disappearing with a growing hatred burning within him.

Chapter Twenty-Five

A great man once said that the human race was simply a virus with shoes.

The human beings that inhabited the planet Earth were behaving more and more like a virus with every single passing moment, consuming all in a path of ruin.

Man had already populated the ground; continents and countries long since lived on and expanded upon but now a change had taken place.

Never before in mankind's history had such violence, brutality and hostility been encountered or witnessed.

Hundreds of thousands of towns and cities were affected.

From the most high-tech metropolis to the lowliest shanty.

Man was moving rapidly toward his darkest hour.

The destruction that had started with the vile actions of the Unclean Six were now running out of control in many parts of the world, yet it was the message that they had planted, the demon seed, that was seeping into the very core of millions of people and affecting them so deeply as to create a wild havoc, whether out of desperation, ignorance or fear. Man's basic existence was being changed forever.

This message seemed to be the real cause of the carnage that was being wrought; the physical acts of terrorism that the Unclean Six had started with merely ignited the touch flame, beginning these series of events.

The world was burning and the fire was raging out of control.

Towns and cities were being destroyed from the ground up, the very fabric of society being torn down.

Mankind was approaching civil war and the level of horror and atrocity was unsurpassed. A mass hysteria had become a mass need for death and destruction.

More of the pilots that had been influenced had taken, unawares, to the skies, before an all out ban on all flights could be instigated, put in place by countries panicked at the amount of death and devastation that had come from above, only to re-route near their landing sites and plunge to the ground kamikaze style.

Reports of the impacts were balanced with news of attempted heroism, even in this adversity; positives were being sought as they were so few and far between.

Seven more major cities had commercial airliners wipe out buildings and thousands of people as they crashed into populated area's, some targets of notoriety destroyed forever, huge regions laid to waste.

Panic reached fever pitch as the people reacted to the terror.

Disbelief reigned as further scattered information of two flights being shot down by fighter jets over the sea and unpopulated area's to avoid casualties and damage, were both hailed as brave and unavoidable decisions or condemned as acts of murder, the furore adding to the conflict that already raged between the populace.

Nine planes reached foreign shores and carried out their deadly missions of massacre, resulting in further problems on the ground for the native population already turning on themselves and stunned by events that had unfolded, whilst also prompting drastic potential retaliation from governments unsure as to whether they were actually under a form of attack and possibly even at war.

The bigger issue was compounded as terrorist groups the world over took advantage of the crisis situation and carried out attacks for their own agenda, confusing an already bewildering series of events.

It was becoming too much.

The authorities could not keep track of who was responsible for what act of violence, could not spare forces to avert possible threats and certainly could not deploy enough manpower to track down all of those responsible. From basic crimes on the street to major catastrophes by terrorist cells, the decline further into chaos was beginning.

As regional politicians struggled with the people, emergency services and the furore encompassing them, they looked to national government for assistance and guidance.

Some regions took matters into their own hands and in an effort to regain control, they installed marshal law and moved troops in to assist and take back the streets.

The scale, diversity and success of the actions taking place took a new twist when the first of the meek could take no more.

In the centre of the very city where it had all began, a mother had reached the end of her tether.

Alone with three small children and unable to cope with the horror enveloping them, the constant reports of disaster and the personal threat that she encountered in her dingy apartment on the hate filled, fiery streets, she took matters into her own hands.

Weeping and trying to console her wide-eyed frightened babies, she gently guided them to the biggest bedroom.

She took the old gun that she had been using for protection during this time of terror and shot them dead, turning the gun on herself, with a shaking hand and then killed herself.

A scared parent, scared children lost in a world gone mad, now lost to eternity.

Chapter Twenty-Six

The cat and mouse game that Gabriel and Yetereal had played out over the course of the next day and a half had resulted in seventeen deaths, multiple injuries to police, and emergency service men and women not to mention civilian casualties. Collateral damage to cars and buildings had been widespread also.

As the pursuit carried on, both Gabriel and Yetereal had become untouchable by the police who had realised that there was simply nothing they could do to stop them and had instead tried to concentrate their limited numbers on the overwhelming task of regaining order.

Never sleeping, never stopping but always centred on what they were doing the elusive chase of two adversaries had moved from one side of the city to the other, through the flames, through the rubble, through the screams.

Gabriel could discern where Yetereal was and had, at first followed at a distance as his wounds repaired steadily and as his mind rationalised what had happened to Jophiel, the world around him and what he had to do.

He was finding it difficult to put aside Jophiel's death and this unsettled him, for he had known that there was little chance of them surviving this savagery. Perhaps it was the fact that Jophiel was as close to him as anyone had been, their previous actions were testament to that or maybe it was the thought that the human race was about to change forever.

Yetereal could also sense where Gabriel was and as he had fled the airport in a fury, he had taken out his rage on the primates still stupid enough to be on the streets at all and even more stupid for crossing his path. He had dispatched them with swift and decisive actions:

Energy bolts had been thrown at a couple that had been fleeing hand in hand, vaporising their fragile forms. Another monkey had stepped out from a doorway, been startled by Yetereal, who had grabbed him with both hands and shook him so violently that blood had begun to ooze from his ears, nose and eyes as his brain smashed against the inside of his skull and pulped, before hurling him across the street and through a third floor window.

Now they were reaching the point that they both knew to be inevitable.

Yetereal had no intention of leaving this world until Gabriel was vanquished and, of course, Gabriel knew the same to be true of himself.

Yetereal had made his way to the largest park and open space that the city had to offer. Even with the rubbish, the wreckage and the odd body littering it, the green environment had calmness to it.

Sitting on a bench, arms and legs outstretched, looking over the grass and the trees in the distance, Yetereal watched as Gabriel walked purposefully toward him.

As he reached the bench, Gabriel paused in front of it, took the time to look around at the peaceful carnage and then sat down next to Yetereal.

Neither of them spoke for the longest of time, each lost for a while in their own reverie.

Finally, it was Yetereal that broke the silence.

"It is well under way. There will be no coming back." His voice was guttural, gravely and low.

"There is always a way back to the Light." Gabriel replied with a hint of resignation.

Yetereal turned and looked deeply into Gabriel's granite eyes and gave a short laugh.

"Then what has all of this been for?" He gestured with a sweeping motion of his right arm. "I cannot affect your perception but even you must admit that this time we have come too far. This is the time that the humans will be made aware, some already are! There is nothing after this," he stood and waved his arms as he turned on the spot.

"Their pathetic little lives are spent on this mud ball and there is nothing after death. There is only service whilst on Earth and this is where and when we will begin to take more souls, more and more will turn to the Lie to the Dark! This is the dawning of the Dark Dawn!" His voice had been rising as he spoke and ended with an emphatic shout.

Gabriel sat and surveyed the figure in front of him. Yetereal had been an ally many eons ago; so long ago in fact that even he found it difficult to recollect such times and had to concentrate to brush the dust of time from the memories.

Now after all of these thousands of generations, all of the tasks that he had performed, all of the deaths he had caused, he was fanatical, he was changed and was almost desperate in belief.

"There is always a way back to the Light. Man will adapt, he will adjust to his environment and move on as he always has. This is one of their best traits. Faith is personal, private and untouchable. Once they have come through this they will be even more resolute in their belief."

Gabriel shrugged his shoulders as he stood to face Yetereal.

"It doesn't matter anyway. Our struggle has gone on for such a time as to nearly seem pointless in some respect. Any victory will be a hollow one . . ."

Yetereal's eyes squinted as he glared at Gabriel, he did not want to elongate the conversation any longer, and he didn't think that there was any need to.

"Spoken like the defeated, pathetic being that you have become, Gabriel."

As Yetereal began to take steady steps back; Gabriel resigned himself to what was about to happen and backed off slowly, facing Yetereal.

Like duellists in the early morning mist, they faced each other with stern expressions, calm demeanours and waited for the other to act before unleashing the form of death that they could dispense that was unique to them. Yetereal began to shake imperceptibly, vibrating rapidly so that he appeared to blur at the edges. He was channelling his power.

Gently, steadily and slowly he rose into the air, arms outstretched, never taking his eyes off Gabriel.

Gritting his teeth, tensing his muscles and strengthening his resolve, Gabriel also lifted himself from the grass, rising easily.

Both of them hovered about ten feet from the dewy blades of grass below and then with the slightest twitch of his face Yetereal revealed that he was about to act, his eyes flicked as he moved to do so.

Gabriel responded to this and both let loose a blue force of energy that utilised all of their might, all of their emotions and all of their will.

The bolts collided between them and smashed with a violent crack that echoed around the park like a cannon shot.

Gabriel lifted his left hand slowly and placed it next to his right, from which the bolt emitted. Both hands focused the power on the one and only objective that he now had.

Yetereal did the same to concentrate his fire and as his vibrating seemed to take on such a speed as to form an energy barrier around him, flowing over his body, he moved forward slightly getting closer to Gabriel.

Gabriel let out a scream as he too edged forward, closing the gap between the two enemies and increasing the intensity of the force that they released.

The unimaginable power between them had to give.

There was a massive explosion, arcs of blue energy streaming from every angle, bolts of electrical power jetting from them as they were blown apart . . .

It was several minutes before Gabriel awoke.

The detonation had stunned him unconscious and now that he tried to regain his awareness, he found that part of him did not want to relinquish his grip on the oblivion that had meant serenity.

He had to make himself focus.

Blood was affecting his vision as it flowed into his eyes from a gaping wound on his forehead. His body screamed in pain as he moved tentatively to seek out Yetereal.

He staggered to his feet, his strength drained along with his mental faculties. He shook from exhaustion as he tried to get a grip on the situation.

Then he saw what was left of Yetereal.

The power of the blast and the energy that they had been able to create between them had taken its toll on him.

Yetereal's grotesque, twisted face seemed to snarl at Gabriel even though the life had mercifully left it.

His body had been distorted, like a plastic soldier melted over a flame, limbs were stretched and deformed to elongated length and his torso slender but twice as long as it was and misshapen in the extreme.

Gabriel stared down at Yetereal's broken body and his shoulders slumped forward, he was drained.

For the first time in as long as he could remember, he felt tired.

His fatigue ran deep to his core and he dropped to his knees, still shaking violently.

As his trembling hand reached into his tattered jacket retrieving two gold coins, tears began to streak down his blackened cheeks.

His quivering hand reached out and placed the coins over what were Yetereal's eyes.

As he sobbed over the body uncontrollably, Gabriel began to realize that he did not feel sad.

He felt relief.

Steven Archer

Chapter Twenty-Seven

The voice was distant at first, a whisper.

Gabriel had no idea of how long he had sobbed over Yetereal's corpse, sobbed for Jophiel and sobbed for himself. Time meant nothing.

His head was clear of all thoughts, he felt a peace that he had not known before.

The voice got louder.

Gabriel was uncomfortable listening to it and he hoped for a second that if he ignored it there was a chance that it may go away.

In the tranquillity of the moment Gabriel knew that he could not ignore the voice.

He knew that he could not ignore his Master.

Gabriel . . .

"Yes, Master."

It is finished.

"Yes, Master."

It is done and now it is time for you to come back to me.

"I know Master."

You have done well Gabriel; you have accomplished what no other could have done.

You have helped me to usher in a new era for man. You have helped me to fulfil the Prophecy.

"Yes, Master."

I am pleased, Gabriel, now . . . come back to my side.

"Yes, Master."

Gabriel wept like a newborn child as he felt unconditional love like a warmth he could never have imagined.

Epilogue

The Truth and The Lie coursed on through time.

The Light and The Dark intertwined together forever.

Good and Evil connected for all eternity, as they always had been and as they always would be.

Man did see out the time of strife, did see out the time of chaos and did emerge stronger . . .

The way had not been easy and it had taken many, many years.

The rebuilding of society, civilisation, and religion in the knowledge that the choice of good and bad had to be seen out on Earth and nowhere else had been difficult.

But it had been done . . .

The Truth and The Lie coursed on through time, Good and Evil connected for all eternity . . .

PART II

CADO EX VENIA

(FALL FROM GRACE)

GADEREAL—THE MUTE ANGELS

ONE

The Gardians are exactly that. Guardians.

Created in the beginning when all was well in the world of the Light, before the troubles, before the uprising and *the* casting down, these creatures would guard places of limited access, goods or on occasion, minor transgressors but they could never have envisaged the role that they would play after the events that changed the Light and created the Dark . . .

Their pivotal responsibility from that point onwards . . . it was as if this was the true destiny that they were fashioned to carry out.

Each of them stood at six and a half feet tall, they were bulky and muscular yet had an agility that belied their great lumbering and cumbersome appearance, with features that seemed squashed and pressed to the cranium, like burn victims, they had piercing black eyes and a habit of cocking their head to the left on their thick tree like necks, as if in an attempt to register some fact that had been imparted to them.

Each wore the same dirty, loose leather-type uniform that gave them freedom of movement but little protection from any of the natural elements that could be thrown at them in the course of their duties, as they had been gifted with the lack of pain. A deprivation of feeling which made them formidable opponents in any kind of skirmish or battle as they would not know when to stop, they would just keep going and going until they were incapacitated or dead. But this also meant that their mental growth was stunted. They understood very little except for any task or mission that was explained to them in detail to ensure clarity. This was simpler to achieve as all communication between and with Gardians was by telepathy, as at birth they had their tongues removed so that they could not give any information away to any body trying to glean it. Over the centuries they developed this sixth sense.

Eight of these Gardians had been dispatched to a small, seemingly insignificant village on the outskirts of Syracusae in what would later become Sicilia and much, much later Syracusa in Sicily. At first their instructions were to remain hidden at all costs and keep a close watch on a husband and wife, again of no seeming significance . . . except for the fact that the wife was pregnant for the first time. They never thought to question the task afforded to them, never queried, they simply got on with the work to be done in as efficient a manner as could be.

Taking up position in a clearing with good ground cover and a short distance from the mud brick and straw hovel that the couple called home, the Gardians took shifts observing the mundane farming life that these people lived, day in day out, watching the lives and the habits that these people had from their various concealed vantage points.

*

Kaben and Josea were young and loved each other very much. Although theirs was, as was the norm in the area, an arranged marriage designed to join two medium sized, middle class families in this case and extend their lands, properties and livestock, they had overcome an age difference (Kaben was eight years older than Josea, who at nineteen, was still a virgin when they were betrothed) and found an attraction to one another.

As the years passed their love grew and bonded them together. Life was as good as it could be for them. It was hard at times, even harsh but they had each other, they had farmland and some livestock and could support themselves with ease, passing on to the family any surplus that they could to help those more in need than they were. The only real blemish, real heartache was the lack of children.

A few years after they had wed, they had tried to have children, not because the family had started to press them for heirs to carry on the lineage, but because they felt the emptiness that a child could fill and make them a true family.

Unfortunately, they were both frustrated by the time that passed without success and without a little one. The longer that this went on the more worried they became that this was something that was not meant to be, that was not meant to happen for them . . . Josea became withdrawn and blamed herself, Kaben tried to reassure her and make sure that she understood that he would always be there for her.

Time passed and so did the visits to the Soothsayer, who looked into the blood fuelled flames that were conjured, the sacred rune stones and the stars high in the heavens in an effort to give them some hope.

Just when the last vestige of hope was about to wane and the sympathetic looks from other villagers became longer and unbearable, the Soothsayer visited Kaben and Josea with astonishing news, late one night.

She had had a vision during the night, a vision of four babies of utmost importance to be born to them. The news lifted their hopes as high as they had ever been over the desolate years of trying and, two weeks later, Josea did in fact find that she was with child. Their euphoria was tangible, their happiness boundless and their lives complete. They could look to a future of hope and opportunity.

From the hidden copse, the Gardians watched these events unfold and reported the news.

*

The Gardians watched, and observed the happy couple going about their daily business with only an odd glance into a thicket or over their shoulder from time to time as if they could sense that they were and indeed had been spied upon for the past nine months, three weeks and three days.

Patience, caution and cunning always kept the Gardians out of sight if not, perhaps out of the minds of their prey.

Meanwhile, Kaben and Josea had spent the time since the amazing news of their imminent arrivals preparing their home and their lives as well as visiting the Soothsayer who could only emphasise that there would be four children of importance but beyond a veil of cloud she could see no more, the visions were perplexing and unlike any she had seen before, this gave her cause for concern and she spent many hours rocking back and forth over an open flame praying for good and for guidance.

Kaben found himself countering the distinct feeling of being watched that had crept up on them both over the past months by calming Josea who was having a hard time rationalising her feelings and fears about the same concern, the only cloud on a clear horizon.

An almost tangible feeling pressed down on them, weighing heavy against the happy day that was upon them. Perhaps after the births, all would be fine.

*

The birth of the children took place in the early afternoon with the sun at its highest illuminating the great day that Kaben and Josea had anticipated and longed for.

Four girls were born in quick succession, with no fuss or trauma to their mother, no complication or delay. The Soothsayer said that this was a sign that they were keen to start their lives and fulfil their destiny, whatever that may be. The sheer joy that everyone felt was infectious.

The family and friends that had gathered to welcome the new arrivals gasped and fawned over the girls, beauty was a word that did none of them justice . . . they were radiant.

The final act before all of the well-wishers in the home of the new arrivals left was to name them, bless them and welcome them with gifts.

Kaben and Josea had chosen boy and girls names and found the thought that they had put in before hand, useful as now they could be a part of the family immediately.

Anne, Anna, Anniy and Aneka were lavished with love, smiles and affection and then each of them given a gift from their parents after the blessing and after a final celebration, albeit quiet as they had drifted off to sleep, the people left and the new family was alone, peaceful and contented.

The sun began to fall in the sky and Kaben could not believe the extent of the love that he felt for his wife and his tiny daughters, it swelled him with pride to look at their sleeping forms, as he too drifted off into a fitful sleep.

*

"If I cannot see my daughters again, then *I do not want to live!*" Josea shouted and cried, tears flowing from her horrified, wide eyes. "If you are to take them, then take me! *Extinguish me!* I have yearned too long for my babies to live without them in this world! Send *me* to the next to wait for them!"

Josea had snapped.

Her mind had fractured due to the kidnapping of her daughters at the hands of these foul demons who had crept up on them as they slept, and about which they could do nothing. They were powerless. Why did no one come to help?

The Gardians had immobilised both Kaben and Josea with a speed that meant that they had had no time to react. They struggled but it was for nought against these giant creatures of the night.

As strong and brutal as they were with the parents, so were they gentle and calm with the infants, who barely stirred from their slumber, and just as well.

Kaben felt a fear so pronounce as to have it stick in his heart like an ice—cold spear-tip. Was he to lose his entire family this night? He said a silent prayer that Josea would pass out or be quiet so that these demons would leave and so that he could then give pursuit knowing that she was safe. He was no coward, but realised that he had no chance whatsoever in the circumstances, but that he could track them and possibly slay them on his terms . . .

The leader of the six beasts leaned close to Josea, causing her to turn her cheek, in disgust at the stench of the foul being as well as at a repugnance of his sweaty, slimy features. The Gardian studied her for a moment and then, having looked over his shoulder at the four children being carried out of the hovel by his allies, and contenting himself that they would not witness his actions, he struck Josea in the side of the head with such a ferocious force as to snap her neck and crumple her delicate face. The mercy was that she died instantly, and could not feel the rage of the blows that followed, pummelling her fragile form to a pulp. Bones snapped and broke, flesh battered and split, under the impact of the massive fists. She had her wish to go to the next world granted.

Kaben, in the final instances of his life now felt a loss and a grief that fortunately would not haunt him for long. As he saw his children taken and his wife killed, so to was he set upon, his held arms wrenched from their sockets by the hands from behind in a firestorm of pain that carried on for a few moments whilst his captor inflicted blow after blow onto and into his unprotected person.

His last thought before merciful, sweet death was of his daughters . . . what was to be their destiny? What would become of his little girls?

*

The beasts had done what the Light had requested of them, almost. The first part of the mission was complete, that had taken time but the next part would not take long at all.

Once they had the infants back to the hidden makeshift camp, swelled by their success and the opportunity to kill, they took the next step.

The small wooden box with dull metal hinges and clasp had been kept safe for the duration of their observations of the young couple, now dead.

All eight gathered as four sat with the little ones in their laps around a small fire and four others took the needles and

Steven Archer

course thread out of the box and heated the needles over the flames.

The babies twitched and rolled.

The needles were heated as hot as they could be and the first child brought nearer the flame. All of the children moved frantically against the immovable bodies of the captures, crying out in the cold, dark night, as if sensing something was about to happen.

One Gardian cradled the first child, the second leaned in and then, taking the needle, threaded it with the course yarn and after pressing the babies lips together between long fat fingers, proceeded to stitch her lips closed.

The stifled shrieks of the first child subjected to that agonising piercing and heat and the crying of the others that followed cut the night sky but not another creature, beast nor man stirred.

TWO

Anne, Aneka, Anna, and Anniy were born to serve.

They knew no other life and nor would they.

They spent their lives in servitude scribing the events that happened between the Light and the Dark.

The Light had formulated the idea to have some events transcribed to keep over the eons for future generations to learn from, for others to interpret and so had developed the plan of the scribes, the innocents to do the work, the girls.

They would be the conduit for the story of the Light and the Dark the tellers of the Truth, the whole Truth and nothing but the Truth . . .

It had taken a while to manipulate events but the right parents had finally been chosen and without their knowledge or consent the Light had affected the embryos within Josea and changed them, altered them to become what they would in time . . .

Along with the Gardians that kept a constant vigil over them, becoming surrogate parents in the process as they had been together forever, they moved constantly.

Part of the method of keeping them secret from the Dark was to move them to a different location at irregular intervals to prevent tracking. Sometimes they would stay for mere days and other times they would establish a kind of routine within the moving that they did when they were rooted for more than a week or two. These were times that the girls cherished as they had time to bond, to inhabit a place for the human body cannot permanently adjust to moving, always.

The girls had no idea of how their movements were planned and they had given up trying to even think about the logistics of it all many years earlier.

Even the memories of parents, faceless due to only a brief meeting many, many years before had faded beyond the point of even an emotional connection, the only thing that they had now, besides a gold coin each from their birth rites that the

Gardians had been instructed to allow them to keep was the work that they scribed and each other.

They would shelter in woods, caves or huts. Some of the habitats that they used had been prepared beforehand for them, some had been created by nature and some had been emptied of their occupants well before they arrived to take shelter for a while, always nomadic always moving.

The packing of their few possessions, the folding of their meagre clothes and the travelling by animal, makeshift carriage or foot had been trying at first on the young girls who had even, on very few occasions been carried by the Gardians but now it was just routine, the routine of moving and hiding.

A never ending life of scribe and movement, never settling, never laying down roots awaited these four innocent sisters who were whispered about at night, talked about over fires in the dead of night and only spoken of in the most hushed tones during daylight for they were the stuff of legend and myth, a paradox that few knew of and even fewer would witness.

The life that they had laid out in front of them was set and established. It could not and would not change, the girls had an idea of this and because they had only seen what freedom was from afar, in the night, they could not form an image or feeling of it and so did not miss what they could not have nor understand. They were the secret they were the shadow. They were the Mute Angels.

The only time that they ever saw another being was when a witness to an event would be brought before them to tell their tale first hand but this was always brief, never elaborate and after each witness had finished, they were killed. The girls knew that they were killed but felt nothing for them for this was part of their role.

*

The girls had grown as all children do in the course of time. They had started life as beautiful, blonde babes in arm, all with strikingly piercing green eyes, which had a sharp quality like emerald. Each still had blonde hair, plaited at the back so that it did not distract them from their work.

As they had grown their lips had all but sealed. The holes that had been created in the horrible act shortly after their births had long since healed, leaving just a tiny slit through which a straw could be placed for them to take in liquid nourishment. The thread that was still used and changed regularly was now more of a symbolic statement rather than actually needing to be used to restrict movement of the mouth.

This did not concern the girls, who had never spoken out loud in all of their lives as they communicated telepathically and had done as naturally as if they did speak to one another.

The physical problems that they encountered from moving all of the time, always being in the dark and eating as they did took its toll. Rather than growing into strong, attractive and athletic women, they had become frail, thin and weak.

The most remarkable indication of this was not their bent over gait, nor their gaunt faces, but the thinness of their pale, almost albino skin, through which each vein and artery could be seen, each heartbeat and blood flow seen first hand.

Yet for all of these physical problems it was obvious to any that should come across them that there was a beauty within them.

And so these poor Mute Angels went on with their lives, designed by the Light to be girls, to be innocents and to be the writers of the Truth. So these unfortunates went about their work scribing the Light and Dark war, year upon year, decade upon decade, responsible for the most momentous secrets in history being written impartially and yet they themselves also hidden and alone save for one another.

THREE

Over time, and much of it, the underground saga of the Mute Angels grew.

This possibility, the chance that the Light did have a team of scribes documenting what occurred between these two immense, unique forces irked devotees of the Dark. The fact that the Light had such confidence in its own righteousness to have these episodes written down was bad enough but the scheming minds in the dark, flattered themselves that this was the case when, in fact they were more concerned and absolutely cynical about the fact that the Light could be influencing these papers, these writings if not out right lying about them. This could not be allowed to happen. It had to be stopped and in doing so one more bothersome facet of the almighty Light would be extinguished, which was all the better, it was the Dark realm that used lies and deceit!

Numerous agents had been dispatched over a long period of time to detect the Mute Angels, supply information and, ideally, kill them.

Many had been sent and none had succeeded in getting close to them let alone exterminating them.

The only clue that the Dark had been able to acquire regarding the Mutes had been from a lowly minion, who whilst on a completely different mission, had come across a fragment of parchment which he had had the intelligence to pick up and keep, trying to barter it in the filthy underworld when he returned from the completed skirmish in which he had been involved for food or liquor, none of which had been forthcoming from any of the sinister community as none of them had any idea what it was or what possible purpose it could serve to them.

The small fragment finally found its way to what was a hall of records, a massive hollowed cave area lined with shelving and volumes of text both discovered and stolen or in the most case forged and made up, this was the Dark's version on what had happened since the casting down, and a campaign that lasted years of disinformation and an anti-history. Torches flared orange and yellow in the gloom, illuminating the works in flickering, skittish light and keeping the vast area dry.

The battered and dirty parchment found a home there, stuffed on a shelf.

It wasn't a disappointment that nothing had really ever come from the search for the Mutes, it was a constant irritation, always there and always stinging.

Finally, the agent with the doggedness to track them down was approached, the agent with the ability to think on a different level and get results no matter how insignificant: Gadereal.

*

After the test of time, alone with his thoughts for such a time as to be meaningless, Gadereal heard the voice of his master echo quietly around the walls of the gloomy and dank chamber in which he had stood for a brief eternity.

These Mute Angels . . . they task me, Gadereal. Do you think that they exist?

"Yes, master, I do." His head bowed beneath his hood, Gadereal kept his reply curt.

Good, then find these creatures for me and dispatch them. Your skills will be of use to you. There is no limit in time as yet . . . simply come back when the work has been done and tell me of it.

"Very well, my master."

Even for one as committed as Gadereal, there were brief moments of frustration, of anger at how little he had produced, pin pricks of negativity. But they were just brief flashes and no sooner had they begun, they ended and spurred him on, perhaps it was the time that was being taken that frustrated him a little for it had been long.

His first line of investigation was to travel to places and times that seemed as though they could have relevance or that had been strong in the myth of these beings as to where or when they had been there.

Prehistoric Amazonian jungles, steaming and hot, European medieval caves which were cold and harsh as well as small huts in tiny villages scattered about the Mediterranean, none had produced anything and it was whilst he stood in one such location, overlooking the Red Sea from the rocky mountain top as the sun lazily fell from the sky above that Gadereal decided that it was time to go back to basics.

*

Gadereal read. He set himself up in the archive of the Dark and by candlelight on a battered wooden desk, he read all that he could think of, that he had heard of and that he had been told of by those few that he had encountered on his travels through place and time.

Volumes of heavy leather bound texts, scrolls which were as brittle as to flake to the touch, sigils that had not been seen by any eyes for ages and the simplest diary entries from those who could be bothered to take the time to impart their knowledge and experiences.

Gadereal read them all and time stretched out before him like an open dusty road, baron and unbroken.

None of these pieces of literature gave up anything that he did not already know, only having the effect of seeming to diminish his crystal azure eyes.

But in carrying out this thankless task he did get a result.

When Gadereal, moved one massive ancient text to read through it, a piece of parchment fell from the shelf to the floor. Pausing and looking down on the fragment lying on the cracked and dry wooden beams of the floor, Gadereal had no doubt that before he even picked it up that this was significant.

Having taken another moment, he replaced the text that he had in his hand and stooped slowly, picking up the parched scrap. Taking it to the desk he sat and held it against the light of a candle and read what little was to be seen;

"When the land was laid to waste, he moved on. When the earth was scorched dry, he passed over. When the sky was drained of colour, he went away. When the air had nothing to lend, no atmosphere, he disappeared never to be seen there again.

In the time that passed after his leaving there was nought. The baron wasteland remained as a testament to his Wrath and Power, the life that had been there once in abundance was no more, nor would there ever be again lest he wish to confirm his ru . . ."

The text was brief but that did not matter. Gadereal had the lead that would take him all the way to his target, for what could not be revealed in the writing would come from the parchment itself. Through the darkness of the hood that he wore, hiding his features from view, his blue eyes glinted in the candlelight.

*

It had taken him a little time to track down the experts that he needed but this was simple in comparison to what he had already done and the work still to be done at this journey's end.

Gadereal's first advisor was on parchment. Sitting in the open air, dusty, dry and warm next to the stream in Niger, The old man with skin as dry as the parchment that he held in front of him spoke. The words came slowly and in a stuttering fashion, but this was lost on Gadereal as everyone reacted to his presence and physicality in the same way, it didn't really register with him the fear and awe that he struck deep within people.

The old man brushed a stray grey hair from his eyes and began:

"This is about the skin, the skin of a goat. All parchment in this area is made from it, all of it. It's in the craft . . ." He allowed himself a quick and furtive glance at Gadereal, feeling that he should go into more detail without hearing the words to do so. It was as if the robed menace was in his head,

Steven Archer

probing his thoughts. He scratched at an undetermined itch and carried on.

"The skin from a newly killed goat is stood in fresh clean water for a day and a night. They are then washed and scrubbed, gently but thoroughly until the water of the well runs clear . . . there can be no dirt. Old lime is then added to a clean trough of water and stirred in to make a cloudy liquid, each person will know the amount to use to ensure best results for the amount of skins to be added. Each skin will be folded on the skin side and left in this solution for eight days and nights . . . Every day they must be stirred with a stick three times. The skins are then removed carefully and passed to the women to remove all of the hair from them. The skins are then placed once again into the lime liquor and left for eight more days, this process takes care, patience and attention as at any point they can be spoiled. After this, the skins are placed in a trough of clean water once they have, again been rinsed in water until the water is clear, for two more days. The skins are then taken out and stretched over circular wooden frames, skinned with a razor sharp knife with great care to get any remaining hair off and then left in the sun for two days. Once this has been done, the skins are then moistened slightly and rubbed with weak pumice so that stretching can be done, over the course of two or three days, the skins should be moistened, rubbed and stretched to the point of use without tearing, this is where the skill comes in to play as many skins are torn and lost . . . Once at their utmost point, they are left to dry. The parchment is then ready for use . . ."

Gadereal did not move. He remained crouched by the man and seemed to watch as he moved his old fingers involuntarily, nervous.

"This is how it is done and has been for many, many years. Different tribes and craftsman have slightly different methods and that is how you can tell where they are from, that and the colour of the parchment as each goat is different from different regions . . ." The old man sweated now as he reached the critical point of information and wondered if his usefulness was about to be outlived. He closed his eyes tightly.

"I would say that this came from Sicilia . . ." His voice trembled and trailed off, his body tensed. After a moment he opened an eye and then spun quickly around on the spot, dirt and dust swirling around him as he did.

His relief at being alone was immeasurable.

*

The Italian professor's hands shook from the cold and his fear as he looked at the parchment and the writing on it. When he had walked into his office in the Tate Gallery, London reading a book as he did, he had almost had a heart attack as the door had slammed behind him, the atmosphere was sucked out of the room and the wraith-like figure that stood before him, leaned into him. The smell, the presence and the oppression that emanated from Gadereal was enough to turn his blood cold. Horror almost made it impossible for him to function but the figure had asked the question, albeit silently in his head and he had to answer . . . he knew that he had to answer.

"This is ancient, ancient . . . the writing is classic Aramaic but it has a twist, a finesse that I have never seen before . . ." Interest in the subject actually caught hold of him for a millisecond before releasing him again to fear.

"There is an element of Egyptian influence also, which I fail to understand. The text would take a lot longer to examine and make sense of but I would hazard a guess that it is a reference to either a plague that covered the land or a mighty warrior after a ferocious engagement a great battle . . . There are other clues like the capital letters used on *wrath* and *power* and also the fact that *when* and *he* is used so much may be a sign or layered message to an informed reader . . . But of course, the most striking thing is that the first capital letter of the page is in blood."

The form in front of him did not move at all, nothing at this revelation. It was as if he had anticipated it . . .

"This is unique, wondrous really . . . I've only ever heard of this once before a long time ago during my studies . . . a tutor had gone into the possibility of a scribe based in Sicilia.

He had a text, a mere page but was positive that the blood of newborns was being used to anoint each page to give a gravity to what were already serious texts . . ."

Professor DeCazio did not finish his remarks. The rush of air, the whirlwind of movement that engulfed the small office sending books, paper and furniture flying about him, causing him to yell out and crouch, hands over head, cowering, caught him completely by surprise. He trembled and shook as the room came to a gradual standstill, whimpering in the corner to which he had crawled.

He did not dare look from behind closed eyes for several long moments and when eventually he did, two things were apparent;

He was alone, soiled and the parchment that he had held onto had gone also with his visitor.

FOUR

Nothing stirred in the immense archive.

Gadereal moved around the perimeter of the room, skirting the shelves and the grey granite rock face before cutting in to wander through the rows of shelves and the thousands of documents that they contained. The only sound was the crackling of the torches that lit the room in an eerie, ever moving glow.

The information from the parchment maker and the professor had been invaluable. It had taken a long time to get to this juncture and there would be more to spend but he knew that this mission was coming to a conclusion. He would soon be able to do what he did best, although the fortitude, persistence and doggedness that he had displayed thus far was an indication of his skills and just what he had become . . . the years and centuries had altered him, changed him from what he once had been but so too had the deeds that he had been a party to and had been requested to do as part of his service. No doubt this would have some kind of affect on him also, no matter how subtle.

In the marriage of these two pieces of information was born clues as to the location of the Mute Angels. Gadereal had looked into the parchment, the amount of goats that had been killed in the area of Sicilia and then had been able to find a more interesting piece of evidence: The deaths of babies in the same place or just on the mainland of Italia right after birth. The connection was made and the fact that the blood of innocents had been used on the parchments and the records made on them was striking to Gadereal, even obvious now but connecting the information could not have been done in any other way. The puzzle was almost complete.

The uneven and jagged rock of the floor, not worn down like the corridors, as there weren't many who felt the need to enter this place, scraped against the souls of his battered feet.

Now that he had the place, he simply had to be a little more patient and discover the *time* that he could find the Mutes.

Steven Archer

FIVE

Gadereal had recognised the Gardians as soon as he had seen them.

He had spent months in the area, taking the form of many, many humans in his search, sensing that he was close but cautious in his approach so as to not jeopardise his plans.

He had been an old, weather-worn merchant, trading goods, as he wandered from village to village pulling his bony donkey along in the dry, arid heat, not in any great rush in his journey to the mainland yet not around long enough to raise any concerns from the locals, never mind his quarry, wherever they may be.

He had been a young goat herder, lanky and lazy sitting in the rough hills and mountains, watching not only his small flock but also everything that occurred within his field of vision whilst appearing to sleep or play with the kids, as they fed on the sparse tundra.

He had been a landowner, fat and colourful from the mainland looking for possible plots to buy for animals to graze on, for his ships to unload on or for his farming requirements. These three and many others had he become in the long months leading up to his find, becoming these humans then watching, listening and waiting . . .

Now he had the fourth of the Gardians that he had seen in the last hours in his sights. The other three that had been outside, maintaining a perimeter had been killed in as straightforward a manner as possible, with darkness as his cover and stealth as his ally, Gadereal had been able to slit their throats before their enormous bodies could react to him. He bled each one of them as if for slaughter and waited with each as their blood spread out over the sandy earth and their life extinguished. The rush from not only finding these creatures and his prey but finally killing them caught up with Gadereal and now he took a moment to prepare himself, his intense blue eyes looking down on his next victim from on high.

It was, perhaps a little odd that his comrade strode up to him early in the morning without an indication or sign that anything was wrong, but not unusual either.

The Gardian that had stood at the small entrance to what must have been a cavern, moved slowly forward and just as he registered that this thing before him looked exactly like one of his own, it realised that there was something different about him that he couldn't quite gauge and now it was too late. Had it been in his movement or his manner it was simply too late for action now and in that split second the Gardian knew that he was dead.

Gadereal moved with a speed and precision of movement that came from a warrior of great capability and belied the physical form that he had taken. The two daggers that he held inflicted three wounds as he rolled past the stumbling bulk of his foe slicing deep into the flesh, tearing it apart and allowing the blood to spurt into the air. The first cut was to the throat, as arms were raised in defence or to try and stem the flow of blood, the second wound was inflicted across his massive chest opening up the cavity that protected organs and as he moved past his right hand moved swiftly again to slice down through the air and then into the lower back of the Gardian which combined with the first two incisive wounds to kill the beast, who slumped to his knees and then fell forward onto the ground dead before he hit it.

Gadereal knew that although there had been little noise it would surely have been enough to alert the others within. He knew also what to expect as to numbers for he had spent two days watching the Gardians from a distance and had decided that he must strike tonight as he felt that they were preparing to move on again. The thought crossed his mind that maybe that was why this had been so straightforward thus far, as the repetition and routine of moving combined with a lack of action had rusted these soldiers' reactions.

As he moved quickly through the entrance tunnel, toward what must open into a cavern or cave in the mountainside,

Steven Archer

another Gardian ran forward, yelling and holding a large broadsword in front of him.

The element of surprise was done. Gadereal acted more now on instinct than on reaction to the unfolding confrontation.

Feet from the body in front of him, moving rapidly, he leapt into the air, twisting his body as he did so that he rolled sideways on into the legs of the brute sending him crashing to the rocky, dusty deck with a heavy impact. A split second later, Gadereal had twisted again, coming up onto one knee and plunged a dagger into the right side of the flailing Gardian trying to get back up, twisting and pulling as he did. He then spun and using his left hand in a backhanded motion that thrust his second, bloody dagger into the stomach of the next Gardian to rush on him. Retrieving the knife from the being on the deck he swung around to strike a cutting wound to the creature's neck but not before it had managed to use its hand spear to lance Gadereal in the left shoulder. Rising and using his momentum after the impact that he ignored, his gritted determination spurring him on, Gadereal pushed the Gardian back and in two quick swipes dispatched him with cuts to the chest and stomach which caused the recipient to bellow loudly as he fell dying.

Turning he stood over the Gardian still trying to rise from the deck and, blade in each hand, arms outstretched Gadereal swung and stabbed into the sides of the enemy, yanking down as he did pulling further on the wounds inflicted.

A pause as he checked the two corpses and surveyed the gore and blood around the walls and bodies was all that Gadereal needed before moving stealthily toward the cave itself, satisfied that both were dead.

*

The scene that awaited Gadereal upon his entry to the cave was neither a shock to him nor surprising.

The four Mute Angels were sat, side-by-side along a wooden table makeshift in its construction but sturdy, nonetheless. They were in front of ledgers open on the page that they were busy with, inkwells, quills and what must have been vials of blood neatly placed on the worktop in front of them, everything in its place and efficient. The four blonde girls sat patiently and calmly looking ahead at Gadereal as he steadily moved into the rugged rounded space, very much aware of the two Gardians that stood to the side of the table, poised. The girls' green eyes following him carefully but serenely.

One of the Gardians stepped forward, lumbering heavily on the rough, rocky floor. The last one did not flinch as if he knew that Gadereal wanted to leave him alive, perhaps it had sensed it in his thoughts and Gadereal hadn't been aware, either way this served him well.

The brute that crouched before him, arms open, beckoning almost was not expecting the transition that Gadereal made. In the second that he started to shake violently and almost imperceptibly at first, the thing was caught in the moment, watching instead of acting and taking the advantage. Just as Gadereal had planned.

Gadereal's Gardian form was disposed of as easily as it had been taken and in the blur of motion that swept his being, re-arranging him, changing him his new form began to appear. Slowly at first the hint of human shape and contour began to structure. The vibration and molecular transition that went with it only lasted a few seconds and instead of being taken advantage of was witnessed by the two Gardians with wide eyes . . .

Kaben lunged and twisted at the same time in front of the Gardian who was transfixed by what he had just witnessed, rooted. It's brain not able to keep pace with the actuality of what had just occurred, nor the speed with which his attacker now moved on him. Twisting and turning back to the spot that he had transformed on Kaben swept his arms and blood stained blades back to his sides as the Gardian blinked, mouthed some silent words, dropped his sword and shield and then looked down at himself.

Looked down at the gaping wounds on his torso, bleeding and seeping his crimson life fluid. One fold of skin actually hung from his side exposing his stomach and intestines as they started to spill from his gut onto the floor. The unbelieving look in its eyes were quickly replaced by blank, expressionless stares as it slumped down into a steaming heap at the feet of Kaben, who rolled his shoulders and looked on impassively.

The final Gardian dropped his weapons and shield and backed off to the sidewall.

Kaben acknowledged the move with a brief nod of his head that indicated that he should stay very still.

The girls did not make a sound or a movement.

It wasn't as if he'd expected histrionics from their stitched lips but he had thought that there would be more of a reaction. The thought crossed his mind that perhaps they had reached the end of the line, the end of their tether and even the release of death was preferable to carrying on in the fashion that they were in this manner of movement and solitude, prisoners of the Light's whim and ego to have all that it was involved in recorded.

Kaben wiped the two knives on his garment and sheathed them then walked cautiously behind the girls, still they did not move, their pale, blue veined faces emotionless.

When he stood behind the first, Anniy, he placed a hand on her shoulder and then withdrew a long blade. Anniy's only movement was to push away the work that she was doing as Kaben brought his hand to bear in front of her face and swiftly, precisely slit her throat open. The only sound in the cave was the gurgling of Anniy's blood as it raced to pour from the wound. She slumped forward, motionless and rigid as blood pooled under her face, matting her blonde hair as it spread, pulsing out of her. Anne, Aneka and Anna did not move, nor react to what had happened, not wishing to prolong the situation, Kaben moved quickly along behind each of the remaining girls and carried out the exact same motion, resulting in the same fashion of death.

Unnoticed to either living form in the room, each girl held, in a tightly gripped hand a gold coin . . .

As he reached the end of the table the Gardian slowly collected up the work that the Muted Angels had been working on, holding the volumes to his chest.

It indicated to a wooden chest near the entrance and Kaben accepted that it must contain more work and nodded to allow the Gardian to take it. The Light could have the spoils and perhaps when this huge minion returned and explained what had happened another set of scribes would be created or . . . perhaps that was the end of it.

As the cave stood silent, the corpses of the girls seeming out of place now in some unearthly way, the Gardian filled and lifted the chest and then with a curt nod left the cave to steal into the dawn.

Kaben moved slowly past the girls, retracing his steps, looking at them one at a time and wondered if his form had given comfort to them, agonised them or even registered with them, he had only picked this body as he collected the image from two of the girls. He briefly wondered who it was. By the time he got back to the front of the table Gadereal had his true form back.

Stooping, as he turned to leave he picked up a piece of parchment that was discarded on the floor. As he walked from the cave, he read a little of it.

Gadereal stopped for a split second as he read part of what had just taken place, scribed by one of the girls. He then went on his way, shoving the page into his robe.

*

I am pleased Gadereal, very pleased.

I admire the time and effort that you have taken, countered with the precision with which you carried out the final . . . dispatch.

"Thank you Master."

I wonder why you chose to let the works be taken away . . . but I do acknowledge the message that you sent in doing so . . . a nice touch.

"Thank you Master."

You have recounted your work well and accomplished the mission satisfactorily . . . I am sure there will be need for your skills again soon . . .

Steven Archer

"Thank you Master."

Having told of his mission, Gadereal saw no need to expand on his replies.

He bowed, turned and with his robes flowing around him left the cold, grey rock walled chamber.

DANYUEL—THE ANGEL THAT BURIED THE TRUTH

ONE

For a being with so many tics and twitches, Jueten accomplished a lot.

There was a confidence within him that countered the physical deficiencies that he had accrued, although they did help him carry out his role more effectively, each had been added like a prop to his abilities and psyche over the years unintentionally creating a better being for his role.

Tall and lean, with a drawn almost gaunt face, Jueten had gone about his work for the Light without fanfare, without fuss for eons. He had been carrying out his work for so long, in fact, that he had become practically invisible. He walked the rugged corridors of the Realm of the Light as every other being that had business there did, and yet seemed to blend into the background, unseen. His work was so good, of such a high quality and had such a success rate that over time his own high standards worked against him as expectation was always high and yet always met.

The human characteristics that he bore were at first of distraction and annoyance to Jueten, but now they were an integral part of his make up. As he had grown into his job, so they had grown on him.

Jueten carried out a unique role for the Light. He was responsible for creating speculation, stirring debate. It was Jueten that ensured that the word and the actions of the Light were highlighted for all to bear witness to and so to discuss and converse on for that was the way that the message would continue on through time. His was a vital role and one that set him aside from all others in service (although he had heard that there was a group of Angels that *recorded* the work that the Light did, scribing all that occurred—he found this hard to believe and felt that they were a diversionary tactic, perhaps to take interest away from him and what he accomplished).

Jueten had hidden the deeds of the Light in plain view, this was the best and most effective way to ensure that success was gained. He had been responsible for some of the greatest examples of the work of the Light ever commented on making sure that the Dark was unsuccessful in its bid to spread the Lie.

Jueten had been the one that had spent months preparing and then placing the shroud of Turin, this was one of his most high profile and continually successful placements. The spear that had pierced Christ's side at the crucifixion was another of his ideas and he had lost count of the amount of nails that he had placed from the same event, too many to remember . . .

He had also been responsible for some of the fables and yarns that had longevity to them, and had indeed in turn been printed as part of the good book or other texts. Noah's Ark was one that he particularly liked as he had taken the time to ensure that there was an element of truth to the tale thus giving it a huge dose of credibility that allowed the story to be retold again and again.

Jueten was the one that had come up with the idea for prayer, psalms and the written word of the Light. But it was his masterpiece, his most brilliant idea that gave him most pride and continued to cause subversive debate centuries after its conception: parables and gospels.

These outline the history of the Light in such a fashion as to be accurate and concise and yet for those with a privileged knowledge, they could unlock an even more important and revelatory body of information for debate and conjecture to mull over. Not bad for this unremarkable and ordinary servant . . . Jueten's idea to weave a second strand to a story by having men or religious leaders, for example be supernatural beings or have real places indicated as Heavenly places gave another layer to the tale being told. One of the best recorded was the star that led the three wise men to the birth of Christ. It wasn't a real star in the Heavens of course, it was Joseph, his father who was the Star of David, leader of the Magians and his political associates visiting his first-born!

The raising of Lazarus was the lifting of an excommunication on a monk that had strayed from the fold!

Even when Jesus had been tempted by Satan, he was in fact having political discussions with Judas Iscariot, who was called Satan, as it was the title given to the leader of the revolutionaries!

How proud Jueten was of this achievement, not simply because it allowed some who educated themselves to grasp the reality of the Light, recorded the true events in an obviously hidden manner and caused a controversy, but it also had a contemptuous edge for those stupid enough to believe all that was put in front of them, the contemptible masses, the sheep.

Jueten had become a master craftsman over the years that he had worked. He was a twitchy, nervous type but had brains that belied him and had a preciseness and attentiveness to details that meant that nearly every task that he turned to was a success. He had travelled to many times, to many places and had achieved some amazing victories with his hunched, thin and frail form and this was partly why he was so pleased with himself and his success.

In his tiny room, darkened and sparse that doubled as his quarters and his place of work, Jueten pondered how next to establish the word of the Light in physicality . . .

Steven Archer

TWO

This time there was a single torch lit.

Danyuel preferred to wait in the darkness, total pitch. The flickering flame occasionally caught his green eyes and made them glint from under the heavy hood that he wore, that they all wore. It wasn't a case of enjoying or hating this waiting, this time spent to prove servitude before being given a task. It was the pointlessness of it that sometimes got to Danyuel. He felt, deep within himself in a hidden private place, that he had proved not only his capabilities but also his loyalty and would rather spend this dead time serving with a purpose, but the time had to be spent, a penance of sorts perhaps or, simply, a test for him and others like him . . . Servants.

How long had he stood in this dank, anti-chamber, there was no way to tell and what did time really matter at all in this place, this Dark Realm, or for that matter, what did time mean anywhere. It was merely a marker, highlighting points in linear time, events and happenings that should be noted, remembered and even visited.

I have a task for you, Danyuel.

The voice did not startle Danyuel, it boomed quietly in every recess of his mind, clear and low.

I have a task suited to your very personal skills.

Rather than reply, Danyuel stood silent, straight and rigid. Ready to serve.

You have heard of the Angel that buries Truth?

"Yes, Master."

You understand fully what it is that he does?

"Yes Master, he has performed his role for many years with great success. Our original agent that performed the same role was terminated long, long ago. I do not know how his successor fares but Jueten has been excellent in his perseverance." Danyuel cut his reply short. The point had been made.

Why do you suppose that he is so . . . successful?

Danyuel's Master asked after pause, perhaps for thought perhaps for effect.

"I believe it is because he is so exact, so thorough."

Yes, maybe this is so . . . I would like you to find this Angel and eliminate him. The problems in finding a replacement of calibre that the Light would have would be of use to us.

"Very, well Master." Danyuel bowed his head a little.

Time is not an issue as yet, but return and tell me of the mission when it is done as soon as it is done.

"Very well, Master." Danyuel took several steps back through the cavernous hall, turned and left down the rock corridor, pleased to have a purpose again.

*

Danyuel tried at first, to get a gauge on his prey by visiting some of the relics that he had placed, some of the places where the history had begun, via Jueten and where he had had his greatest successes. It didn't help.

Danyuel knew of much that Jueten had put into place, and saw a few that he hadn't known, but the only thing that he gleaned from these numerous visits in time and place was to underline the fact that he already knew: Jueten was thorough. He was one of a very few that the Dark knew of in any role and what he did, yet he evaded capture or contact . . .

He was thorough and clever.

Danyuel knew that he could not underestimate this Angel, this being for he would prove to be a worthy adversary. He also knew that the slaying of this Truth burier would be the *easy* part of his task. The hard part would be to even get close enough to do it.

After some thought, Danyuel realised that the best way to get to Jueten was to have him come to Danyuel.

Why would he come to Danyuel? To check a piece of history, a piece of contentious history that Danyuel would place with care and attention to get Jueten to try and verify it as real, human real at least or . . . change it to suit his needs.

Danyuel was pleased with the idea in principle, but the question was what to use as bait?

THREE

It had taken Danyuel a long while to come up with what he thought would be a contentious subject, worthy of debate and conjecture for time to ponder over. He knew that it had to be something that the humans would believe to be true but was as equally aware that he should not treat the humans with the disdain that he felt for them. This had to work as he would only get one chance and so he had to balance his opinions of the apes with the need to make sure that his plan worked, as Jueten would surely spot a fraud, and would certainly not fall for a second attempt. Danyuel knew that he had to be very aware of the mission, the humans and especially the target.

That was why he settled on the knife.

Travelling to Milan, Italy in 1498 had not been a problem. Placing himself within contact of the great Leonardo Da Vinci and gaining his confidence had been slightly more difficult, but not impossible.

Danyuel had taken the form of a wealthy industrialist from Europe and took to the streets of Milan around the area that Leonardo had his famed workshop, as it was so large—a converted barn—and so well known, this had been easily located.

Days were spent in the local taverners, where Leonardo would turn up from time to time at all hours, as he was renowned not only for his brilliance, but for his boredom threshold, his wandering attention span, his temper and his liking for an occasional drink. Once Danyuel had traced the great man and followed him for several cobble-stoned streets from his workshop to a tavern that he frequented, he put his plan in motion.

History already reflected that the great one had a passion for tinkering and for trickery at the expense of not just his wealthy benefactors but also anyone who would view his work. The subtleties with which he added messages and blasphemy to his work was staggering and showed the contempt of the genius and the lengths to which he would take his mocking, especially of the church. Danyuel thought that this side of Da Vinci was something that Jueten would appreciate.

Danyuel was able to buy his way into the small group that sat with Leonardo in the heavy beamed room with fine wine and over the following hours turned the conversation to the painting "The Last Supper" which Leonardo was currently working on, and that was one of the most debated works ever. Leonardo bellowed and laughed his way through the list of twists that he had added to the painting already, relishing the chance to impress some of the locals and have his ego stroked as much as he stroked his full, grey beard, rolling with laughter.

Danyuel kept the most expensive wine that was available in the mediocre tavern flowing into the early hours and made sure that Leonardo was enjoying every drop. Few questions were being asked of him and he was able to give a potted history of his fake human-monkey life and why he was there in Milan before Leonardo bored of him to a degree and returned the conversation to that which he enjoyed talking about most of all, himself and his work.

Danyuel imparted his idea.

Quietly and discreetly he planted the seed, he planted the idea of a phantom hand holding a knife in a manner so as to cause outrage in such a descriptive narrative as the painting of the last supper. A knife that clearly did not belong in the scene.

It worked. Having pressed the suggestion on Leonardo during the evening and the early morning, of course being careful so as to let the great Leonardo believe it to be his very own idea when he left, drunk and seeking his bed, Danyuel was certain that it had worked.

It did.

Leonardo painted the celebrated painting with the addition of the hand and the knife and the rest was history.

This priceless piece of art became one of the most talked about ever, but had the realism and factual background to make it as authentic as it could be.

Now Danyuel had to wait.

Steven Archer

When he saw the results of his labours with Leonardo, Danyuel was very pleased. It was perfect. Of course, he was the only one who knew about the change in the painting as to everyone else, the timeline had had the knife in the picture from the very beginning and that should include Jueten.

Danyuel now had to stay as close to the painting as possible so that he could wait for Jueten, who surely would be inquisitive about this piece, for although the timeline had this knife in from the conception, Jueten would feel there was something about it and would want to investigate it for himself as it was work that he hadn't done or been involved in manipulating.

And so the real chore began for Danyuel, the real test. Following the painting through time, waiting to catch the Angel that buries the Truth.

*

It's not like living another lifetime.

It's not as if Danyuel actually lived through the ages, aging as he went.

Keeping the painting within his reach was akin to an out of body experience for Danyuel. He was able to maintain a sort of ethereal existence that Angels in the timeline could get used to. As he could only remain for a short period in any given time, he made multiple visits to times along the line but broke the monotony by alternating the route.

Danyuel was sure that this was going to work and because he did he was able to have a confidence that he would, at some time meet Jueten.

And so time passed . . .

*

The stooped man looked like a banker, his dull grey suit was like a sort of uniform and his overly shiny shoes somehow discreet.

He had been standing in the Grand Gallery on the pristine wooden parquet floor for two hours, staring at the same painting, unmoving.

It was not unusual for tourists to stand in front of the more unique and famous pieces in the gallery for a while, especially after "The Da Vinci Code" book and film but two hours was long enough, even for such an exalted place as The Louvre, Paris.

In the security office off Napoleon Walk, Chief of Security Bastin reached for the radio. He could see one of his staff had sensibly been monitoring the thin man from a discreet distance and was going to have him investigate further.

"Bravo-two-twenty, bravo-two-twenty, ask the gentleman you have under your gaze if he has any intention of moving on today, we should be winding down in ten minutes and I do not want him hanging around until then . . . he seems . . . different. Take care of it Alain." Bastin had a suspicious sensation run through him as he straightened and pulled on his impeccably ironed dark navy uniform jacket. He was aware that even the most innocent of situations could turn bad very quickly.

"Very well, bravo-two-twenty out." The reply was tactfully spoken into a mic on the collar of his uniform and Bastin watched, pleased with this new recruit's awareness and approach to the situation. He liked the new guy and he seemed to have this under control. His anxiety lifted slightly and he moved to survey the other monitors covering the Louvre in its entirety and all of his officers, his precise confirmation that all was well around the rest of the world famous building took no longer than two minutes. He returned his full attention to making sure that the hunched man looking at "The Last Supper" had been moved on and was surprised when he found that both he and his officer had gone, vanished.

*

As the security officer had approached the thin, frail looking man, he had turned and anticipated what he was going to ask. In clear French he said: "I have finished here, I will move on

Steven Archer

now, its beauty enraptured me for a time . . ." Jueten started to move away, smiling.

"I understand, it is a marvellous piece . . . but we are about to close . . ." The guard said, returning the smile and taking up a position just behind and to the left of Jueten, who began his journey out of the Louvre, satisfied with his findings and aware that something was amiss, he could sense it.

Before he had the chance to realise that it was indeed the guard that escorted him along to an exit, Danyuel had leaned into him and immobilised him with a dose of cocoa and cocaine doused on a handkerchief and placed over Jueten's face, an ancient but efficient anaesthetic.

"Everything is all right. He just needs some air . . ." Danyuel said to the few people still around at this time, placating them with comments on the man he carried fainting and knowing that nobody in the Gallery would interfere as they were all far too polite and perhaps a little wary too.

As they turned the corner, the coast clear, Danyuel smiled as he made good his escape. His time had been well spent.

FOUR

As his blurred eyes focussed, Jueten knew that it was over. He had been caught.

His body felt as weary as his mind in that instance and he also felt a numbness that throbbed through his veins.

He knew that it was also his own fault that he had been captured and so, instead of feeling scared, concerned or panicked, he felt a sense of relief, calm. There was a small part of him that wondered whether or not he wanted to be caught meaning that he let his guard down, had he sabotaged himself?

Even when his eyes cleared and he looked down, shaking off the groggy sensation filling his head to see that he had been strapped to a wooden chair with leather binds he didn't panic.

But when he then saw the blood draining from him from the deep, open cuts made to his bare forearms he did have a rush of fear, a moment of clear panic. He struggled against his bonds, but the leather seemed to tighten and bind him closer to the wood of the chair, cutting into him. His gripped hands released, his tensed shaking relaxed for Jueten knew that it was useless, that there was no point.

"Acceptance of your fate would make the next few moments easier . . ." Danyuel said from behind him.

There was a still quiet as Jueten looked again at the wounds inflicted exactly on his forearms, he guessed that the way his blood was seeping from them and the tiredness that he felt could only mean that he had minutes left. He thought quickly about all that he had done in his service, a picture book of memories reminding him of all that he had done and of the brief time that he had had before becoming the Truth burier . . . and he had no regrets, perhaps that was why he felt so calm now that and the fact that perhaps it was his time . . . actually, it was definitely his time and he felt it as surely as he felt his life draining away from him.

Steven Archer

"I didn't think that you would wish to prolong the inevitable and so I took the appropriate steps while you were under." Danyuel said moving to the side, so that with lifted head, Jueten could see his robed figure and covered form as it passed before him to take up a close position in front of him in the dry, sandy cave where they appeared to be.

"You have performed admirable service in your time, achieved many great feats . . ." Danyuel passed the comments with an honest edge but without any feeling or compassion. It was a simple respect for one that had done great deeds. "Our agents have searched for you for a *very* long time . . ."

"Yes, perhaps . . . but not so good so as to be able to avoid you and your dogged pursuit, I wonder how long you have dedicated to me . . . I did not realise that you were so close to me until it was too late. Your work on the painting . . . masterful, subtle . . . how . . . ?" Jueten's voice trailed as his concentration wavered.

"Done by the man himself. I thought that if I were successful, that you would appreciate the effort and I also knew that you would be a difficult catch, that it would take something very special to lure you."

"Where are we?"

Danyuel took the time to wait to emphasise the point, as he knew that Jueten did not have very long left. "We are in what will be Wadi Qumran. I have decided to place you in a cave where you, yourself will become a relic, a great find to future man, right in the region of the Dead Sea Scrolls find. You will give them cause for debate . . . I thought that you would enjoy the irony."

Jueten used all of his remaining strength to lift his head and gaze around the cave. He then slumped and his view fell to his feet where the expanding puddle of blood got darker and clotted, mingling with the sand.

He did appreciate the irony and he was glad that in time he would possibly be the topic of some conversation just like some of the items and words that he had planted himself. He could scarcely have thought of a more fitting end himself.

"I'm alone here, then. This will be the end of me . . ." There was no tone or sentiment in his voice just an acceptance, which wasn't lost on Danyuel.

Danyuel didn't see much point in replying and so contented himself in his moment, staring with shining green eyes at his captive. This was his payoff, what his work and thought and careful planning had led to.

It took Jueten another fifteen minutes to die. Danyuel enjoyed them all.

Danyuel stared at him, standing still in the silence for over three hours.

He then took the time to seal the cave; its passageway and the entrance using small charges to dislodge the rock but that would leave no trace of his having been there.

Time was indeed a tricky concept he thought as he left, his job done.

*

Sealing him in the cave . . . that has an irony and a level of malevolence that is fitting for one such thing that tampered with time. You have done well Danyuel . . . I am sure there will be need for your skills again very soon.

"Thank you Master, I would like to serve again."

And I am sure that you will . . .

YETEREAL—THE WILD BEAST

ONE

The pride that Ferus Bestia felt at killing so many Dark agents had diminished over the centuries since the rebellion, which saw him fight with honour then, as now for the Light.

Time could do that.

What had not diminished was his capacity for violence, his passion for the fight and his willingness to take on any challenger or battle that was placed before him. He had been fashioned as a fighter, a creator of havoc and was single-minded in this pursuit.

His years as a champion of the Light were soaked blood red. It was all that he knew and all he ever would be . . . a warrior, a gladiator . . . a beast.

Ferus Bestia had served with little acknowledgement prior to the rebellion, and the casting down of Lucifer and his allies. The only thing that set him aside was his physique, which was commented on often and just as often led to the speaker being injured in some manner, as the comments were seldom flattering.

Squat and solid at only five feet and five inches, he was muscle layered on muscle. His broad shoulders and thick neck tapered to a thin waist, which went on and down to legs as thick and dense as tree trunks. His build was chiselled and muscular, which gave the appearance of bursting at the seams from his skin.

To say that this figure was formidable was an understatement. The very size and shape he had only hinted at the power and sheer strength that was contained. The other element of this construct was his hands. These were twice the size that they should have been and lent to the striking stature that he had. They looked and were, capable of crushing bone.

The body was terrifying enough, awesome in its build and might but his head, his features were what really struck fear into the heart of many if not all of his enemies and had seen many of those run, literally in the face of terror.

Long and drawn, the best description would be of a rugged and worn bull's head with the forehead, eyes and ears of a man. Complete with rough and used lethal horns, a thick brass ring through the thick snout and a fearsome look that could almost turn a being frigid with fright, Ferus Bestia was in himself a grotesque spectacle to behold.

As if this were not enough, he had also been cursed or blessed depending on the viewpoint by another element to his body which added not only to the macabre nature of his being but amplified the look of his true self.

In his calm moments, infrequent as they were, or if seen first hand from afar Ferus Bestia had the look of a man.

Although the head did seem out of place on such a hulking body, nevertheless there was a face with delicate human features that caught those that saw it completely unaware, especially when his primal form was revealed in all of its ugly glory.

Ferus Bestia was unique. He was a soldier of the Light yet as close to being one of the Dark as it was possible to be. He had served with distinction in some of the most unforgiving battles and frightening situations that it was possible to be involved in, yet never sought or got acknowledgement.

With a low centre of gravity and a heavy frame, he had recorded some spectacular victories over ages against some of the most brutal of agents and beings that the Dark could find and was now, for all intent and purpose, a champion of the Light, awaiting the next challenger to arrive and test him.

These challenges were fewer and further apart as there was not a creature that would not hesitate before even thinking of a challenge, and the Dark had bigger issues to deal with than what could be seen as an impotent and pointless position. It wasn't as if there was outright war in which to be engaged and so, the beast found himself left lonely more and more, yet rising to any challenge to his animal dominance with a vigour that would not lessen.

In becoming the Beast with no equal, starting with his ferocious defence of the Light during the rebellion all the way through to the annihilation and ripping apart of many in single combat and the chaos that he had wrought on the Dark, he had become the worst kind of victim to his own success . . . and one that still yearned to serve.

TWO

The cold accompanied the darkness as it always did, even with the meagre heat from the one, lit torch, like friends that had been and would be together for eternity. Cold and darkness were a partnership, a team.

As long as could be remembered, they had worked in tandem to send a shiver down a multitude of spines and facilitate the spreading of fear and anxiety through all that they came in contact with . . . nearly all of them.

Yetereal felt neither, fear or anxiety.

He did not know how long he had stood, but he had an inclination that it had been the longest time that he had spent waiting to serve, waiting for the Master. He felt that he was about to be given a mission of importance, but was expected to earn it as always, in this hellish solitude, in the resounding silence.

None of this mattered to Yetereal, all he wanted to do was serve and to use his abilities to do so. He could sense that this would be a task fit for him, fit for his skills and fit to test him.

He knew that he was raw and that he had a power that was yet to be tested completely, he knew that he could mould his being and his abilities but that he needed to be pushed to be able to gauge just how far that he could go. He wondered, momentarily if there were any challenge that would be ultimate and, of course, what happens after that.

Thoughts and processing were put to one side, compartmentalised. He was back in the reality of the present, of the chamber, of the cold, of the foreboding pressure that came just before the task.

*

The time of Ferus Bestia has long since gone, wouldn't you agree?

Yetereal's conscience came back to the moment like a being walking from a fog to a clear copse.

"Yes, but that is only because he has conquered all that were worthy to challenge him, he is not to be underestimated."

True. He is a symbol of the old ways, he harks back to purer times, perhaps simpler times and is one of the few constants. I debate the need for a champion to challenge him as his time has passed and he is in danger of becoming a relic, but then does that not mean that he becomes a kind of example, an aspiration . . .

"I would be able to give him a final battle, I will be able to defeat him and in doing so dirty his reputation, but there would be another possibility . . ." Yetereal left his words hanging in the cold air, knowing his thoughts were being read anyway, but waiting for the words of confirmation.

That you defeat him and he becomes some kind of martyr, that he was past his best and that this did not need to happen and yet . . . and yet, I do believe that his accomplishments could benefit from tarnish.

Bowing his head in understanding, Yetereal replied: "I will make it so, Master."

*

When the messenger entered the beast's small, sparse quarters at the heart of Granite Mountain, he was out of breath and dishevelled. He had come a long distance and so took a second to compose himself before rapping on the heavy wooden doorframe that led to Ferus Bestia's dwelling place. Just as he raised his hand and was about to knock, a black shadow crept toward him, causing him to take an involuntary step back when he heard the scuffle of dirt as well.

The beast was here. He looked down on the tiny, frail messenger and held out a massive hand, into which a small parchment was placed by a shaking claw.

The beast knew that if this were a challenge, it had already been sanctioned and that he had permission to take it as he saw fit, he also remembered that it had been some decades since his last test. He gave the messenger a look that informed him to wait and so he did, standing in the same spot, trembling and too scared to twitch, awaiting the reply that he knew he had to stay for.

Ferus Bestia walked back into his abode, paused before looking at the parchment, savouring the feeling of a challenge to come and then perused the information. He stiffened, tensed.

Taking his time after immediately deciding to take on this scum, he flicked through a small, crisp volume. This contained the many trials that he, as the challenged, had the right to select from for both he and his aggressor to partake in, to prove that they were worthy to stand toe, to toe in mortal combat. This was the chance for the challenged to choose two ordeals that may weaken his opponent, if they made it through at all, and so give him an edge . . . not that he had ever felt that he needed one, but in combat, every advantage should be taken. Breathing the dry dusty air as slowly as he turned each page, Ferus Bestia made his choices.

He wrote on a small parchment one word acknowledging the event would take place and then two numbers, the trials to be undertaken by both parties. He felt a surge through his veins as he thrust the message into the waiting minion's claw and watched as he scurried off toward the small oval of light at the entrance to the mountain.

Ferus Bestia felt the warmth of usefulness heat up to the fire of anticipation at what he was about to take part in, these were the moments that he lived for and stopped simply existing in-between bouts. He was a warrior, he needed the challenge, he was a soldier and needed the battle, Yetereal would give him this and in return he would crush him, pulverise him over hours to pulp . . . one final challenge before he had to accept that there were no more gladiators, there would be no more duels . . . and that was the empty sensation beginning in his stomach, that he will have outlived his usefulness, he would become a relic, a thing of the past.

But that also fired him to new levels of confidence, as he would make sure that he went out undefeated and with a spectacle that would live through the ages.

Steven Archer

The trials that the beast had chosen were ones that he was, of course familiar with but ones that he felt might best test his foe: The Trial of Fire and The Trial of Cold Water.

The duel was confirmed, his training and preparation began.

*

Yetereal had had time to prepare. Once the duel, the challenge was extended and accepted via tenuous links of communication between Light and Dark and both had agreed the oath of not using any unique powers (some possessed mind control, or invisibility skills that would, naturally, give that being an advantage and had been outlawed eons ago so that each event was as even as it possibly could be and each participant relied on guile, spirit and strength alone) the date and place were set, agreed by both parties.

Neither upbeat or down about the choices of Trial that had been picked, Yetereal simply moved on with his preparation with a determination that matched his desire to take this opportunity to move forward in his level of service . . . he would succeed and these were mere obstacles in his way.

*

All Trials are straightforward. There is no ambiguity to them at all, they are simply designed to test limits, whether they be physical, mental or both.

The Trial of Cold Water was first.

Iceland: 732bc. The river that would become the Glera (the river of glass) in years to come was chosen for obvious reasons. Within the grey, rugged, granite-like mountain region this river cut through the landscape and had a temperature of minus 15 degrees. The cold air that they breathed stung their lungs and the temperature was dropped even further by the wind that howled about them in a whipping frenzy.

Combatants lay in the river, close to the bank on their backs submerged in the freezing water, using a reed to breath.

There was no winner or loser, it was simply required that each being last longer than four hours, if not they could not go on to competition.

This was when the two protagonists had the chance to see each other for the first time and weigh each other up, gauge the opponent. Both arrived at the same time with their seconds and both, silently prepared themselves for the freezing plunge, never taking their eyes off one another, grim expressions covering both of them.

If Ferus Bestia was surprised or taken aback by Yetereal's form when he took off his cloth robes, he did not show it. His face was like the stone and rock that surrounded him, cold, unmoving and hard.

After disrobing and stepping into the river, through the broken ice covering and preparing themselves, they nodded to each other and placing the reeds in their mouths, submerging themselves.

The absolute shock to the system is electric.

It is enough to stop some hearts.

After the initial freeze, the being is beyond sense, beyond feeling; the only way to survive is to allow the mind to shut down as the body quickly does, into a state of hyperthermia. Almost but not quite.

The body needs to keep one tiny vestige of it awake, alive in order to live . . . that is the test.

After the four hours had elapsed, the seconds dragged their champion to the bank, struggling with the size and form of each.

Ferus Bestia was first to open his black eyes after two and a half hours.

An hour later, the orange eyes of Yetereal opened and came into focus. When he was able to see clearly, he realised that he and his second were alone. The beast had gone, he had survived and had gone to ready himself for the next task.

Yetereal, shivered as he moved undaunted by what lay ahead.

*

Steven Archer

Western North America: Prehistoric Mesozoic era, a desolate and harsh environment, which would become The Cascade Range of Mountains in Northern California.

The heat from the volcano was terrific, it parched the atmosphere and dried the air itself making it difficult to breathe even at the distance from the crater that they were at.

The four figures stood some two kilometres from the crater, which pulsed and spewed black and orange lava, tinged with yellow and gold both into the air and over the lip of the volcano. Sparks and splashes of liquid were fired intermittently into the crackling air, booms and echoes of sound filled the area to deafening degree, showing just how powerful and raw nature could be.

None of the four beings at the base of the stony, living mountain took any notice. They were oblivious to their surroundings, as dramatic as they were. All of them were locked into the moment that they were in and the task at hand.

They were simply there to carry out the duel that they had to participate in, as seconds and as the two that had to actually do The Trial of Fire.

The Trial was an endurance test over twenty feet. Not a very long distance to accomplish, but the fact that the walkway was white-hot rocks and that each participant had to also carry a rock in each hand, did make it more of an ordeal, indeed this practice was spoken of over the years and carried on through to the middle ages as a test for witches and heretics . . . the outcome of which is obvious.

Here and now this was the second and final task before the duel that would take place between Yetereal and Ferus Bestia, once both had got through what lay before them.

Both of the beings taking part, walked to the start of the walkway. This was eight feet across and so gave them plenty of room to stand alongside one another.

The ground was hot all around so that balance had to be shifted from one foot to the other and this was giving them an indication as to what to expect from the scalding hot rocks that stretched out before them.

Yetereal and Ferus Bestia did not acknowledge or look at each other. They simply readied themselves by stripping down to loin cloths and standing in between the two rocks that they would pick up to carry the distance that they had to cover, these had been placed by the start in small wells dug to ensure that they would be as hot as they could be for their short journey.

The two stood in silence, looking ahead with a tunnel vision, blocking out all else, concentrating on what they had to achieve and how to best do it.

They had reached a level of concentration that was almost meditating.

With the grumbling and growling of the volcano in the background, one of the seconds gave the signal to go with his dropped arm.

Ferus Bestia and Yetereal stooped without pause and picked up the rocks at their sides. They then strode out onto the white-hot rocks, their feet searing the sound and smell of burning flesh instantly filling the air with its pungent odour. Each walked with purpose, each looked straight ahead and each had a determined look etched into their features, into their unblinking eyes. The distance seemed far, their feet blistered and burned as did their hands, but they moved on and covered the distance in an agonisingly slow ten seconds.

Once past the end and indicated by the second minion on hand, they dropped the rocks from their shredded hands and stepped into the cool mineral water baths, with healing properties, that were near by to help start the healing process.

They had done it.

As their seconds attended them and prepared them for the journey back to their camps, still neither said anything or looked at the other.

That was until Ferus Bestia cast a quick glance over at Yetereal, who felt the look and did not return it, giving him some consolation to his body's damage as that was the slight sign of weakness that he had not expected . . . was the beast about to fall?

THREE

It took only five days for the two opponents to prepare themselves and heal ready for the duel. Each utilised the best medical treatments available to them, each used secret and mythical applications at their disposal and, of course, each meditated and took advantage of their bodies quick healing ability.

The determination that they had, the drive and the passion to win was strong in both of them for different reasons. Both of them were as ready physically and mentally as they could be and both knew that it would be the strength of the mind that would steer one of them to victory, as each knew that when the body could take no more, the mind and their will would have to force it to gain the win each craved.

Word of the placement for the duel reached the two competitors and each looked forward to the meeting and becoming the substance of legend, this was a chance to go down in history and yet, this was for both beings a long second to the sweetness of victory.

*

The combatants stood in the haze of the early afternoon heat, dry and arid and climbing in degree every minute.

Both seemed relaxed and as ready for battle as they could be. The efforts of the two trials did not seem to have taken too great a toll on either of them, but as the fighting went on for any length of time, fatigue would surely be a factor. They moved from side to side, foot to foot, shaking themselves in preparation for what was to come.

The two warriors wore similar battle dress that afforded protection but also gave maximum range of movement. The body armour was sturdy but light and each had also been given a short sword and a spear. There were no shields, no other protection for either soul.

The seconds retired to a ridge nearby whilst the moderator explained what he expected of the two foes.

The rules of engagement were simple; this was a battle to the death and no powers could be used. Both gave a shallow nod of understanding and compliance to these basics and then it was time.

In the sandy, dry desert of Upper Egypt, south of what would become modern-day Cairo, the battle was about to commence.

When the raised arm of the moderator was lowered, the two enemies jerked into action, Ferus Bestia smiling as he rolled shoulders. This was his moment and he was going to savour it.

Yetereal gave nothing away in his own motion only his orange eyes hid something behind their glare.

The two figures moved slowly and purposefully around each other, arms swinging, legs stretching and minds working on the first part of a changing strategy that they would employ as the fight went on. Moments passed without a blow being struck or an advance being made as if there were a game between them as to who would make the first move in an attack.

Ferus Bestia was the one to make the move. He lunged at Yetereal when he thought there was an opening hoping to make an early contact with his short sword but Yetereal countered and took the power out of the blow with his right arm and his own short sword, using the big opponent's own momentum to send him past him and almost stumbling with an appearance of ease and confidence. These early encounters went on for several minutes as they prodded at each other to work out a weakness and hopefully inflict the first wound, for both knew that an injury would drain a fighter quickly and could easily be the road to death . . .

*

The fight entered the pantheon of legend.

It became the stuff of myth within in both the Dark and the Light Realms and even entered human lore as a fable (slightly distorted into what would become the tale of David and Goliath) accentuating the fight between good and evil.

The battle went on for two days and nights, each competitor taking advantage and having it pulled back from him as the terrain, the skills of each and the wounds inflicted told on each of them.

They moved toward Alexandria from Rosetta, taking in the rugged landscape with more difficulty as each tired and as each took hits to their person. The speed with which they covered the land in giant fifty-foot leaps and sprints of up to forty miles per hour began to falter as time went on without either really being able to force their dominance on the fight.

Drops from cliffs and earth shattering landings that accompanied them took them on and on to Jabal Al Tariq, near to what is now Gibraltar, where the final act of this battle would take place.

*

Exhaustion was upon both creatures, weighing on them like a rock to be carried as a penance. The utter strength needed to carry on, wielding their weapons and using them to try and finish off their rival was unimaginable.

Each took turns to scream their frustrations to the rain soaked heavens of the night as they both endeavoured to end this conflict and take the rest that every fibre of their being wanted desperately.

Yetereal had been forced toward the edge of a cliff. As the lightening struck loud in the blackened and blue sky above he paused and looked his foe directly in the eye.

Ferus Bestia made his mistake. He took this to mean that he had the advantage and that he could finish off his enemy. Neither of the two had broken any rules of engagement, but now, Ferus did. He unfurled his massive wings, tensing them so that they broke the ties that held them in place to restrict this kind of use and rose up into the air.

This was when Yetereal took his shot.

As the huge figure of the beast loomed toward him, Yetereal quickly stooped, picked up a rock and as he rose, threw it at the dark shape, striking it in the face.

The shock and pain of the rock's impact shook Ferus Bestia. He still moved forward, flailing his arms and his short sword and as he did so, Yetereal lunged forward and plunged his spear into his stomach.

He then gritted his teeth, yelled at the strain and at the sky and dragged the bulk of his foe over him and on over the cliff, the beast's own momentum assisting him to defeat him.

As the champion of the Light plunged, in a waterless swimming motion toward the sea and the crashing waves and the jagged rocks below, Yetereal sank to his knees and cried in relief that this epic encounter was at an end.

Ferus Bestia was beaten. There was no way that he would survive the fall, let alone the spear in his gut.

Yetereal sobbed for a few moments as the thunder crashed, the lightening flashed over the Heavens and the rain poured down like tears from loved ones . . . He had done it.

Steven Archer

FOUR

Yetereal did not know how long he had lain out on the top of the cliff, the rain soaking him and easing his aching body. He did not know how long it had taken him, with the mediator creeping behind him, to climb down the cliff to where the beast had fallen.

It had taken several hours to find the spot where the beast had landed and when he did, Yetereal stood silently gazing at the scene before him, finding it hard in his fatigued state to comprehend what he saw at first.

The blood that was all around, the skin and gore indicated that this was the impact point, along with his broken spear but what also made it obvious, was the phrase: "Iam vos es Bestia" crudely written in blood in a slightly more sheltered part of the cove on which he stood, which meant: "You now are the Beast . . ."

Yet Ferus Bestia was nowhere to be seen.

From that day forward, he was never seen or heard from again.

Yetereal, turned, slowly and looked at the mediator who simply nodded his victory, then he turned to leave for where he called home.

*

Do you understand the strength that you have demonstrated?
"Yes, Master."

Do you understand why I tasked you with this particular challenge?

Yetereal paused for a moment not thinking but reflecting on the recent past and the change in him that had occurred, slight as it was, "yes, Master".

Good . . . Good. Then you are ready to move on to tasks that I have to be completed Ferus Bestia . . . Yetereal.

"Thank you Master." His eyes glowed orange and bright in the gloom of the cavern.

ARMEAN—THE INFILTRATOR

ONE

The high pitch squealing was pitiful but did not illicit any response from those that stood around the being making the noise.

Its wiry frame stretched, strained and pulled against the rough rope bonds that bound ankles, wrists and his middle section to the wooden board that was in the centre of the cavern.

The disbelief at being in this situation had passed, the denial of what it thought that they were going to do to him had just gone but the fear as to what they were going to do now was engulfing the messengers bony, long and scar strewn form.

If any of the three figures in the room felt any hint of emotion for themselves or for the wretched thing that they had captured, they did a good job of being impassive as the screams and yells carried on for hours, becoming ever more pleading and ever more hoarse in projection.

They all waited.

Eventually, two figures entered the oval, rugged cave and stood at the side of the support board, next to the crying and wailing being.

The first of the two ran bony fingers over the creatures form, taking his time, feeling all of its person, especially its face. After a few minutes it stopped, slumped in the shoulders slightly as if not completely satisfied with what it had discovered then turned to the second figure who dispassionately took a small step forward.

Steven Archer

The first being placed its left hand on the forehead of the captive, who after pausing, started to scream again, pleading. He then placed one hand on the head of his colleague.

For an instant the noise in the room evaporated and all that was left in the quiet was the crackling of torches. Then a low hum emanated from an unknown source in the cave and as it rose slightly, a couple of the guards tilted their heads to the left to hear better and the prisoner on the board again started to cry and again started to scream as his body began to shake uncontrollably without his own efforts. Muscles contracted, bones moved in and out of sockets and tendons stretched to the breaking point.

As it shook more violently with every second that passed a glow got brighter around the form of the second being that had entered the cave, he stood rigid, the light shimmering about him.

The screaming, the crying and the hum reached a crescendo and then all stopped.

The glow faded from the second form and the hand of the first to enter the room who appeared to have been a conduit, for the sounds had died out when the prisoner had died, a shrivelled, aged and frail version of the creature that it had been mere moments before.

Stepping back the conduit spoke: "You can be him now, Ramyel."

Ramyel shakily took a step back and concentrated. His head began to vibrate and shake, a blur materialising around him like an aura. Slowly his features changed to that of the being that had been killed seconds ago, clear for all in the room to see and then back to his true form.

"In time you will learn how to use this gift Ramyel, for longer periods, with slight changes to the features and even, as you absorb more essences, combinations of them. Once you have done that, you will be ready for more."

Ramyel couldn't help but wonder for a second what more there could be.

TWO

During the Battle of Gettysburg in July 1863, there was a battle going on within it.

The turning point of the American Civil War came about with Major General George Meade's army defeating repeated attacks by Confederate General Robert E. Lee's Northern army and so ending Lee's invasion.

The battle, at Gettysburg, just outside of Pennsylvania, had the most amounts of casualties of the Civil War and so, was the perfect place for Light and Dark to have some of their troops sequester to fight a battle within a battle, to partake in a conflict simply designed to have one side try and reduce the numbers of the other.

It was during a skirmish at Little Round Top near the Devil's Den that Ramyel took advantage of a situation whilst fighting for the Light.

He and two others had captured a confederate soldier, caught behind lines and dragged him off to the small and battered structure that had once been an outhouse (the farmhouse and barn obliterated and burning from enemy fire) where they could keep him for their purpose.

Whilst the rifles fired, the canons roared and the screams of the nearly dying echoed around them from all sides and not too far away, they bundled into the small confine, bent on their purpose.

"Kill me!" The agent of the Dark revealed his true form, that of a cohort, as soon as they were out of sight of human eyes.

"Kill me! There are no prisoners for us in this battle! There are no captures today! Kill me and be on your way!"

The two soldiers held him firm and pushed him to his knees, struggling, shaking their heads at his comments.

"Quiet now . . . what is your name?"

"My name, what does that matter? Kill me, you fiends of Light!" The cohort continued to writhe in a misguided attempt at escaping.

With a nod of his head, Ramyel signalled the two soldiers holding him. They forced him lower to the floor.

"I am Ramyel. I have never killed a Dark agent whose name I did not know, I ask you yours in accordance with Order 60: the seventh Sigil. Tell me and you will be dispatched . . . quickly and painlessly." Ramyel allowed the captives gaze to linger on him for a few seconds.

"Sevo . . . my name is Sevo. Why recount a Sigil that has not been used for centuries?" The cohort queried. Fear now gone as was resistance and a quizzical look in their place. Surely today was about the battle at hand only.

"Because I need to use it so that I can use you . . ." Moving fast, Ramyel placed his hand on top of Sevo's head and closed his eyes. Sevo began to shake, faster and faster as an eerie glow surrounded him and Ramyel's hand. The screaming was loud and shrill but the battle outside was home to such sounds and welcomed it to the din.

As Sevo died in a bone stretching agony, his muscles contorting and his features changing, he took on the appearance of Ramyel and Ramyel took on the look of Sevo.

Once the dead form of Sevo, with Ramyel's face, slumped to the wooden floor, Ramyel, now with Sevo's features took a step back, stretched his itching, tingling face and spoke through a different voice . . . Sevo's voice.

"Take him and leave him where he will be found. It is time for me to go . . ."

With those last words, Ramyel left and having checked the area quickly, went to rejoin the fighting but this time as an agent of the Dark, as a spy. His orders were clear as he had had many years to understand them and his mission, its complexities and its perils and now it was time to put it into action. He had a purpose and was clear on the execution.

He would be the first infiltrator of the Light into the Dark Realm.

THREE

Ramyel had been an agent of the Light holding the form of a dead Dark cohort for many, many, many years.

He had held the form of Sevo for so long that he had almost forgotten his own face, his own features. Time was taking its toll on him.

When he had first got into the Dark Realm and learned, carefully, who this Sevo was and what he did within the Dark, he had gone to lengths to blend in as carefully and unobtrusively as possible for decades, not only out of fear of capture but to try and ensure that he could operate effectively as a spy within the Dark for as long as possible.

He was invaluable.

At first, he had taken the opportunity to change his face to his own once in a while, so that he did not forget who he was nor get out of practice of facial manipulation, he certainly did not want to stay in this form forever, but now maybe he would, for he had integrated so well as to be a part of the Dark.

Yet his mission went on the real reason for his being here at all was to spy.

Ramyel's role in the Dark realm was to kill prisoners. A simple job and one that Sevo (ironically, having himself been captured and killed by Ramyel) had taken great pleasure in. It had taken him only a short while to discover that Sevo had come up with many different ways to kill agents of the Light in varying fashion and varying lengths of time and utilising various tools. He really did enjoy his work . . . and so Ramyel had to dispatch agents of the Light, some of which he had known, and learn to live with it and like it.

Before his mission had begun, he had been tutored at length to understand that part of him being able to survive in the Dark was to be like one of the Dark and if that meant killing an agent of the Light, then he must do so, without a thought. He must not pause.

"Besides," one of his tutors had said, "if an agent of the Light has been captured, he has failed and if he cannot escape, you will be doing him an act of kindness in ending him and at the same time, possibly stopping the Dark from learning something useful."

But that had been a long time ago and nobody could have imagined that Ramyel would have to kill so many agents of the Light in this kind of service, even though he had been given clearance to do so, even though his slight conscience should be clear, there had been so many . . . so many.

Once, a prisoner that Ramyel had recognised had been brought to him to be killed in his tiny grotto that he used as a chamber and for an instance, before dying, Ramyel was sure that he had been recognised by the Light operative.

This had lived with him. That look of recognition.

His mission went on, he was valuable after all.

And what was his mission? Simple.

All Ramyel had to do in the disguise of Sevo, was to whisper.

Whenever he had the opportunity to speak to a weak minded being of the Dark, he whispered. Whenever he was alone with one of these Dark things he whispered and spread the words. Small simple seeds, little thoughts and tiny questions that led those he whispered to, to question and ask of their leaders.

"Why did we have to do that?"

"Who tells him what to say?"

"Why don't we travel in time more?"

"Who are the Light?"

"Why do we have to stay here?"

"Where is Lucifer?"

Over many, many, many years, Ramyel stayed as Sevo. Over many, many, many years he whispered in ears. Subversive and seditious he carried out his task as though he were one of them . . . acting like one of them . . . being one of them . . . at times Ramyel thought that he may actually *be* one of them.

FOUR

Armean's yellow eyes glinted in the light of the torches that paved the way along the corridor. If he was stiff or ached from the days that he stood waiting for this task, he did not show it. It had been the longest time.

His gait was long and purposeful. He was pleased to have work and was even more pleased with what he had to do, as it was something that he could relish. His manipulative skills would be well used now for the task ahead. That's why he had to wait so long; he didn't mind as he wanted to serve, to do his best.

He strode back to his standing room only cubicle of sorts, carved into the rock of the corridor down which he had walked, this was one of many at different levels that ran in a giant oval, with creatures quarters allocated within them. Armean preferred to be in with the minions, sprites and cohorts not out of a sense of superiority but that his needs were simple, just like his compartment.

Armean shuffled on the spot to get as comfortable as he could in the small confine and then moved his robes to have himself wrapped in their length and then began to formulate his plan of action.

How would he tempt and capture this spy?

The first that had been able to get into the Realm of the Dark and the black sanctuary never mind be able to operate for so long, undetected.

This was a mission that he could not and would not fail. This would be the next step to being able to stand even longer in the chamber to prove that he was worthy of the greatest of all tasks that could be given to agents.

He was as close to being pleased with himself as it was able to get from such a being.

Thinking, thinking, thinking . . . how do I catch this cunning thing?

Armean was sure of two thing's: time had no meaning in this task and secondly, he would have to be very cunning, very

Steven Archer

cunning indeed to catch one that had been submerged in this filthy culture for so long as to be invisible, amazing really but Armean would put an end to this.

*

His discontent was etched on his face.

Standing on the plain in the Canadian countryside that would become part of British Columbia, Armean stared down at the contemptible being that knelt before him, arms over his head, shaking. His blade raised, he was about to dispatch the creature for failing to capture and kill cleanly an agent of the Light that had nearly escaped, until Armean himself had stepped forward, struck the thing with a blow to the throat after a brief chase over the knee length grass and then snapped his neck with both hands gripped on the flailing thing's head.

Instead of delivering the cutting blow of death, Armean flinched, tensed for a millisecond and then struck the grounded minion with a fist so hard as to send it sprawling backwards, bleeding from the mouth and shattered nose.

"Don't let that happen *again*." Was all that Armean said as he walked off and the two other beings along on the mission looked from him, to the thing on the floor, writhing in agony but living and then at each other . . .

*

Thinking, thinking, thinking . . . he would have to be so cunning.

*

Holding the knife to the throat of the creature in the darkness of the night and the cover of the forest in Borneo, Armean knew that he should kill the stupid messenger for killing the captive that they had too soon.

They had not been able to get the information from him that they had been sent to retrieve.

Instead, Armean threw the thing down to the ground, flinching and turning his back in disgust as he did.

Walking away, Armean knew that the three would follow, albeit quizzically. They, as others recently, had never seen behaviour like this but Armean was already thinking . . . he was already being cunning, even if it was against his nature and judgement.

*

Payoff.

It had to come sometime and sure enough it had, and a lot easier than Armean had thought that it would be.

He had been on a simple retrieval mission with two other troops and upon completion, successfully, Armean had escorted the captive to detention with the two agents. Once they had delivered their target, he had dismissed the two out of hand and started off. One had followed behind, a few paces.

Armean could sense him and had a feeling that the thing wanted to speak but left it to him, carrying on, steadily to his alcove.

"Why do we do this?" The question stopped Armean dead in his tracks and so, the thing behind him.

Payoff.

There was no way that any minion, troll, messenger, troop, cohort, beast, agent or creature would ask such a question of one ranked as Armean. *Maybe* among themselves in secure peer groups but not like this.

Armean turned and without a word, took hold of the thing and with a tight grip and tighter smile across his lips he walked and shoved the thing back to detention without another word and very little resistance.

His cunning and thinking over the past couple of years had paid off handsomely, the last detail he had to remember was finding those that he had reluctantly spared during this period and killing them as soon as possible.

FIVE

"You are Sevo and yet you are not Sevo." Armean stood leaning against the rough wall of the small detention room across from the figure on the floor, bloodied and battered.

He paused.

"I knew Sevo . . . just a little . . . and you are not he." There had been no need for the torture, for the beatings inflicted but Armean had decided to spend some time making his intentions clear, venting frustration and, almost enjoying himself. He had made himself stop when he had heard the first bone snap. It wasn't a big one, just one in the left forearm but still, he had thought that he should stop at that point and he had.

He paused, strolling the perimeter of the room.

"I once did a task with Sevo. He was . . . competent . . . useful to a degree but otherwise unsurprising. You have done well to conceal yourself for so long . . . very well." The figure lay inert, motionless save for the slight movement that came from breathing. Rising and falling. Rising and falling.

He paused looking down at his captive with a glint in his yellow eyes.

"Why don't you let me know and see who you are? Is there any point to this anymore? I am going to *kill* you, but wouldn't you rather be in your true form . . . instead of this husk?"

Once again, he paused, but now he wanted to make a move.

Pushing away from the wall, Armean moved toward the figure, picked up his pace and kicked out at it as hard as he could, right into the midriff. The thing coughed and spluttered, spat some black, congealed blood out over the floor and then rolled over, wheezing into a seated position against the wall, legs out straight. The thing that was Sevo sat and shook.

"You may be right. I would like to be myself again . . . I'm not sure if I remember what I looked like. I know that you would like to see . . . ."

"You've been in that shell for that long . . . ?"

"Yes. A long, long time. I have started to forget my true self . . . I remember being with Ferus Bestia at the time of the rebellion. We fought together. We fought together long and hard . . . I miss him . . ."

"You are indeed a paradox. Here before me is the body of a minion, a thing, low and disgusting and yet you are a warrior, a soldier for the army of Light now just a *spy*. Now a *caught* spy . . . where did your honour go? When did you feel it leave you?"

"I have honour, I am in service!"

Armean leaned close to the thing, nearly touching and whispered: "whose service?"

Ramyel jerked his head to look directly at Armean. The despair in his eyes revealing a wound as bad as any physical blow could leave.

As Armean took a step back, the form of Sevo started to shake, quicker and quicker. The shaking became a vibration and then a blur. Armean was aware of a hum in the cell but ignored it, looking straight at the change that was happening before him.

*

No sooner had Sevo turned to Ramyel, back to the true self, and then Armean wanted to act, to make sure that this spy suffered and knew real pain before being dispatched.

As Ramyel stood, shakily, weakly and reached his full height he stretched out his wings. That was when Armean struck, no hesitation.

The shaking had stopped, the vibration had stopped and the humming had stopped, now after a split second of quiet, the screaming started and the horror began.

Armean spun Ramyel around and pushed him into the wall his features fairer than that of the small, hunched creature he had inhabited for so long, his body fuller. Ramyel's face struck the wall with a dull and heavy thud. Armean pressed it further into the wall, stunning his weakened prey even more.

Steven Archer

In that moment, he placed his knee into the small of Ramyel's back, grabbed his left wing at the shoulder and pulled.

The screaming started high and got lower, the pain that Ramyel endured started low and got higher to his threshold as he felt his wing separate from his body, the agony intense and hot.

The sheer force and power that Armean exerted was tremendous, but even so he was aware that Ramyel was not putting up any struggle at all. He continued to pull, to tear the flesh from flesh, the tissue from bone and sinew from muscle.

Once the wing stopped flapping involuntarily and detached from the shoulder the worst was over.

Blood spurted out in a spray ending in a fine red mist. The wing made a gut-wrenching snapping sound as it came free from the socket of the shoulder to which it was attached.

Ramyel slumped to the floor, trying to reach behind him to stem the flow of blood, reaching but not being able to get near. He sobbed, rocked backwards and forwards and realised the waste that his life had been. In serving the Light as a spy for so long, he had lost himself, he had practically become part of the Dark . . . what had he lost?

His essence was gone. He cried.

Armean stared down at this being in front of him, lost and distraught, feeling empathy for an Angel that had simply wanted to serve but in the course of doing so had lost himself . . . He did not offer any information at all that Armean could use nor did Armean even ask.

In one swift motion, he reached behind him for his blade, lunged at Ramyel, who seemed to turn to him and present an open target as if knowing what was coming and slit his throat from side to side. Stepping back, Armean watched for a second as the Angel of the Light faded in front of him. As he left the room, he heard the final gurgling and spluttering of life.

*

That was a very difficult task.
"Yes Master, harder than I thought it would be."

The actions to capture him were well laid.
"Yes Master."
The capture was sublime and the dispatch . . . excellent.
"Thank you Master."
Looking that closely into a being gives . . . insight.
"Yes, it does Master."
I think you are ready to move on to other things now . . .
"Thank you Master."

AZAZEAL—THE INNOCENT

ONE

Bodies were piled up on top of one another.

Some of them moaning and some of them silent. Twisted and thrown together in a sculpture of horror.

The ground was soaked with blood in some places, making a red-brown mud that stuck to everything it touched.

The smell of rotting flesh, smoke from the fires that burnt constantly and sweat filled the air with thick invisible clouds, which could almost be choked upon.

Still on the acres of land that the battle covered there was skirmishes, fights. The conflict had raged for days and seemed as if it still had some way to go yet.

Thousands upon thousands of troops had been employed by each side, Light and Dark. What had started out as columns of soldiers now was a raggle-taggle of individuals, fighting in small pockets, frantically, with comrades against the enemy. Every being fighting through the fatigue for survival.

All that could be used had been used: cohorts, messengers, lackeys, minions, scavengers, trolls, creatures, beasts and . . . Angels. All of them had been thrust into action on this massive battlefield, which could have been anywhere, at anytime. Long sweeping green fields, edged with rock wall boundaries, flowed up to green hills and beyond, mountains capped with snow under an appropriately sombre and still, grey sky.

Among all of the carnage, all of the bloodshed, all of the horror, the fighting went on with a frenzy that was tangible, real.

It is easier to destroy than to create.

TWO

Deta had been an Angel of The Watch for some time.

This had been service of a varied nature for him, undertaking missions and tasks through differing time zones and with differing cultures.

Invariably, the task would be elimination of a transgressor or Dark agent, sometimes capture but not very often. He had realised that one of the skills that he possessed was a taste for battle and so that was why he had requested, and was granted leave to fight in various conflicts where his skills could be utilised and his appetite sated.

Conflicts like the one that he found himself in now.

He stood on a small hillock, surrounded by five Dark creatures that he had slain and was surveying the battle, breathing heavily. It was difficult to tell at the moment who was winning, and was there ever really a winner in all of this? He took huge gasps of air to get oxygen to his tired and aching muscles, screaming from the constant use and battering that they had taken over the last few none-stop days and tried to spot his comrade, Thaddyus.

The smoke and the greyness of the day made it difficult to see over the vastness of the field of conflict and it took him several moments and several horrors to spot his friend.

When he did he was stricken. Thaddyus was pinned against a rock, facing three foes and wounded. He fended with his shield using his badly cut left arm, trying to fight them back with his sword, but he was weakening and tiring as the three picked and stabbed at him like the Jackals they were.

Deta ran.

He cut a swathe through those that were in his way and ran as fast as he could, deciding against a brief flight, as he may be more vulnerable in the air.

He ran until his lungs burned as much as his muscles and then harder, Thaddyus all the while, fighting, fighting but taking another blow to the side that spun him around against the rock, weakening him.

Deta saw the final blow.

He saw the thrust that killed his friend and felt his legs go weak . . . he was too late.

The figure in front of the wide-eyed Thaddyus lunged and punched through his chest cavity, pushing the defensive move to one side as he retrieved Thaddyus' still beating heart, watched it turn to cold, grey stone and then smashed it against the rock in front of which they stood.

A blank expression fell upon Thaddyus' face and he fell to his knees, blood streaming from the hole in his chest, as the Angel that had killed him picked up his sword and ran off to hunt more soldiers, more victims, screaming as he did in a bloodlust frenzy.

Deta couldn't look, he turned away and stood a mere hundred yards from his friend and for a second he was invisible . . . the war went on about him as his heart sank and so did he.

The ache that he felt, the loss was like nothing he had encountered before.

*

The fighting went on in sporadic patches.

Deta cradled his dead friend and rocked back and forth, shaking uncontrollably. He had lost comrades before, many of them in many different places and times over ages, but not as close to him as Thaddyus had been. They had been comrades, friends for eons during some of the worst experiences imaginable.

How could this happen?

How could this be allowed to happen?

He looked upon his friends grey features, ignoring the killing wound in the periphery of his vision.

What was the point?

Deta shook and sobbed. The battle went on around him and he did not pay it any heed, nor it him.

He sobbed and changed within his heart.

What was the point?

THREE

Could this be the first time there had been a question?

No. That was what had led to the rebellion so long ago, but perhaps not since then. At that time Deta knew exactly where he stood . . . who did Lucifer think he was? How could he imagine himself to be anywhere close to a God?

But now Deta had queries.

Questions rolled around in Deta's head as he slumped against the rock face with his dead comrade, his friend in his lap.

Why does he kill for the Light? The truth?

Isn't the Truth good?

Deta did not become aware of the figures moving over him for quite a while and when he did, he saw that they had recognised a shift in him. His expression gave it up, the conflict within, the questions and the lack of answers.

Was he going insane? Was he retracting into himself, or was he about to die. Perhaps, for the very first time in his existence Deta was not resolute.

Deta didn't care. Deta could barely function, his head and mind spun.

"Take him." One of the Dark Angels, Azazeal said to the others.

Deta was in such a state of shock, flux that he did not recognise that Azazeal was the one that had killed Thaddyus and indeed, held his etched shield. His eyes were open, staring but they saw nothing and informed his brain of nothing. He was too busy trying to answer questions without answers and watching memories of his life over and over.

Azazeal watched as two of his minions pulled Deta up, threw his friend's corpse to one side and then dragged him off. His purple eyes puzzled by the state of Deta.

FOUR

Deta had been a prisoner in his own mind for decades.

He had been taken back to the Dark Realm as a prisoner, he would normally have been killed without pause, but Azazeal had seen something in him, he felt it and sensed that there was something more to Deta now.

He had spent decades in a tiny cell but as he had retreated further and further into himself, the agents of the Dark stopped locking the door. He had become numb. He had become a harmless, pitiful wretch.

He had become so oblivious to the environment around him, that he became something of a sideshow freak, to be occasionally stared at and taunted but after more years passed even that stopped.

Sometimes Deta would stagger about the corridors of his prison, returning, gibbering to his home, for that was what it had become, a sanctuary and not a cell.

There wasn't much to be done with him and so he was left to search his own mind for the answers that he so desperately wanted and craved.

The only constant was time. Time kept moving forward at a pace that would never stop, but Deta was oblivious to even this. Time had no meaning . . . nothing did.

He was empty, hollow.

*

Deta found himself in a small boat, slowly travelling over a never-ending sea clouded by a fog that hovered over the surface.

The lapping sound of the water on the hull of the boat was hypnotic.

He did not steer.

He did not row.

Deta simply sat while the small wooden craft in which he sat rocked gently in the endless sea and moved steadily on . . . and on . . . and on.

Deta stared ahead into the vastness, blank.

He finally realised that the mist was clearing and instead of the lapping of the sea against the boat there were gentle thuds and bumps.

It took Deta a while to comprehend that the sea on which he travelled; the tranquil ocean had become a nightmare.

The sea was filled with corpses. Hundreds of thousands of rotting, stinking corpses, everywhere that the eye could see.

Deta stood with a jolt, the boat rocking more and nudging against the closest bodies, bloated and scabrous after time in the water.

It was then that Deta recognised some of the swollen features as friends, comrades and even those that he had killed in battle. All of them rolling and ebbing, arms entwined with legs and faces that stared to the blank sky.

Deta tried not to look, felt his pulse race and tried to look away, cover his eyes . . . but he couldn't. He had to watch the corpses.

Then he saw Thaddyus.

That was when Deta awoke, in a sweat, in his stinking cell . . . screaming.

*

As Deta walked through the forest, feeling the cooling breeze on his face.

The sun, hidden by the forest's canopy, shone through the gloom in streaks of light, fluctuating continuously, moving and changing as he strolled on, thinking, pondering, questioning.

The first sound was like a whisper.

It sounded like a voice, just out of earshot. Deta could not work out what it said or what it meant. He continued on, asking his questions over and over as he did, his mind never resting.

The whispers grew louder. There were more of them, discontent.

An unnerving sensation crossed over him as he tried to make sense of these bodiless voices, these ghoulish sirens.

The voices got louder and louder. The whispers grew in tone and sound and got louder.

As Deta moved quicker trying to block out the sounds, trying to reach the end of the forest so the voices rose to a shrieking, a shouting cacophony of voices of the damned. They were screaming at him and about him, never letting up, never stopping.

Deta joined them.

Deta began to scream in a high shrill voice.

Again he awoke in his cell . . . still screaming.

*

As the wind rushed at him, Deta realised that he was falling.

Arms out, legs flailing he fell . . . fast.

There was no sign of land or earth below him and onward he rushed, faster and faster.

He looked at his wings and winced at the problem.

As he fell, the thick feathers and plumage on his wings was falling off, stripping down to the flesh below, pink and raw.

His eyes filled with tears as he continued to speed downward, spiralling and tumbling out of control . . . down . . . down . . . down.

Still Deta had his questions rushing around his mind at the same rate but that did not stem the rising fear he felt the faster he fell, the longer he fell. He had no control.

He was about to fall through giant grey rings that had formed in the sky like heavy grey spectral clouds. But Deta knew that they were not clouds.

As he approached, ever quicker, he knew exactly what they were and he started to sob.

They were memories. They were spectres of the past that had taken form, as fragile as they were for him to gaze upon as he fell, and fell, and fell.

He could not stop, he could not look away, he swiftly fell down and down, taking in these ghosts of times and friends past. His brain could not compute the images in their entirety and so they repeated, allowing him to take them in again and again. His questions sped around with them and his mind felt as though it may explode.

He screamed. He screamed as loudly as his voice and lungs would allow him. Then he closed his eyes tightly.

When he opened them he was back in his cell, still and unmoving and screaming. Screaming until he was sick.

*

Time and the agony of asking questions to which there were no answers took its toll on Deta. He changed.

His mind finally reached a place were it was content to dwell without the torture that it had endured anymore.

He was blank. He was a blank canvass.

Deta was the Innocent.

FIVE

Azazeal had looked on Deta with disgust as time had gone by.

He questioned why he had ever thought to bring this innocent to the Dark Realm in the first place.

Now he had been tasked with returning him to the Light.

After the longest of waits, he had been given this service. He could not see the point, did not want to do it and wanted to kill Deta instead. He sickened him.

Azazeal had not been able to approach Deta for a while; he needed to get his thoughts collected and a plan of action to make this task as easy and as straightforward as possible. It was hard.

Azazeal watched Deta from afar and observed how pathetic he was. He observed while Deta wandered around the darkened corridors a blank expression on his face. Others would stop and cross away from him for they did not know how to deal with him now. He was a breed apart.

Deta had become a kind of link between the Light and the Dark and it made the creatures uncomfortable.

It made Azazeal hate him.

After a day spent following this being, this *thing*, Azazeal entered Deta's tiny cell immediately after he had entered.

"I've been expecting you." Deta's tone was even, quiet and calm.

Azazeal simply looked at him.

"I won't go back. I don't want to go back . . . or to anywhere that you may have been tasked to take me to. I don't think that you are to kill me, I've been here too long and I have become . . . different, changed. Don't make me go away."

Azazeal was surprised by the fury that rose in him while this vile thing talked at him.

"I'd rather stay here. I know my place here. I am content here. I have a semblance of peace. Can you imagine what that's like? Can you ima . . ."

Azazeal's blow to the throat stopped Deta's words in his mouth. As he raised his hands to his airway and fell to his knees, Azazeal did not wait for another second. He hit Deta.

He hit him with all of his strength, all of his might.

Azazeal struck Deta with hate and with revulsion. His fists were a blur. His feet were a blur. He pummelled Deta with a force that he had not known that he had possessed turning the Innocent into a bloody mess.

The thing that had been Deta, the Light Angel that had become the Innocent and was now a pulped, crushed mass of bone and tissue and blood and gore.

After the frenzy, Azazeal stood back against the cool of the cell wall and dispassionately stared at the body, like a child looking at an ant they'd stood on. The distance in his purple eyes was as wide as the hatred that he had felt for this thing and now he knew his limitations.

Although the rage scared him a fraction, a smile spread across his lips, tight. He had created this innocent when he had ended Thaddyus and now he had killed his creation.

*

Did you know the point of the task when you were given it?
"No, Master, it . . . caught me by surprise."
Do you understand what you have done?
"Yes, Master I realise completely what I have done.
You have taken a large step, Azazeal.
"Thank you, master. I do feel . . . different."
Good. Now for more pressing tasks to come . . .

TUREAL—TIME TAKES ITS TOLL

ONE

The first time it happened could have been at any point in history.

Perhaps, it was inevitable.

Evolution affects any colony, culture or group in differing ways. Even in a dictatorship there will be progress and there will be change. Attitudes and conceptions will become different. As time passes and masses interact, there will be change.

Nobody could have seen this coming, and even if they did . . . how would it be stopped?

The first time that an agent of the Dark killed a being of the Light and then absorbed part of its soul was long, long ago.

This was taboo, unspoken and if found out treated with zero tolerance, simply meaning the thing that did this foul but addictive deed would be killed, no reprieve. The killing of an enemy (and even a comrade) was expected as well as tolerated but to take any of the victim's soul was not to be done . . . ever.

It was an urban legend a myth.

Whispers around darkened corridors spoke of the high that could be derived from the taking of a soul, even just part of it. Not only was there a brief rush of well-being and strength, but also to be able to look into another creature's life and feeling it, *experiencing it* first hand was the stuff of legend.

The troops, the hordes had been fighting and killing for centuries. Some dealt with this constant bloodletting but some got caught up in the frenzy, the high of the kill. It was all that they registered in their meagre existences.

Simply put, some of the population had reached a point of being not only psychotic but also addicted to killing. That was when one had taken the next step and sampled a part of another's soul.

The never-ending passage of time in this Realm had manipulated some of the servants into fiends, but even in a hellish place like this, there had to be control, there had to be a semblance of order over the chaos.

Addictions to this, the most powerful of drugs had to be stopped. And the killing for killing sake had to be policed otherwise; there would be no future for the Realm. There had to be respect, either that or fear.

TWO

Jacques De Molay, the respected Grandmaster of the Knights Templar screamed as the fire licked its way up the dry tinder.

He screamed as the flames began to burn his skin, making it sear and blister in an agony of death with shuffling on the spot against the post to which he was tied rather than the death dance he would have preferred to do, to try and combat the intense pain. This was useless.

Here, in France, 1312 on Friday the 13th (a day that would become taboo for many human's in the future) Tureal had overseen the downfall of one of the most significant forces of the era, the Knights Templar. He and two others had spent eight months manipulating events to get to this point, he and Mannus and Sillus had schemed with royalty, government officials and the Knights themselves to ensure that they would go down in history as a renegade band brought down before they became too powerful and ushered in a new dawn of prosperity and invention.

That could not be allowed and so, Tureal had been given the task of tumbling this order.

He had relished the mind games more than the strategic killings, and had noticed that his comrades had enjoyed the killings more than the manipulations, and had been happy that at the end of it all the thing that brought down the order was greed. The greed of the King of France, to be precise, in debt and looking for wealth, Tureal had served it up for him.

Now the three of them stood and enjoyed the fruits of their labours.

Skirmishes broke out on the streets and arguments turned to beatings, which rapidly turned to killings. Mannus and Sillus had gotten too involved in this, beating passers by and even making the effort to stab them which meant Tureal had to have them all leave earlier than he would have liked, for the Dark Realm, he would have preferred to savour the moment for longer, but their behaviour meant that he could not. Mannus in particular had taken on a gleeful attitude to injuring these monkeys.

It was time to go.

*

When the three got back to the Dark Realm, Mannus was still hyperactive.

He and Sillus argued over who had killed more humans and helped in the mission more. Tureal was content, in his own environment to see where the debate led. It amused him somewhat but it was becoming an annoyance.

The pushing and shoving between the two started and soon escalated to a brawl. Mannus and Sillus traded blows, punches and kicks, each becoming more enraged and angry.

Tureal stood back and watched.

It wasn't long before Mannus pulled his blade and during a clench that had them rolling around the floor, he stabbed Sillus in the side. The jerk that followed told Tureal that this had been a well placed blow and would be the death of Sillus, although he struggled on, lashing out at Mannus, who then proceeded to repeatedly stab him in the stomach, a manic expression on his evil features.

Tureal was pleased that it was over quickly and that the outcome saved him the trouble of killing one of them, which he would have had to have, done as an example.

Sillus lay inert now, blood weeping from his many wounds and one major gash. But what bothered Tureal was that Mannus continued to lie on the deck also, shaking.

Tureal lunged forward and dragged Mannus back when he realised what he was doing . . . taking part of the soul of Sillus, the essence of him.

Mannus was weak, imbalanced and staring vacantly, blood covered him from Sillus's wounds.

Tureal thought quickly and dragged Mannus off to his hovel. He wanted to see the effect of this action and then he wanted to get information from Mannus.

When they reached the pathetic, sparse little space that Mannus inhabited, Tureal threw him to the floor and watched. He watched as Mannus experienced some of Sillus's life and the high that he got from it.

Disgusted and yet unable to look away, Tureal watched, his golden eyes blank.

THREE

The hours went by quickly.

Mannus had rolled around unable to get comfortable, moaning and groaning as he did.

His twitching and jerking a dance of the macabre.

He seemed to be lucid at points but distant and babbling at others.

It was apparent to Tureal that he was moving through the emotions given from the experiences he had taken from Sillus.

When Mannus came around he was unsure at first of where he was. It took him several seconds to get a grip on his faculties.

"How many times have you done that?" Asked Tureal in a tone that immediately got Mannus's attention and let him know that there would be no chance of avoiding the problem that he stupidly created in his very presence.

Mannus looked at Tureal, deep into his golden eyes and decided that he had to be direct.

"That was my third time."

"How did you start?"

"I watched another do the same thing to a human and watched him react to the experience before we returned to the Realm . . . there are more that do it than you could know."

"What is the effect?"

"Its . . . its . . . relief. It's a relief for a brief time. The feeling of power is strong also, physical and mental . . . but it takes hold . . . it takes you, makes you want more. The cravings just seem to get worse."

"So that you want to do it again . . ."

"Yes."

Tureal took a couple of steps toward Mannus and knelt in front of him. He placed his hands on his face and looked directly into his eyes. "Then a message needs to be sent. Who did you watch that first time?"

"Amone . . . it was Amone . . ." Mannus's eyes pleaded in a way that he could not do verbally, but it was to no avail.

Tureal tightened his grip on Mannus's face and as he squeezed, he gave a quick jerk to the left, snapping his neck and extinguishing him instantly. Tureal wiped his hands on Mannus's clothing, dirty as it was to get rid of some of the being of him. He stood back and looked down at the lifeless shell.

He then did something that surprised even him.

He leaned close to the dead form and drained part of its essence. Breathing it in, deep and long.

*

Tureal had no idea how long he had been unconscious.

It had been as though he had been dreaming. Images of places and events that he had never seen before, people and beings that he had never met had rushed around his mind in a swirl of colour.

The experiences had been both vivid and vague but the element that Tureal now contemplated was just how real they had been as if they had been *his* memories.

The residual power of the happening still had a hold on him and made him feel stronger and vital.

Now he walked with a purpose to find Amone.

Tureal had conflicting thoughts about what he had done, about whether it had been right or wrong but he decided that he would have that debate with himself at a later date, right now he wanted to send the message.

He saw Amone in a centralised area, a junction between levels speaking to four other creatures. Perfect. That meant that he could make his point and kill him.

Tureal strode straight up to Amone and looked at the others, silently indicating that these minions should step back to avoid any trouble and then not move. They got the message.

In the flickering light of the torches dotted about the rock face walls of the junction, Tureal's eyes shone vibrantly.

"I need to send a message that taking the essence of those recently dead is to stop."

"I don't know what you mean . . ." Amone did know what he meant and realised that in saying what he had, he'd just made things worse, he stood rooted, scared and shaking.

"Everyone around here will spread the word that this is what will happen if I find any culprit of this crime."

The few that stood around moved back slightly as did the others that had entered the crossroads on route to other places.

Tureal stepped close to Amone and without any resistance put his hands around his neck, gripping.

He lifted Amone off the dirty, stony floor and squeezed.

All of the minions around watched with gritted teeth as Tureal strangled the life from Amone, one of his eyes leaving the socket because of the massive pressure he was exerting. It only took seconds for Amone's form to tense and then relax in death.

Tureal held him for some moments longer, having his rage evaporate before throwing the corpse against the furthest wall.

He turned to those watching uncomfortably and made eye contact with each.

"Clear?"

*

You know why you had the task with those two agents now?
"Yes Master."

I am pleased that you achieved both tasks set out on that mission.

"Thank you Master. I only want to serve."

Serve you will, Tureal for now you have begun to understand things beyond you. You have shown that you can deal with issues that are not always obvious.

"I am pleased to have fulfilled your expectations, Master but you knew that I would . . . try the . . . essence."

Of course, Tureal. That was the whole point. You are unique. You are able to do this thing and not become a pathetic addict. You will learn to use this skill over time and then you will be able to move on to other tasks that I have planned.

"Thank you Master, I understand."

GABRIEL—THE PARTING OF THE WAYS

ONE

Emptiness is a void that is difficult to fill after such an event.

To have been one of the most revered of Angels . . . to be a part of the Kingdom, the Truth. But then to have witnessed the change after the brief rebellion that saw Lucifer cast down . . .

Change was immeasurable, so many affected now and for time to come . . . all of time to come. It was difficult to comprehend, the loss, the emptiness.

How do you serve when your belief, your faith is tested to such a limit?

Now Lucifer was in his prison, the rebellion crushed, his allies all but killed or cast out over nine days and the same fate awaiting Lucifer.

Gabriel did not want to be here, he did not want to guard him, there was no need for it at the moment, Lucifer was in transformation he was metamorphosising into a new being, a new life and Gabriel wanted to be as far from it as possible.

His emotions rolled and swirled, his conflict was inside. He wasn't sure whether he was more angry at having to fight with former friends and allies, by the situation, disgusted at Lucifer and his ways, saddened by what had now come about and what would happen in the future or shamed at the thoughts that he was having about whom he should serve: the Light or the Dark. For now there was Dark.

It was unbelievable, incomprehensible to think that there was even a choice.

*

Gabriel remembered. Head in hands, he thought back. Thought of how Lucifer had been the Shining Star, one of *the* most trusted of the Angels. The energy and verve that he had was incomparable. But then he had changed. Slowly at first, almost imperceptible to all but not Gabriel, Gabriel had seen it in Lucifer's eye.

He had spoken to him as his manner and behaviour had changed on several occasions, each time being laughed off by a Lucifer who put an arm around him and assured him that all was and would be well. How long had it taken to affect this change, to notice it and to be aware of it?

He had literally unleashed Hell.

Lucifer had become arrogant. Over time he had shown conceit and finally in the focal point of the maelstrom, he had displayed pride . . . to even think that he could be more than an Angel, more than what he was created to do and to even consider that he should be at the hand of God . . . and equal!

The reaction had been swift, the lines drawn and Lucifer and his allies taken on in the first and most Holy War, having spent time whispering among themselves, advocating change, now there was action. For some, the decision whom to fight for was clear. Others struggled and many, like Gabriel fought and then wrestled with the consequence. The carnage that was left on the battlefield and in the psyche of every servant of the Light and those still surviving that had been banished was awesome, the repercussions felt forever.

And now Gabriel sat and watched over the catalyst.

Gabriel had never wanted to be in the situation that he had to pick a side. Deep within, he knew that he would always serve the Light but now how thing's had changed . . . how different they would be. He served but he had lost something. Innocence? A naivety or belief, even his faith. How long could he serve when the questions remained unanswered and the irony that was not lost on Gabriel was not that it was only he that could supply answers but that Lucifer had given him a choice . . . a freedom of sorts.

Gabriel's face was drawn and pale, looking like so many of the others that now struggled with the same issues with varying degree of success. The whole of Heaven waited for the casting down to draw a line so that they could move on and start to heal . . . but the pain, the conflict and the scars that they left . . . this would remain for a long while.

TWO

His time in captivity was brief by some standards but solitary.

He had to remain on his own without any contact before he was banished. That was what had been commanded. Angels that still had the conflict inside of them wished him gone, gone but surely not forgotten. His vile stain would be upon the Light forever.

Many had taken matters to hand and tried to get to Lucifer so that he could be killed, but none got past Gabriel, in actuality not many even came to blows once they got that far.

Six hundred and sixty-six days in a hole.

That was when Lucifer would be allowed out and immediately banished.

Gabriel contemplated the sounds, screams and rantings that Lucifer had yelled from his prison, with only one night remaining.

He had denied his role in the battle, the rebellion, he had shouted that he had grown, that he had shown that he could be different to his original template and perform beyond that of his creation. As he shouted his defiance, so he had asked questions of the silent Gabriel, choosing to answer them for himself and almost reaching the point of realisation that he had transgressed, only to draw back.

Lucifer had been defiant. He extolled the deeds that he would carry out on his new mission now that he knew of the casting down and this he would use to his benefit for he would wreak havoc on man. The humans who had been given a soul by God would be the ones to suffer from this, he had been right and now, without the finality of death, Lucifer would torment the humans.

Gabriel listened, sometimes intently to the debate that Lucifer had with himself, sometimes tuning it out to get on with his own thoughts and recovery. The anger that vented from the hole, that dark, damp, stinking hole was almost tangible. The venom with which Lucifer spat words about the things that he would do and naming some to be on the receiving end were fierce and had a finality to them. The rage, the temper and the wrath that was demonstrated was so deep and prolonged as to even give Gabriel pause for thought.

After a silence, an introvert time of contemplation, acceptance had been on the lips of Lucifer. He had done what he had done. There could be no change, no going back. He would not do anything differently given the opportunity and so, he accepted his role, his future and his task. His own personal mission of opposing the word of the Light with the will of the Dark.

If he could not have a voice in Heaven then he would rule in Hell.

Gabriel wept at the tone and determination behind the spoken words.

*

"I know that you can hear me Gabriel. I know that He has placed you there to escort me to the end . . . soon. I knew he would choose you. Who else could be here and listen to me without a word. Who else could listen for so long . . . and how is your own turmoil, your own little dispute? I ask, although I know too that you will not answer and perhaps that is for the best."

"I couldn't help or deny it, could I? What kind of a being would I be if, once I had realised the change in myself, as small as it were, I ignored it or suppressed it? How vain of Him to think that I could really be a threat. That speaks volumes . . . that tells a tale that a mere Angel can change, can improve itself only to be accused of Pride and cast down after a small solitary lesson. Once I was aware, I had no choice; I could not deny it or myself. Isn't it natural to mature? Isn't that what He expected and perhaps even wanted?"

"I haven't felt His warmth for so long now . . . Haven't enjoyed His attention. I can't even hear his voice anymore. The point that I have realised, in here ironically, is that I don't miss it. I don't miss Him. I thought that I would, but I don't. What a revelation. What a comfort I can gain from understanding that there is more beyond this Realm, this Kingdom. I can live without his love. I can survive without Him being there, and perhaps it is only survival, but it is better to go on surviving than to be a traitor to yourself, to ignore what you are . . . I am different now, aren't I Gabriel . . . do you think it was inevitable that one of us would evolve?"

"I'm going to make Him suffer. I am going to make man suffer as I have. I will take out my vengeance for an eternity on those monkeys, those things that He saw fit to bless with a soul that they do not deserve and did not earn . . . how can they have been so worthy of His love after no time at all, no effort and no penance, well, I shall make them pay. And the strange thing is that I couldn't really care less about them, but being cast down . . . what choice do I have, what would I do? This is the best way to get at Him. The extraordinary thing is that he would banish me to Earth so that I can torment, but then wouldn't that be a part of His plan, so that they turn to Him for solace, for assurance and for help? Am I playing into His hands? Am I part of an elaborate strategy? I don't care anymore for over the eons I will bend man, I will manipulate him and in the end create such a scar of apathy and distrust in them that He will have to act and bring me back, back to His side . . . Is that my Pride again? I should really be more careful who I speak to, don't you think?"

Steven Archer

THREE

Gabriel walked behind Lucifer.

He was not chained or tied. There would be no need. Lucifer walked with a steady pace through the dark and gloomy passageways without another being to be seen. There were just the two of them.

Gabriel didn't speak, nor even feel the need to. His heart and soul were heavy and hardened. He thought that this would be the case for a long time to come. Time is the greatest healer, he thought, but what pathetic and scant consolation that was.

He wished that he had not had to choose, he wished that everything had stayed the way that it was forever, he even wished that man had not come about to begin the end, the end of all that he knew. And even in having these thoughts he knew that he had changed too.

Yet there had been change and there would be more. Gabriel had to get used to that fact. He felt a sorrow so deep as to touch his very core like an icy finger. He felt wretched and sick.

He had not heard his Master's voice for a little while now and wondered why. Was he being left alone to sort out his own opinions and state? Was everyone?

Even as they approached the opening to the cave, and saw the rocky outcrop ahead, when he was at his lowest ebb, he began to feel a twinge of something. A tiny spark in the blackness of his misery and sadness.

They reached the end of the outcrop and both looked over the edge. All that could be seen were swirling grey clouds, whipping around beneath them in a storm, the odd lightening strike flashing across. Below that . . . Earth.

The isolation of this place was not lost on either of them, the remoteness. Lucifer looked into Gabriel's eyes but did not speak anymore. He had said all that he wanted to.

They stood for a moment before Gabriel approached Lucifer and put his arms around him. Lucifer did not move but bowed his head.

"Lucifer, before you complete your change . . . before you become . . . Satan . . . goodbye . . ." Gabriel held on tight for a moment longer and then stepped back, their eyes locked once more in an exchange of expression for a long second and then Satan stood to one side.

He looked over the abyss and without pause, he leapt.

Legs together, arms out and wings spread wide he rushed, spiralling to the Earth from Heaven. Gabriel watched as it only took seconds for him to disappear into the cloud. He was gone . . . forever. Lucifer was no more.

Although Gabriel shed a tear, he felt the tiny spark within him flicker.

Steven Archer

FOUR

After the beginning there was the parting of the ways.

There had been Lucifer.

With the ejection of Lucifer from Heaven, came the creation of Satan and the casting of the shadow. The darkness that affected the Light.

And so began the conflict over time and place . . . forever?

JOPHIEL—BORN AGAIN

ONE

The third time that a dead body was found outside of a speakeasy was Jon J Norton's second time on duty with the Fed's.

Still, in the pouring rain and twisted in a disjointed way that made the corpse look as though it had been moved to test the bodies limitations, Norton looked down on it and wondered at the coincidence.

He had been seconded from the 34th precinct to help the FBI monitor the speakeasy's in the area and so, clamp down on the illegal sale of alcohol, which was just plain funny as they made few arrests, did fewer stakeouts but all drank as heavily as any man he knew. It was his knowledge of the local area that had gotten him this posting. He didn't mind it as it was a change of pace and gave him a new challenge . . . for what it was worth.

Norton had been on the force for fifteen years and considering he was only thirty-five years old, that wasn't bad going for an officer, considering all that was to be seen on the job.

"Move it along, Norton, you're here for watchdog duties *only*. This don't concern *you*." One of the Fed's pushed Norton back as he spoke, looking at the body and not him.

Norton shook his head a little, pursed his lips and then took one more look at the body on the cold concrete deck, gauging where the wound in his side must have been to allow the blood to flow out.

"Just get back inside and finish off ya shift . . ." The Fed remarked as Norton walked off to the rear entrance of the speakeasy, pulling his trench coat tight around him.

There wasn't any more action inside the dive as everyone had left in a hurry when they had realised what was going on outside.

Norton had sat at the back of the smoky room and left himself for home shortly afterwards, not seeing any point in letting anyone know he'd gone.

As he strolled along the wet pavements of downtown Chicago, his home since birth, he pondered the two dead men that he had seen so far and the similarities. After forty minutes, the walk into his apartment block and entering his shabby front room, all he could think about was sleep.

*

"Okay, Jon. I'll make the call . . . I don't think they'll go for it but what have I got to lose? You'd be doin' me a favour actually."

Norton watched from the chair in which he sat in his Captain's office while the big barrel chested man chomped his cigar, spoke to a Fed on the end of the line and pushed papers around with his free, fat fingered hand all at the same time.

Norton smiled. He'd known Mac for a long time and he was one of the few people that he trusted, in or out of the department anymore.

He had barely had time to take in some of the photograph's charting Mac's career and weight gain dotted around the office, before he was through.

Before speaking he replaced the telephone to its cradle slowly and raised his eyebrows.

He looked at Norton and his quizzical expression. "They couldn't give a fuck. As long as you wanna check it out while with them and still pull some surveillance time for them, they couldn't give a fuck, so you got the case. You *are* doing me a favour, 'cos I thought I'd have to assign somebody, so everyone's a winner. That's gotta be a first. What time are you on?"

"3.30" Norton smiled and wondered why he was so glad to get a murder investigation. He'd been there, done that and got the medal but there was something about this . . .

"Why d'ya want it so bad?"

Norton shook his head and feigned a mock frown: "Just a feeling . . ."

Mac picked up the phone again. "Lucy . . . Lucy! For pity's sake listen. Get me everything on the speakeasy murders from the past few weeks that we have and bring it in here, quick . . . I know it ain't much but be a sweetheart and bring it anyway." He put the phone down. "You need to do your homework and then get to work. Keep me posted and we'll do a catch up in a coupla days when you wanna move on."

"Great, thanks Mac, that was easier than I thought."

"Yeah, great, well done ya got a murderer to find . . . enjoy."

*

Lucy had been right.

There wasn't a lot in the files.

Norton had poured over them before he had gone to work at another club downtown, on the west side.

All of the victim's were men. He knew that.

All of them had been stabbed outside a speakeasy. He knew that.

The stab wounds were just about in the same place, in the left side just above the third or fourth rib. He could have guessed that.

All of the men were in their thirties. He didn't know that.

Two of them were married, one single. He wondered if that was important.

All three were working, which was good going in the current economic climate.

There didn't seem to be a struggle in any of the cases as if they had known the attacker. He hadn't known that.

All evidence had been bagged and tagged and was back at the 27th, so he'd have to check that out tomorrow, then he would sit down and formulate his next move.

Norton placed the files in neat piles, on the neat desk and reminded himself to go over the pictures in more detail tomorrow as well.

He shrugged on his coat and left to meet the Fed's.

*

The place was lousy with people, swimming in booze and heavy with smoke. The piano music loud enough to be heard but not to disturb the babble of conversations between the men and women chatting, dancing and smiling at one another.

Norton sat at the back of the warehouse that had been emptied of stock and filled with barrels of booze, chairs and seats and people who wanted to and could afford to get drunk. Times were hard and people needed a release, so this sort of dive had opened its doors.

Norton had been working with the Fed's to try and find a main supplier for two weeks, they had been successful in the previous endeavour before that, even though these government guys seemed as happy to let things slide as catch someone at it, but that one had fallen in their lap. The guy had literally delivered while they'd been there. Even the Fed's couldn't ignore that kind of idiot. This time was taking longer . . . the word was out.

Norton stretched and indicated subtly to his colleague at the far end of the bar that he was going for a smoke. The man nodded slightly and he got up and left after taking a leak.

*

He'd just stepped outside; let the door swing closed behind him as he cupped his hands to light his cigarette.

That was when Norton got killed.

As he felt the sharp, hot pain in his neck where the knife entered, he saw the body of the man to his left. As the knife was pulled out and he fell to his knees, dropping his lighter and cigarette, his neck lolled forward and then he felt himself pushed to the ground, unable to react and another pain in his lower back, then another, then another then blackness and then nothing.

Jon J Norton was dead.

TWO

How long had he stood here, in this place?

How much longer would he have to?

His feet felt numb to the ankles, his knees trembled, his arms jerked sporadically and he was sweating.

Was it going to be worth it?

Was standing so still for so long in this pathetic manner really going to be worth doing a task?

Yes it would be. After God only knows how long, another irony in this place, getting used to his new home, its meaning and its environment and more importantly, his part in this Realm, Jophiel was struggling.

He had decided that it would be better to serve, to be active and perhaps use the skills that he had from when he was alive (he was still, after all of this time coming to terms with death) rather than wander this location forever, in a torturous world of inactivity, a limbo of sorts.

It was probably at around the time that he had started to get used to what every being called him when they needed to instead of his real name, that Jophiel had made that decision.

He'd been warned about this test, well, informed of how hard it could be to simply stand.

He'd underestimated just how hard.

How long now. How long had he been standing now? How long to go?

Jophiel felt himself go light in the head, his body unfeeling and then he collapsed.

There'd be no task this time.

THREE

He could not and would not fail this time.

Not this time, not again.

Jophiel had to do this thing for himself now as much as to be given a task.

Twice more he had failed after that initial attempt, in which he had been shocked to find that he had only been within the dark chamber for twelve hours. It had felt longer. A lot longer.

Now he was better prepared. He tried to occupy his mind with anything that would keep him on his feet, silent and waiting, with only the crackle of the torches in his ears.

Memories of people, places, good times and bad were relived in as much detail as he could remember. Songs, school and his childhood. Joining the police, anything to keep him busy. Anything to keep him on his feet.

Then he had seen the dirt. It had made him think and it was then that context hit him. In this tiny space, in this Realm that he now inhabited, he would make up stories in his mind about the dirt.

Just dirt.

*

It had not seemed that long when he heard the voice. It was all around him and in his head.

You have proved yourself and so you will be given a task.

"Er, thank you, thank you." Jophiel tried to get a grip.

You will be sent for and when you are, be ready to go, ready for anything. You will be sent on an observational mission first. Do not interact. You will have your task given to you after the observational visit.

"Yes Master. Thank you."

*

Jophiel had been called what must have been days later, after yet more waiting. Was this part of the process or more of the test. Now he entered a cavern, following a messenger who had not said a word throughout their brief walk from Jophiel's abode.

The messenger indicated a round platform approximately four feet round.

Jophiel hesitated and then stood in its centre.

There wasn't anyone else in the cavern, Jophiel felt unease but comfortable at the same time. He was dressed in a suit that he would have worn when he was . . . alive. The minion had given it to him on his entry into his small quarters.

Jophiel wondered where the hell he was going. What he hadn't thought of was *when* the hell was he going?

*

Once the sound of wind rushing around him had died away and the flashes of purple light had faded and so had the blurred colours in his eyes, Jophiel had to convince himself of where he was.

He pushed himself back against the cold and wet wall of the back alley. It could have been anywhere, but he knew it to be the very alley in which he had died.

What kind of fucked up trip was this?

A shiver ran down his spine and his mind tried to reject what he was seeing. Before he could take in any more information and rationalise what was going on and why he was here of all places, the door to the big building on his right opened with a bang. It was the side door to the old warehouse he had been in, the speakeasy.

Two figures tumbled out, into the alley, supporting each other and laughing.

It was a man and a woman. They wasted no time in pulling down clothes and pulling open shirts and blouses.

The man pushed the woman against the wall opposite the door that they had exited. She liked it. He kissed and fumbled through her camisole top.

The woman made sounds of pleasure as he busied himself, caught in the moment.

It was then that the woman dropped her right hand and Jophiel saw the knife. He took an involuntary step forward but remembered that he was only supposed to observe, as hard as it may be, as difficult as it was to see. This was his test.

He continued to look through unbelieving eyes.

The woman moved her hand and as her lover busied himself with her body, fumbling and rubbing still as she stabbed him. She had paused to aim and then shown poise before striking ensuring a good hit. When the man lurched back, eyes wide enough for Jophiel to see the whites and the horror, he reached for his side and she stabbed him again in the chest.

He crumpled to the deck, dead before he hit.

Then something made the woman motionless. A sound.

She rushed to the door that she had come through moments before and pressed herself against the wall.

Jophiel was shocked to see himself walk out of the door that swung open and even more shocked to see the woman move behind him and stab him.

Jophiel turned and looked at the ground, he was reeling. His senses whipped around in his head and thoughts of his life intruded on him, making him nauseas.

He held his hand against the cool of the rough brick wall and sweated. He felt bile rise in his throat.

Did everyone have to witness their own death?

Was this still part of the test?

His eyes stung with tears of sorrow and regret as the reality of this unreal scene struck him, his mind feeling as though it would fracture from the pressure.

It had been a while, but soon he was able to look. He composed himself and then staggered to the place where he lay, dead.

The woman had gone and he didn't know where, nor did he care at this exact moment, this was something he had to see for himself.

Standing over Jon J Norton, Jophiel took a deep breath and held it.

He was dead, but here he was, alive and some sort of thing in an afterlife.

How strange, he thought, to feel such a deep sorrow for yourself, to feel loss.

The sound began as a whisper and rose in volume as he himself started to wail. The purple lights pulsed and flashed around him brighter and brighter and Jophiel was pleased to be leaving this place, pleased to get away, pleased to go . . . home?

FOUR

Jophiel was surprised at how much better he felt, stronger.

He still had contradictory feelings about quite what he was doing here and what his role was, but since he had got back from watching himself die, he felt a sense of closure. Perhaps this was the new start he needed in this place. Maybe that was the reason that he had been allowed to view his own death . . .

Now you can complete the second part of this task.

The dismembered voice made Jophiel flinch a little. He wasn't used to the quiet booming and the fact that it came so unexpectedly.

"Very well."

You will be taken as you were before. You will know what to do when you get to your location.

"How will I know?"

Silence.

"You said that I'd know what to do. That's it? No further instruction?"

Silence.

Jophiel was perplexed but knew that he could stand here forever and not get a reply.

He left to wait for the task to come to him, acceptance making an easier companion than being quizzical.

*

He was back in the alley.

The hairs on the back of his neck stood up.

Palms flat against the wall again; he looked from side to side and wondered what the fuck was going on.

Jophiel gritted his teeth and let his instincts take over. He had to see what was going on and react or be proactive in whatever it was he was going to witness.

Steven Archer

He was sure that this was the same alley again, the one in which he had died. It was. He was positive.

Then the door opened again and the two figures tumbled out again.

Jophiel was not struck by deja-vu. He was watching these events as they unfolded in real time, he was aware of the difference.

It was then that Jophiel felt that he knew what he had to do. He smiled.

Quietly, he moved down the side of the building until he was as close to the couple as he could be without being detected.

She was about to stab him.

Jophiel looked the other way and as he observed the empty alleyway and the street beyond, the buildings, the fire escapes, the trash cans and the litter-strewn floor he felt different.

He had changed a little and perhaps it was in his soul, for that's how profound that it felt to him.

Looking back at the woman who was now pressed against the wall herself about to kill him, or rather, Jon J Norton, he felt stronger in body and mind. He was focussed, like he hadn't been for a long time and he was enjoying the fleeting feeling.

As she pounced on him and stabbed him to death, Jophiel ran, crouching across the alley, light of foot and fast of movement. Just as she straightened, he struck.

Jophiel hit the woman with a force that sent her crashing against the wall next to the door. She fell to the floor, sprawling and stunned.

She had dropped the knife.

Steadily, Jophiel picked it up and without a thought, he leaned forward and thrust it into her stomach, her expression as she watched the man that she had just killed, that lay dead beside her, was unique and Jophiel savoured it for a moment.

As she tried to scratch at him, he twisted the knife and her face twisted with it in a silent scream, expelling only a last breath.

Jophiel pulled the knife out and then watched as she slumped to the side. He knew that she was dying; her blood spilled from her stomach and would leave her dead in minutes.

Rather than finish her off quickly, Jophiel decided to let her suffer. Why not?

He looked over at himself and then with a spike of icy coldness, he placed the knife in Norton's cold dead hand.

Satisfied, Jophiel stood for a second and then walked off down the alley enjoying the beating of his heart and the sound of his feet on concrete.

*

Time would show that Detective Jon J Norton was killed in the line of duty.

He had managed to find a serial killer whose male victim's had all been killed at the rear of speakeasy's.

An only child, her father had left her and her mother at an early age and to survive, the killer's mother had turned to prostitution to survive. The girl endured all of the shocking details of her mother's trade as well as some of the abuse, verbal, physical and sexual that she had taken in the years that passed.

Finally, when her mother had died, the girl had taken several low paid waitressing jobs and then set about exacting her revenge on the men she hated and that had hurt her so.

Det. Norton had disturbed her during one of those attacks, suffered fatal injuries but had managed to kill Mary-Ann Hoskins before he perished.

He was posthumously decorated.

He was single and left no surviving relatives.

*

You knew what to do.
"Yes . . . I did know what to do."
You have abilities that can be of use here.
"Yes Master."
You may be called upon from time to time to use them.
"Yes Master."

THE END

Steven Archer

Unclean Six Authors Notes

This story has taken a long time to get from conception to completion.

I don't normally add notes like this to a story that I've written because I think it is very important for the reader to make up their own mind about the content and, of course, whether or not they like the text and ultimately the idea.

In this case, however, I wanted to just get a few points across as this has been the most serious and difficult piece that I have written to date.

It is very personal, very contentious and hopefully, thought provoking.

I have never amended a piece as many times as I have this one whilst writing the text.

*

This idea started when I was reading many books about Freemasonry, which led to the life of Jesus and then onto even more weighty books like the Bible, the Dead Sea Scrolls and Pesher technique (translating psalms and parables to reveal a hidden meaning).

It was then that I had the idea of God being both good and bad, both God and Satan. Basically being a schizophrenic.

This is the core of part one of the story that you have just read.

Once I had the thought, I started to research using various pieces of literature and the Internet and whilst doing this I read about The Unclean Six.

That was it in a flash.

I had the title that hooked me and more of an idea of how I wanted to structure the story that I had in mind. The Unclean Six were six men who had been outcast from the faith and so referred to as unclean but to me they were the spark.

I took some artistic license and decided to have the Six be Fallen Angels and part of a rebellion that had taken place in the early days of Creation, part of the war between Good and Evil and lend to the myth of Satan.

This meant that I could also introduce a "hero", Gabriel and a partner for him to take up the cause for Good.

This also allowed me to try and get across points on good and bad whilst hinting on terms such as the Truth and the Lie in reference to script.

During the course of the book, one thing became more and more important to me, the fact that I had to keep the narrative, the action and my idea vague so as to let the reader really use their imagination to create the world of the story, in keeping places and people as non-descript as possible but at the same time accessible and interesting enough to have the reader keep on reading I had to do many re-writes.

I stripped the idea to the bone over many months.

Some of the deleted and never to be read parts of the story included:

Gabriel and Jophiel conversing with their Master (also in an italic form like the Unclean Six conversations) but I felt that this detracted from the reveal at the end that they, in fact, had also been working for the same Master as the Six.

Extra chapters explaining in more detail about the research I had found on the Truth and the Lie, Good and Bad, faith and belief as well as context in religions. These chapters were deleted for obvious reasons; they detracted from the fictional story, they were far too deep and I wanted the reader to maybe find out more for themselves at the end of the tale.

A seventh "bad" Angel called Uriel was deployed to track the two hero Angels from the onset of their mission, hindering and at one point attacking them to thwart them in their task. I deleted this character and removed all traces of the story arc (at great pain to myself as I was just warming to him!) as I started to realise that, obviously, the story is called The

Unclean Six, not the Unclean Seven and I also wanted to keep the good/bad conflict as simple as possible.

Upon introducing each of the Six and Gabriel/Jophiel, I had written a small flash back piece on each of them, to fill out the character, give them more depth and especially in the cases of the Six, describe other evil deeds that they had been party to as a way of ensuring the reader got not only how good and evil they were, but also how long they had been around and a physical idea of their appearance.

At one point, reading these synopsis would be a choice left up to the reader but that got binned as it detracted from the flow of the story and the pieces I had written were deleted as I, again, wanted the reader to imagine their looks and also I started to wonder if, maybe, these could be short stories in themselves at some point in the future and possibly add to the story already told, not like a trilogy as such, but as stand alone adventures of Good and Evil that add to the world created.

This morphed once again into the tome that you have just read as these histories on the main characters were too good in terms of ideas to lose and so, they were added to the story as "part II".

I felt that this rounded out the characters very well, allowed me to have a complete story in this world that I had created and use what really should be notes for a prequel in a, hopefully, unique way.

Finally, I had a lot of city narrative giving more feel to the human world that they had entered and were involved in but, again, upon reading the early drafts I decided to trim this down as I didn't want the detail of their surroundings to detract from the story, only that the city be, potentially, any in the world.

I got the idea for the story in January/February 2005.
I started writing this in November 2005 and had completed it in May 2007. This had been the hardest story that I had written and the only one, so far, that I have changed so many times

during writing, normally, I let the story unfold to conclusion and then re-read it and edit slightly.

If all of the above had been in the finished article and not deleted (bar the short story histories), I don't think it would have been as lean and straightforward as it reads now.

Cado Ex Venia Authours Notes

Short stories about the main characters of The Unclean Six

I didn't enjoy writing The Unclean Six.

The idea, as it expanded into that story, interested me, challenged me and made me think that if I were the reader, it would be the type of yarn that I would enjoy. Not only was the structure of it refreshing and paced to suit the action but also the very premise that God could be Satan was, I think, a little different. It's almost boundless, really. Yet it was a nightmare to write.

Even when I was writing that story, I had ideas about sequels and prequels because the world of The Unclean Six, the environment, the atmosphere was compelling to me (not least the ability to place characters in any time frame or period away from the underworld and folklore that they inhabited) and I realised that to remain true to the story that was being written, I couldn't get too carried away . . . but the seed was sown.

Once I had finished the story, I decided to leave it well alone as it had been more demanding than I had thought.

However, over time, I came back to it, I couldn't resist it.

After re-reading notes and writing down ideas, I finally ended on a premise that I was happy with, that satisfied all of my desires as to this work. Forget prequels and forget sequels. I wanted to know more about the main characters of that fable and in learning a little about them expand the mythology of the world of The Unclean Six.

This is why I decided to give each main character a short back-story that can be added, rather like appendices to the original Unclean Six without taking anything away from it.

It took three years on and off to come up with strong enough stories for the participants and to elaborate on ideas, as I didn't want to start until all were ready to go. Each of the histories lends to the character from the original story, putting more flesh on the bones so to speak, but in a subtle way as I didn't want to let any reader not work on it themselves in their own imagination but also and just as importantly, gives more of a look into the world that they are from. I haven't forced these, it's been quite a long and enjoyable process coming up with and expanding on ideas for each one as well as doing some research to help.

I hope that these are as interesting to you as they have been to me.

The bulk of the ideas and musings about the above eight stories are contained in a red book that I carried around a lot of the time and added information, thoughts and suggestions too as I went on over the next three years.

This filled out the world of the Unclean Six and finally gave me the stories that made me want to write what you have read to accompany the Unclean Six.

You will notice that these chapter notes are different again from the end result because, once I had the basic premise and added to it, I then went back and cut back as I wanted these stories to be as concise as possible, really hitting the characters above all else and not detracting from the Unclean Six.

Anyway, here you can see the thoughts behind it and the final outcome in this one book.

I hope that you enjoyed all of it as much as I *eventually* did.

Time to go.

Steve Archer.